THE AZTEC PRIEST MURDERS

Volume 1: Zen and the Art of Investigation

ANTHONY WOLFF

authorHOUSE®

AuthorHouse™ LLC
1663 Liberty Drive
Bloomington, IN 47403
www.authorhouse.com
Phone: 1-800-839-8640

This is a work of fiction. All of the characters, names, incidents, organizations, and dialogue
in this novel are either the products of the author's imagination or are used fictitiously.

Published by AuthorHouse 03/10/2014

ISBN: 978-1-4918-5521-8 (sc)
ISBN: 978-1-4918-5520-1 (e)

Any people depicted in stock imagery provided by Thinkstock are models,
and such images are being used for illustrative purposes only.
Certain stock imagery © Thinkstock.

This book is printed on acid-free paper.

Dedicated to Christopher deW. F.

PREFACE
WHO ARE THESE DETECTIVES ANYWAY?

"The eye cannot see itself" an old Zen adage informs us. The Private I's in these case files count on the truth of that statement. People may be self-concerned, but they are rarely self-aware.

In courts of law, guilt or innocence often depends upon its presentation. Juries do not - indeed, they may not - investigate any evidence in order to test its veracity. No, they are obliged to evaluate only what they are shown. Private Investigators, on the other hand, are obliged to look beneath surfaces and to prove to their satisfaction - not the court's - whether or not what appears to be true is actually true. The Private I must have a penetrating eye.

Intuition is a spiritual gift and this, no doubt, is why *Wagner & Tilson, Private Investigators* does its work so well.

At first glance the little group of P.I.s who solve these often baffling cases seem different from what we (having become familiar with video Dicks) consider "sleuths." They have no oddball sidekicks. They are not alcoholics. They get along well with cops.

George Wagner is the only one who was trained for the job. He obtained a degree in criminology from Temple University in Philadelphia and did exemplary work as an investigator with the Philadelphia Police. These were his golden years. He skied; he danced; he played tennis; he had a Porsche, a Labrador retriever, and a small sailboat. He got married and had a wife, two toddlers, and a house. He was handsome and well built, and he had great hair.

And then one night, in 1999, he and his partner walked into an ambush. His partner was killed and George was shot in the left knee and in his right shoulder's brachial plexus. The pain resulting from his injuries and the twenty-two surgeries he endured throughout the year that followed, left him addicted to a nearly constant morphine drip. By the time he was admitted to a rehab center in Southern California for treatment of his morphine addiction and for physical therapy, he had lost everything previously mentioned except his house, his handsome face, and his great hair.

His wife, tired of visiting a semi-conscious man, divorced him and married a man who had more than enough money to make child support payments unnecessary and, since he was the jealous type, undesirable. They moved far away, and despite the calls George placed and the money and gifts he sent, they soon tended to regard him as non-existent. His wife did have an orchid collection which she boarded with a plant nursery, paying for the plants' care until he was able to accept them. He gave his brother his car, his tennis racquets, his skis, and his sailboat.

At the age of thirty-four he was officially disabled. His right arm and hand had begun to wither slightly from limited use, a frequent result of a severe injury to that nerve center. His knee, too, was troublesome. He could not hold it in a bent position for an extended period of time; and when the weather was bad or he had been standing for too long, he limped a little.

George gave considerable thought to the "disease" of romantic love and decided that he had acquired an immunity to it. He would never again be vulnerable to its delirium. He did not realize that the gods of love regard such pronouncements as hubris of the worst kind and, as such, never allow it to go unpunished. George learned this lesson while working on the case, *The Monja Blanca*. A sweet girl, half his age and nearly half his weight, would fell him, as he put it, "as young David slew the big dumb Goliath." He understood that while he had no future with her, his future would be filled with her for as long as he had a mind that could think. She had been the victim of the most vicious swindlers he had ever encountered. They had successfully fled the country, but not the range of George's determination to apprehend them. These were master criminals, four of them, and he secretly vowed that he would make them fall, one by one. This was a serious quest. There was nothing quixotic about George Roberts Wagner.

While he was in the hospital receiving treatment for those fateful gunshot wounds, he met Beryl Tilson.

Beryl, a widow whose son Jack was then eleven years old, was working her way through college as a nurse's aid when she tended George. She had met him previously when he delivered a lecture on the curious differences between aggravated assault and attempted murder, a not uninteresting topic. During the year she tended him, they became friendly enough for him to communicate with her during the year he was in rehab. When he returned to Philadelphia, she picked him up at the airport, drove him home - to a house he not been inside for two years - and helped him to get settled into a routine with the house and the botanical spoils of his divorce.

After receiving her degree in the Liberal Arts, Beryl tried to find a job with hours that would permit her to be home when her son came home from school each day. Her quest was daunting. Not only was a degree in Liberal Arts regarded as a 'negative' when considering an applicant's qualifications, (the choice of study having demonstrated a lack of foresight for eventual entry into the commercial job market) but by stipulating that she needed to be home no later than 3:30 p.m. each day, she further discouraged personnel managers from putting out their company's welcome mat. The supply of available jobs was somewhat limited.

Beryl, a Zen Buddhist and karate practitioner, was still doing part-time work when George proposed that they open a private investigation agency. Originally he had thought she would function as a "girl friday" office manager; but when he witnessed her abilities in the martial arts, which, at that time, far exceeded his, he agreed that she should function as a 50-50 partner in the agency, and he helped her through the licensing procedure. She quickly became an excellent marksman on the gun range.

As a Christmas gift he gave her a Beretta to use alternately with her Colt semi-automatic.

The Zen temple she attended was located on Germantown Avenue in a two storey, store-front row of small businesses. Wagner & Tilson, Private Investigators needed a home. Beryl noticed that a building in the same row was advertised for sale. She told George, who liked it, bought it, and let Beryl and her son move into the second floor as their residence. Problem solved.

While George considered himself a man's man, Beryl did not see herself as a woman's woman. She had no female friends her own age. None. Acquaintances, yes. She enjoyed warm relationships with a few older women. But Beryl, it surprised her to realize, was a man's woman. She liked men, their freedom to move, to create, to discover, and that inexplicable wildness that came with their physical presence and strength. All of her senses found them agreeable; but she had no desire to domesticate one. Going to sleep with one was nice. But waking up with one of them in her bed? No. No. No. Dawn had an alchemical effect on her sensibilities. "Colors seen by candlelight do not look the same by day," said Elizabeth Barrett Browning, to which Beryl replied, 'Amen.'

She would find no occasion to alter her orisons until, in the course of solving a missing person's case that involved sexual slavery in a South American rainforest, a case called *Skyspirit,* she met the Surinamese Southern District's chief criminal investigator. Dawn became conducive to romance. But, as we all know, the odds are always against the success of long distance love affairs. To be stuck in one continent and love a man who is stuck in another holds as much promise for high romance as falling in love with Dorian Gray. In her professional life, she was tough but fair. In matters of lethality, she preferred *dim mak* points to bullets, the latter being awfully messy.

Perhaps the most unusual of the three detectives is Sensei Percy Wong. The reader may find it useful to know a bit more about his background.

Sensei, Beryl's karate master, left his dojo to go to Taiwan to become a fully ordained Zen Buddhist priest in the Ummon or Yun Men lineage in which he was given the Dharma name Shi Yao Feng. After studying advanced martial arts in both Taiwan and China, he returned to the U.S. to teach karate again and to open a small Zen Buddhist temple - the temple that was down the street from the office *Wagner & Tilson* would eventually open.

Sensei was quickly considered a great martial arts' master not because, as he explains, "I am good at karate, but because I am better at advertising it." He was of Chinese descent and ordained in China, and since China's Chan Buddhism and Gung Fu stand in polite rivalry to Japan's Zen Buddhism and Karate, it was most peculiar to find a priest in China's Yun Men lineage who followed the Japanese Zen liturgy and the martial arts discipline of Karate.

It was only natural that Sensei Percy Wong's Japanese associates proclaimed that his preferences were based on merit, and in fairness to them, he did not care to disabuse them of this notion. In truth, it was Sensei's childhood rebellion against his tyrannical faux-Confucian father that caused him to gravitate to the Japanese forms. Though both of his parents had emigrated from China, his father decried western civilization even as he grew rich exploiting its freedoms and commercial opportunities. With draconian finesse he imposed upon his family the cultural values of the country from which he had fled for his life. He seriously believed that while the rest of the world's population might have come out of Africa, Chinese men came out of heaven. He did not know or care where Chinese women originated so long as they kept their proper place as slaves.

His mother, however, marveled at American diversity and refused to speak Chinese to her children, believing, as she did, in the old fashioned idea that it is wise to speak the language of the country in which one claims citizenship.

At every turn the dear lady outsmarted her obsessively sinophilic husband. Forced to serve rice at every meal along with other mysterious creatures obtained in Cantonese Chinatown, she purchased two Shar Peis that, being from Macau, were given free rein of the dining room. These dogs, despite their pre-Qin dynasty lineage, lacked a discerning palate and proved to be gluttons for bowls of fluffy white stuff. When her husband retreated to his rooms, she served omelettes and Cheerios, milk instead of tea, and at dinner, when he was not there at all, spaghetti instead of chow mein. The family home was crammed with gaudy enameled furniture and torturously carved teak; but on top of the lion-head-ball-claw-legged coffee table, she always placed a book which illustrated the elegant simplicity of such furniture designers as Marcel Breuer; Eileen Gray; Charles Eames; and American Shakers. Sensei adored her; and loved to hear her relate how, when his father ordered her to give their firstborn son a Chinese name; she secretly asked the clerk to record indelibly the name "Percy" which she mistakenly thought was a very American name. To Sensei, if she had named him Abraham Lincoln Wong, she could not have given him a more Yankee handle.

Preferring the cuisines of Italy and Mexico, Sensei avoided Chinese food and prided himself on not knowing a word of Chinese. He balanced this ignorance by an inability to understand Japanese and, because of its inaccessibility, he did not eat Japanese food.

The Man of Zen who practices Karate obviously is the adventurous type; and Sensei, staying true to type, enjoyed participating in Beryl's and George's investigations. It required little time for him to become a one-third partner of the team. He called himself, "the ampersand in *Wagner & Tilson.*"

Sensei Wong may have been better at advertising karate than at performing it, but this merely says that he was a superb huckster for the discipline. In college he had studied civil engineering; but he also was on the fencing team and he regularly practiced gymnastics. He had learned yoga and ancient forms of meditation from his mother. He attained Zen's vaunted transcendental states which he could access 'on the mat.' It was not surprising that when he began to learn karate he was already half-accomplished. After he won a few minor championships, he attracted the attention of several martial arts publications that found his "unprecedented" switchings newsworthy. They imparted to him a 'great master' cachet, and perpetuated it to the delight of dojo owners and martial arts shopkeepers. He did win many championships and, through unpaid endorsements and political propaganda, inspired the sale of Japanese weapons, including nunchaku and shuriken which he did not actually use.

Although his Order was strongly given to celibacy, enough wiggle room remained for the priest who found it expedient to marry or dally. Yet, having reached his mid-forties unattached, he regarded it as 'unlikely' that he would ever be romantically welded to a female, and as 'impossible' that he would be bonded to a citizen and custom's agent of the People's Republic of China - whose Gung Fu abilities challenged him and who would strike terror in his heart especially when she wore Manolo Blahnik red spike heels. Such combat, he insisted, was patently unfair, but he prayed that Providence would not level the playing field. He met his femme fatale while working on *A Case of Virga*.

Later in their association Sensei would take under his spiritual wing a young Thai monk who had a degree in computer science and a flair for acting. Akara Chatree, to whom Sensei's master in Taiwan would give the name Shi Yao Xin, loved Shakespeare; but his father - who came from one of Thailand's many noble families - regarded his son's desire to become an actor as we would regard our son's desire to become a hit man. Akara's brothers were all businessmen and professionals; and as the old patriarch lay dying, he exacted a promise from his tall 'matinee-idol' son that he would never tread upon the flooring of a stage. The old man had asked for nothing else, and since he bequeathed a rather large sum of money to his young son, Akara had to content himself with critiquing the performances of actors who were less filially constrained than he. As far as romance is concerned, he had not thought too much about it until he worked on *A Case of Industrial Espionage*. That case took him to Bermuda, and what can a young hero do when he is captivated by a pretty girl who can recite Portia's lines with crystalline insight while lying beside him on a white beach near a blue ocean?

But his story will keep...

MONDAY, OCTOBER 5, 2009

It was one of those old "historical society" designated houses that by some obscure custom was referred to with a definite article: The Hollyoak. The iron gates were wide open, and judging from the vines that climbed the balusters, they had been standing open for months. Beryl Tilson couldn't even guess the property's acreage. Hedges and stands of trees kept the surrounding areas from view.

She turned onto the cobblestone driveway and studied the building, wishing she knew more about architecture. She liked the stonework, the stained glass bay windows and oriels, and the slate roof that was penetrated by groups of chimneys; but all in all, she thought, it had a cold, aloof kind of look that said that as a house, it had no friends or neighbors and preferred it that way. The lawn and shrubbery hadn't been tended in a year at least. It had just stopped raining and a breeze was blowing. The weeds swayed, top-heavy with water.

Beryl could see that no matter where she parked, she'd have to walk through puddles. She recalled a verse in the Hagakure: "If you're walking along and encounter a rainstorm, you can try to dart under eaves and trees, but you'll still get just as wet as if you continue walking with determination." It didn't say that people watching - as there just might be in the big house in front of her - will think you're an idiot for trying to avoid the unavoidable - which wouldn't be a good first impression for a private investigator to make. She got out of the car and tried to show Samurai resolution, walking through muddy puddles as if they weren't there.

Ivy on the entryway pilasters mingled at the top in a kind of triumphal arch. A gust of wind made the leaves tremble and the raindrops on them glittered like so much confetti. She hoped that the call that brought her to the address hadn't been a hoax.

Standing on the wide doorstep, she banged the brass knocker against its striker plate, smoothed her skirt and began to stamp the mud off her heels. The door opened, loosing a wave of warm, stinking air that made her recoil as she stamped her feet.

"You're selling dancing lessons?" asked the bearded young man who pulled the door back far enough for her to see the source of the stench. Mounds of litter - pizza boxes, food-to-go bags, greasy hamburger wrappers, chicken buckets with bones and skin spilling out, beer cans, wine bottles, and french fried potatoes scattered like curls on the marble floor. She covered her nose and stared at the garbage. "You the detective?' he asked.

"No, the Rat Police. You're under arrest."

He swung the door all the way open and stepped aside. "Come on in. You'll need your sense of humor. I'm Groff Eckersley." With his foot's instep he soccer-kicked some trash aside.

"Beryl Tilson." She followed him into the foyer. "Maid's year off?" she asked, looking around in disbelief and wincing at the smell.

"It's so hard to get good help. One must be self-reliant." He waved some flies away from his face. "I emptied the wine cellar last month. Would you care for tea?" He gestured toward the living room doors and a garbage-strewn couch positioned near the room's far end. She treaded her way across a Persian rug as though she were walking through a minefield. He stepped ahead of her and pushed a tangle of trash off the cushions, clearing a place for her to sit.

Movement in an open pizza box caught her attention. "Christ!" she shouted. "There are maggots in there!" She turned and waved her arms, gesturing "No way!" and headed to the door.

"No!" he pleaded, grabbing her arm as she plowed ahead. "Look, you're here now. The whole place ain't like this. Come on. We'll go upstairs."

"You must be mad!" she hissed. "Get your hand off me!"

"Please," he spoke softly without letting go. "I'm not going to hurt you. You know that. As I told you on the phone, my grandparents told me my mom's dead - which just doesn't make sense. There's a reason I've been cooped up in here for months. It's like... I'm desperate." He seemed to be on the verge of crying. "Help me. Please. I don't know what to do." He pointed to one of the staircases that flanked the foyer. It was remarkably clean. "I'll take you up to her room. It smells good there."

Beryl's shoulder bag had been tailored with a special gun slot that made her Beretta readily accessible. She knew her gun was still there, but she patted the bulge to be sure. As she stepped onto the first step she stopped to look at a full-length portrait that hung on a panel between two doorways. It was of a modern army officer, possibly handsome and of some high rank. Hunks of pepperoni, mushrooms, chicken skin, tomato slices and other unidentifiable oily slop stuck to the portrait's face or slid down the canvas to lodge in the frame or fall onto the floor.

Groff Eckersley stepped up beside her and whispered in her ear, "You the camp-following type?"

She pushed him away. "One of your heroes?"

"Yes. Dad. The late and long overdue Colonel Dalton Eckersley. Conquerer of nubile pussy. A chest that just demanded fruit salad. I did the best I could."

"Work on your aim." For some reason, she felt more secure and continued up the stairs.

The second storey of the house was immaculate. Beryl's heels wobbled in the deep wool pile of the hallway runner. Eckersley led her to a door that opened to reveal Madeleine Eckersley's huge bedroom, a fantasy of pale green silk and ebony wood, white marble fireplace with ivy draping over the mantle, and andirons that gleamed beneath a polished brass peacock screen. As if on cue, shafts of sunlight suddenly pierced the diamond-shaped panes of stained glass in an oriel's casement windows, casting complicated patterns of color on the walls.

Groff pointed at a portrait that hung above the bed's headboard. "My mom, Madeleine Eckersley."

The portrait, Beryl guessed, had been done when she was in her thirties. She was regally dressed in white velvet, sitting with her hands in her lap, holding a prayer book and rosary. Her dark hair was pulled back, accentuating the diamond tiara, necklace, and earrings she wore. Beryl suddenly felt embarrassed by what surely seemed like excessive admiration. "I was just visualizing Dana Andrews doing a *Laura* number. Your mother is beautiful," she said, looking at Groff. "You have her blue eyes."

Groff didn't understand the remark. He knelt on the bed and attempted to straighten the painting that was already perfectly aligned. "She's wearing some of the missing jewelry." He got up, closed the bedroom door and walked to the oriel to open one of the casement windows. "Sit in here," he said, indicating one of the two chairs in the alcove. "Please. Be comfortable." He sat down and watched her.

Beryl stayed at the vanity, examining several crystal perfume bottles, each with a crochet covered pump bulb. They were completely full. "This bulb style allows a lot of evaporation. Have you been keeping them full?" She smelled the first. "*Joy.* Jean Patou. Nice." She tried the next. "*Chanel Five.* I'm convinced. She used great perfume." She replaced the flask and went to join him. "What's the third one?"

"Creed. *Spring Flowers.* You know your perfume."

"Not my perfume. Too expensive for me. My familiarity is academic. It's yours that's interesting. Most sons couldn't identify their mother's perfume let alone keep the flasks correctly filled."

"And what is that supposed to mean?" he said aggressively.

Beryl was surprised by his sudden change in tone. "I meant that most sons couldn't identify their mother's perfume. If I wanted to mean something else, I would have said it. I don't get clever with my clients. That is, if we sign an agency agreement and you become my client." She looked around. "This room is gorgeous. It's bigger than my whole apartment." She laughed. "I sound like a backwoods hick."

"Well... it is beautiful. She is beautiful. That portrait was done ten years ago. But trust me, she didn't age in those ten years." His hair had been tied in back with a rubber band. He pulled the band off and shook his head and bent forward, flipping his hair over his face. Beryl wondered if he could possibly be starting to cry, but he abruptly tossed his head back, grabbed his hair and tied it again with the rubber band. He stood up.

"I'll show you another part of the mystery. Look at this other portrait with its green-feather headdress." He went into a dressing room and brought out an unfinished portrait. "The artist brought it here. Fortunately, it had already been paid for. I knew enough to recognize an Aztec headdress and asked him why she was wearing it. He didn't know. He said she didn't talk much. And he never saw her wearing the headdress. She gave him a photograph of it. He had finished painting the feathers on and was waiting for her to come in for finishing touches when he heard that she had died."

Beryl studied the portrait. Madeleine's face was surrounded by long, green iridescent quetzal plumes that radiated from a beaded crown. A slight and somewhat mischievous smile informed her expression. "It's unusual," she said, "but beautiful." She tried to read the artist's signature. "Who painted it?"

"Damned if I know. I was stoned when he delivered it, and he didn't talk much."

"I recognize the headdress, too. The photograph he copied was probably Moctezuma's headdress. Long quetzal bird tail feathers. I think it's in the Prado or maybe Vienna. What is she doing wearing an Aztec headdress?" She took a notepad and pen from her purse.

"That's what I want you to tell me. There's more weird Aztec stuff - these two ceramic pieces—" as he turned, he glanced out the window. "Here! Look! Tell me what you see. You thought I was being paranoid when I told you they spy on me constantly."

She stood up and looked out the window. An elderly man was looking at the rear of her car, writing something in a tablet. "Who is he?" she asked.

"Half of the reason I can't leave this place. The other half is his wife. They're old family retainers, the Trasks. They live in the carriage house behind the stables. They report everything I do to my grandfather - my father's father, Lionel Eckersley, the one who thinks he's the original Philadelphia Lawyer. They're dying to get in here, but I don't let them get past the kitchen door. Incidentally, all the doors have keyed locks and interior bolts. For the record, I don't even have a key to any of the locks."

"Before you tell me more about all this, are you sure you're old enough to sign a contract, and also, while I don't want to seem crass, is hiring me and my partner something that your grandfather is not going to be happy about?"

"The old man won't like it, but I'm twenty-two, and that's old enough to sign a contract. There is a question about the retainer..."

"We usually get money up front. So maybe we should settle that before we get into the mystery of things."

"I must be scrupulously honest. I've got about twelve dollars in cash to my name. Ok. That may be an exaggeration. My grandfather is trustee of my money so you'll have to get your fee from him. My mom used to keep a stack of bearer bonds hidden in here. They're gone, too."

"Ai, yai yai. Investigative work involves a lot of time and expense. I need to have an agency contract signed so don't tell me any of your family secrets. It's a tad premature." She returned the pad and pen to her purse and stood up.

"Come on. Take your shoes off. Relax. I'll sign your papers. And please let me tell you all the family dirt. The more dirt you know, the more likely you are to have Lionel throw money at you. He'll go crazy wondering what you already know, and he'll probably double your fee to find out - and, naturally, to get you to turn against me."

Beryl found herself laughing. "I haven't known you for half an hour. We had a two-minute phone call. I spent an hour driving out here only to have my health threatened by vermin and paranoid delusions. And then I'm told that not only don't you have money to pay my agency for an investigation, but I should be prepared to get our fee through extortion."

He pretended to be offended. "It was clean garbage. Fly larvae are nature's sanitation workers. And I am not paranoid. I own this house. I was getting ready to come back to it when my father was killed. My grandfather may be the trustee, but that's temporary. I'm the heir. Look,

I'll give you a bill of sale. One dollar for anything you want in this room except my mother's portrait. The rug alone is worth ten grand. Take it with you. Just hear me out."

Groff had left the door to the dressing room open; and as she glanced in at the rows of hanging garments, she saw her reflection in a full-length dressing mirror. There was something appealing about the way she looked, standing there framed in the bay's casement windows. She said, "What the hell," and sat down again. "It's not an open police case. But first the contract."

Beryl looked around for something to write on. On the floor beside Groff's chair lay a large silver-and-blue calculus book by Tom Apostle, a famous mathematics' professor. She pointed at the book and gestured that he should hand it to her. "Yours?" she asked.

"No. I gave all my books to one of the guys I knew in Switzerland. He was a year behind me. This is a great book. Slide rule era, but the concepts are well explained. My very own father used it to amplify his West Point text. You should read some of his marginal notes." He stroked the book, making an obscene gesture. "Dear old dad."

"How far did you get in math?"

"I was intimate with LaPlace and Fourier," he said suggestively. "Want details?"

"Just hand me the book!" She found it impossible to be angry with him.

"All right," he said. "You've seen where I live. Fair's fair. I've been away from this part of the universe for so long that I can't remember anything about it - except the statue of William Penn above City Hall. I remember that from a certain angle it looks like he's taking a piss on the town. Please tell me that he's not pissing in your 'general direction,' as they say. I know your office is in the city. Is it near where you live?"

Ordinarily she would side-step personal questions; but he was nervous and clearly suffering from "cabin fever." She smiled. "No. He's aiming elsewhere. Our office is in Germantown at the northern edge of town. It's the downstairs of a two-storey, store-front row house on

Germantown Avenue. My apartment is the second floor. I just have to come downstairs to get to work."

"I pictured it like those film noir B-flicks... your name painted on the smoke glass of an office door... a blonde receptionist who files her nails and chews gum."

"My desk is the one that's out front and I don't file my nails and chew gum. George Wagner's desk is behind the partition. No privacy. It's a nineteenth century building designed for nineteenth century commerce. Maybe it used to be a gentlemen's hat shop. I don't know. It definitely wasn't designed as an office for private investigators. It used to have gaslights! I'm serious. The electrical wiring isn't built in. It's all in tubes and sockets that stick out. If we didn't have our name printed on the *clear* glass door nobody would know what we did. We keep sick orchids in the display windows."

"Why sick orchids?"

"George raises orchids. He says he's a 'default orchidologist' because his wife dumped her collection on him when they were divorced and she moved to California. So the display windows have become his orchid hospital. He brings in sick plants that he needs to keep his eye on."

Groff Eckersley was smiling at her. "How many people have you told that your office used to have gaslights?"

She laughed. "I don't think I've ever told anyone that. You have the distinction, the singular honor, of being the first."

"You like me," he said. "I can tell that you like me. You're sitting there with your goddamned semi-automatic sticking out the side of your purse, and you're telling me about the wiring in your office. What is your apartment like?"

She laughed, pushed the Beretta deeper into its slot, and checked her watch. "Thirty seconds of background baloney. No more. Part of my apartment's been renovated in a Zen style. Tatami platform floors and shoji screens in the meditation room. And in case you absolutely need to know, my Zen Buddhist priest is also my karate Sensei and associate investigator. His temple is down the street. It, too, is part of the line of row houses. Time's up. Now, can we get on with your problem."

"Don't take notes. Just sit there and talk to me. I am so thoroughly fucked up I can't think straight as it is, and if I have to look at the top of your head while you write shit in a notebook, I'll be completely incoherent."

"I won't take notes. Continue giving me your back story."

"Ok.. the short version of my life. Mommy and Daddy. My father... that officer and gentleman you saw hanging on the wall was what you might call, 'the martinet type.' He was a drunken, womanizing prick who used to, let's say, 'discipline us' regularly. Life at home - wherever home was to our little military family - was hell. When my mother had enough of his shit she got us both away from him by telling my grandfather... dear old Lionel Eckersley... that I had a few psychological problems that warranted my being sent to a special 'funny farm' in Switzerland. The institution offered an assortment of cottages for those fastidious individuals who prefer to be privately insane. We rented one. Two bedrooms. I tell you this to disabuse you of any suspicion that we lived in it in a conjugate manner."

"I am disabused, thoroughly so. All right. You were a 'closet' sane person. Where did you go to school?"

"I took high school courses through accredited online British schools. My mentor was the finest man I ever met. By the way, I'm serious about that. He really was a great guy. He died of a heart attack last November. Before he went nuts - major bipolar - he taught at Oxford. Jesus College. He lived in the cottage next to ours. His first name was Donald. I called him Don Don. Every now and then he'd try to base jump the north face of the Eiger, but otherwise he had a mind that was pristine in its clarity. I think he had a thing for my mom. My Jungian analyst had a thing for him. Funny how that happens. Anyway, I spent twelve hours a day being hammered with Wittgenstein... not in the beginning, of course. In the beginning one must be tickled by Aristotle. Where the fuck am I going with this? What else do you want to know?"

"Did your mom stay with you... like... full time?"

"Yes. She has... had... relatives in Europe, so she sometimes visited them. But even when I was jamming my American accent into

Puritanical English Speakers' ears, she was keeping my supper ready back in the funny farm. I loved living there. I thank God every night of my Episcopalian life that she could afford to indulge me. I was happy for the first time in my life. She was happy for the first time since I had a life. The only time we came back to the States was to be with my grandfather on my mom's side. But that wasn't in this house. That was in New Hope, Pennsylvania. We spent time with him as he lay dying of cancer and then for the funeral."

"How old were you when you first returned to the U.S.?"

"Eighteen, but since I was within such easy reach, my father and his father took an interest in my welfare. I guess because the newspaper account of my grandfather's funeral didn't report that I was running amok trying to bugger statues or shit on graves, they thought that I had cleaned up enough to go to school here. They wanted to send me to Prep school." He grinned. "Is there a Prep school for defectives?"

"I hesitate to ask. What, specifically, did they want to Prepare you for?"

"Neither of them had seen me once between the time I was thirteen and eighteen, yet they knew me well enough to order me to choose between the military and law. Can you see me as a Ranger? Do I strike you as the barrister type?"

Beryl laughed. "You probably would be a good lawyer. If you could convince me to take your case after showing me the squalor you live in, you could convince a jury of anything. So what do you want to do with your life?"

"I don't know what I want. I know what I told them I wanted. I informed them, in rather colorful language, that I intended to remain in strict training to become a bum and that they shouldn't disrupt my academic progress. Naturally, they permitted me to return to Switzerland with my mother."

"And college?"

"I already *was* in college. That's the joke! They stood there and lectured me about getting myself under control so that I could attend Prep school.

"I had taken online accredited college courses; and, being a glutton for erudition, I matriculated. I logged a trillion miles flying back and forth from Zurich to London. Don Don owned a nice house midway between London and Oxford, so he would accompany me. They put me in Exeter which I liked. I met truly sincere people there. And some goddamned smart ones, too. My tutorials were lessons in humility. I did not socialize... ever. Exeter recently granted me a bachelor's degree which qualifies me to do absolutely nothing. Do not let that B.A.get around. It would damage my reputation. A bum must not only be useless, he must appear to be useless."

"Smartass. Caesar's wife. I get it. And then something happened to... to..." She waved her hand. "I'm trying to move the story along. When did your problem begin?"

"Last December. I don't know how or why... just *when* things changed. Don Don had died. I was bummed out. The Michaelmas term ended so we did a little traveling. I met an Irish girl in Cairo. She stole some of my mother's jewelry and returned to Ireland. My mother came home here to The Hollyoak, and I went to Ireland to get the stuff back, and I managed to get myself into trouble. I broke into her apartment and found the necklace and bracelet she had taken, so I immediately mailed them here.. bubble envelope, ordinary air mail. My mom received them. Then I went looking for the girl and found her wearing my mother's ring, so I took it off her finger and forced it onto mine, and a lot of bad shit happened. Her friends beat the crap out of me. I won't bore you with the details since they don't concern the matter at hand. I wound up in a hospital. During the fight my finger got swollen and they couldn't get the ring off. The doctors did get it off and I immediately mailed it home and told my mom I was in some legal difficulty. My grandfather came to straighten out the mess and pay the bills. I limped back to Zurich in a somewhat depressed state of mind. My grandfather got me a shrink who put me on anti-depression medications. That was at the end of January."

"Where was your mother?"

"Oh, she gave me lots of excuses and consoled me on the phone, but she didn't plan to return to Switzerland until Easter - which happened to fall in the middle of April. Yes, I felt hurt. I called her and my calls went to voice mail. Usually I'd get a brief call back but she just wasn't the same. In March I sent her flowers for her birthday. This time she called back and was more talkative. She told me that she'd be seeing me soon for Easter. I did my Oxford gig, and when I saw her just before Easter Sunday, I thought she looked a little too thin and tired. She said she had been dieting, but she was in good spirits while I both looked and felt like shit. Anyway, she seemed upbeat but sort of preoccupied. My shrink suggested that perhaps her joy was caused by my romantic failure in Ireland."

"What did that mean? That your mother didn't like the Irish girl or that she was glad she still had you to herself?"

"Incest seemed to be his special field of interest. I didn't want to pry. He'd put his hand in his pants' pocket whenever the subject came up. It came up too much as it was. Besides, going to see him was part of my deal with my grandfather. I didn't want to stop seeing him because I was selling the prescription drugs I got for spending money.

"While my mom was there at Easter, my grandfather called to tell us that my father, the Colonel, had been killed. He was at our hunting lodge, having sex with a teenaged girl, when the young lady's father showed up and shot him in the ass with a rather large caliber weapon. My widowed mother returned immediately for the funeral, but I didn't go back. Too bad. I had wanted to put the 'fun' back in 'funeral.' They preferred to keep 'the Pond' between us."

"And who can blame them?"

"Not I. That was the last time I saw her. Three days after Easter, she called to report the details of Daddy's funeral and told me that she'd be back just before Memorial Day at which time she'd have a great surprise for me. My spirits were much raised - no doubt elevated by my father's death - and I spent the Trinity term in-house. I tried to call my mother, but all I got was voice mail. When Memorial Day came and went and I still didn't hear from her, I called my grandfather. When he finally returned my call he said that he'd be coming to visit me in a week or so and that he'd explain everything when he saw me. He would call me with his flight information and that was it. I finished the term and went back to Zurich. I didn't like the sound of his message, but whom else could I call? I had no friends back here. And I'm an only child.

"In June, my grandfather arrived in Zurich and casually told me that my mother was dead - supposedly of natural causes - and that her body had been cremated. There had been no ceremony. I reeled. I called him... you don't wanna know what I called him."

Beryl sat up. "Ouch. No wonder you're upset. So, you saw your mom in April and she's thin but emotionally fine... but your father is murdered... and then a month or so later, your mom is dead allegedly from natural causes. Do you have the feeling that you're next? Is this why you've barricaded yourself in the house here?"

Groff Eckersley got up and walked to the fireplace. "I don't know. Lots of things occurred to me." He put his fingers into the grape ivy pot and decided that it needed water. He went into the bathroom, brought out a glass of water for the plant, and totally occupied himself with the task. He pinched off a few of the new tips and returned to the bathroom to flush them down the toilet. When he returned to the chair his concentration had gone and his eyes darted around in confusion. "In Zurich, my grandfather told me that I had inherited everything, but that he was the trustee. He was in total control of the assets and said he'd dole them out to me liberally if I stayed in Switzerland - but I had to stay inside the hospital, not in the cottage I had occupied with my mom. I had to be an in-patient and get therapy, and to force me to comply with that requirement, he closed all my accounts - all my credit cards and bank accounts. He paid up the lease on the cottage, turned in the Mercedes I drove - which was leased in my mother's name, cancelled my phone service, and got me a nice room in the big booby hatch. And I was standing there in a state of shock. Stunned! I didn't believe it. I didn't even know she was sick, and he says, *en passant*, 'she died in May of natural causes and was cremated.' But he gives me the full court press about commitment! Then he says 'Sayonara' and comes home here and shuts off everything, except the utilities which also go to the servants' quarters."

"What did you do?"

"I responded to his ultimatum by hocking my Longine, paying off a few personal debts, and flying home... economy class as suited my status in life. I was busted."

"And how did your grandfather take the Prodigal's return?"

Groff laughed. "Not very well. No fatted calf for *moi*. I didn't have enough money to pay for a cab ride all the way out here, so I called him. He said he'd send his man for me... the limo. So I waited... and waited. I called again. Voice mail. A lady gave me a map and instructions for the bus and train. I had a lot of luggage so this was a royal pain in the ass. But, having learned humility, I was helped by the kindness of strangers. I didn't have a key to my own house and his spies wouldn't let me in without his approval. I flagged down a car and asked the driver to call the cops for me and a sheriff's deputy came. He knew my mother and my father and he called my grandfather who then told the Trasks to let me in.

"My mom told me where she kept a bunch of bearer bonds... in shoe boxes in her closet. I looked. I found shoes but no bonds. And none of that jewelry I had returned to her. And so here, amidst all this splendor and garbage, I have no phone, internet, TV, credit cards, cash, car, house keys, or bank account. He says he had to close the accounts for probate purposes. He wants me out of here! And I know that if I leave the house, those caretaker spies will come in and lock me out."

"How do you get your food?"

"He reimburses the caretakers. I tell them what deli or fast-food to order, and they call it in and come to the gate to pay the delivery man for it. Then they leave it on the front door step and knock, just as you did. A few days ago I decided to get help. I got your number from an old Yellow Pages and went out and waited for the pizza guy. I borrowed his phone."

Beryl sighed "This is October and you've been locked in here since the end of June? What do you do all day?"

"I read. We've got shelves filled with the classics down in the library. Some, if you can believe it or not, still had to have the pages cut! What a kick to read while holding a letter opener. Mostly I got stoned and listened to 33 rpm vinyl classics."

"Stoned? Where did you get the money for dope?"

"What are you now? The D.E.A.? I'll get to that later... if we have an agreement, that is."

She shook her head. "Well, it is mysterious and you do need answers. I take it that you want me to find out if your mother is really dead. If not, where she is. If so, how she died."

"Yes. I want to know details."

"And you want to know the disposition of the bonds and jewelry."

"Yes."

"All right. Let's sign the agreement. I'll take the case. But there are conditions. Your grandfather will have to agree to pay us. As you've said, he controls your money. And, I am not coming back to this filth. You get your ass in gear and start cleaning up the downstairs. Pristine. It has to be pristine. The portrait free of slop. No maggots or flies or trash of any kind. Clean floors. Do you understand?"

"Yes."

"I'll pick you up a disposable phone... a 'burner' prepaid cellphone you can use. But it will be limited. There will be only a certain number of calls you can make and I'd like you to confine its use to contacting me... not harassing your relatives. Do you understand?"

"Yes."

"I'll be back tomorrow. I'll take the feathered portrait with me to see if I can locate the artist. Meanwhile, you've got work to do."

George Wagner whistled. "That's significant! Getting one of the Eckersleys for a client! What's the house like? Hollyoak?"

"You're supposed to say, 'The' Hollyoak," Beryl corrected. "Don't ask me why. It's beautiful. Stone.. hard wood... marble... stained glass... velvet... crystal... maggots... flies... garbage... beer cans, soda cans, and wine bottles. Downstairs, anyway."

"I like the case already."

"Groff signed the contract, but if we want to get paid, we have to present it to the old man and get him to initial it and give us our retainer."

"Should I call Percy and ask him to come down to hear about the new client?" he asked. "There's no point in telling the story twice."

"Sure. Ask him if he wants peanut butter sandwiches."

Sensei Percy Wong, karate master and Zen Buddhist priest, immediately walked the half block from his row-house temple to their row-house office. He entered by the rear door that opened into the utility kitchen. "I've brought bearclaws for dessert," he called.

While they drank tea and ate the sandwiches and pastry, Beryl described her afternoon at The Hollyoak. As she finished outlining the case, she asked, "What was it Tolstoy said in *Anna Karenina*? 'All happy families are alike, but each unhappy family is unhappy in its own way.' This is one uniquely 'unhappy family.' What really amazes me is that Lionel Eckersley treats the kid like he's crazy or mentally deficient. My Jack is his age. I know kids his age, and this kid is not crazy. He says he's not taking any drugs, and I believe him. His eyes are clear and his mind is sharp. My kid has a few friends I'd think twice about, but Groff? He's confused, but he's definitely not nuts."

"This won't be an easy case," George said. "His mother has no paper trail and he has no friends, and his only relatives are hostile." He thought for a minute. "We're gonna have a lot of fun dealing with that old man. He's a tough cookie."

"He must be a hard man. He's got the caretakers spying on Groff. While I was there one of them came out and took down my license number! I'm serious!" She laughed. "The wonder is that the boy's managed to stay so sane with all this."

They agreed on assignments. Sensei would get a copy of the death certificate and check the morgue files of several newspapers and George would check with the police in Lehigh County to get background on Colonel Dalton Eckersley's death in his hunting lodge.

Beryl picked up the portrait and removed the sheet that covered it. "Take a look at this and tell me what you think."

Sensei whistled. "It looks like Moctezuma's headdress!"

"Yes. Bizarre and beautiful. I'll take it around to a few galleries to see if the artist can be identified. We also need to make an appointment with Lionel Eckserley."

George volunteered to make the call. "I saw her once. Years ago the President was in town for a Labor Day celebration and I was part of the security detail. Eckersley and his wife Madeleine - he was a major then - were part of the president's party. She was one good lookin' gal."

Beryl sighed. "You guys would've done a Dana Andrews number, falling in love with her other portrait, the one he hung over her bed. You should see that bedroom and that portrait. Beautiful."

She covered the portrait. "I'm gonna go upstairs and soak in the tub. See you in the morning." She started up the stairs to her apartment.

George began to whistle *Laura*. Beryl could hear him jokingly break into song, *"but she's only a dream,"* as she closed her apartment door.

TUESDAY, OCTOBER 6, 2009

With Madeleine Eckersley's "feather" portrait safely covered on the floor behind her, Beryl turned onto Roosevelt Parkway and headed downtown. Rush hour was over and the traffic had lost its tense congestion and moved along at an alert but relaxed pace. An early morning shower had cleaned the air and the sun had not yet had the chance to dry the tree leaves. They glistened, red and yellow, along the roadway's edge. It was a Mozart kind of morning, she thought, and she pushed Concerto 21 into the CD slot.

She parked in a public garage and carried the painting a few blocks to a Walnut Street gallery that specialized in selling the work of local artists.

The art dealer easily unscrambled the signature in the painting's corner. He smiled. "That says, in what only appears to be hieroglyphics, 'Ernesto Duran,' and even if it said something else, I'd know by the brushwork that Duran painted this. Why he painted it, over and above pecuniary considerations, is another story. It's certainly strange. But he has handled the feathers beautifully." He gave her directions to Duran's studio which, she was relieved to learn, was only a few blocks away.

Duran, thin and taciturn, was, as Groff had said, "not exactly garrulous." He smiled only once - when Beryl removed the portrait's covering.

She sat down, but he stood; and during the entire time they talked, he dunked brushes in turpentine and wiped them dry with a disposable diaper. He spoke in clipped sentences: the portrait was done for a guy she was nuts about; she never gave his name; the portrait was a fun gift; it was an inside joke thing; the real headdress was in a museum in Vienna;

feathers are difficult to paint; she paid cash up front, thirty-five hundred dollars; he started it in the beginning of February; he took a bunch of Polaroids; photographs keep the hairstyle from changing; he threw the pictures away; it was good that he took them because she cancelled all her appointments for a month; he worked from the photos; she sat only a couple of times after that; her son accepted the painting.

"Did she tell you why she couldn't keep those appointments?"

"She said she was healing from an injury."

"For a month? That's interesting. And she did come in after that."

"I saw her again toward the end of March and a few times after that."

"Did she appear to have lost weight?"

"As a matter of fact, she did. I didn't acknowledge the change."

"Is it unusual for an artist to deliver a portrait?"

"Sure. When she didn't show up for an appointment, I waited a couple of months. Then I heard she had died. I never had her phone number. She was secretive. Then I remembered that she called her house, 'The Hollyoak.' I asked around and found out where it was. I drove out there and gave it to her kid." He shrugged. "The countryside," he allowed, "definitely put me in a landscape mood."

"One more thing," Beryl said. "She's wearing unusual jewelry... these black stones?"

"Obsidian. Volcanic glass."

"Did she ever talk about them?"

"She said they were 'smoky mirrors' that you could see your sins in. I never saw anything but slightly translucent stones set in silver. Tough to paint."

It was noon when Beryl reached The Hollyoak. Trash cans, garbage bags, and a row of wine boxes that had empty bottles in their twelve cardboard sections, lined the shoulder of the road in front of The Hollyoak's wall. She pulled into the driveway and saw that many of the casement windows, both upstairs and down, were fully open. The front door was open, too.

Groff, clean shaven and barely recognizable, was mopping the foyer's marble floor.

She hesitated in the doorway.

Groff spoke in a falsetto voice. "That's right. I work my fingers to the bone to get these floors so clean you could eat off them, and you want to walk all over them with your filthy feet!"

"Suffering is good for the soul." As she tiptoed across the room she noticed that the living room was clean and orderly. She took her shoes off as she stepped onto the carpeted staircase. Even the Colonel's portrait was free of slop. "Ah," she said, "I finally get to see him. You look like him."

Groff mopped away the marks they had made in the wet floor as he followed her to the stairs. "He undoubtedly paid the artist to alter his features so that they more closely resembled mine, out of spite. That's the kind of man he was." He took Madeleine's portrait from her and led the way upstairs.

"How did he know what you looked like?"

"He used one of those computer aging programs... you know, how they age photos of missing kids."

Beryl gave him the prepaid phone and reviewed the rules he had to follow. She took out a new, small spiral tablet. "Ok," she said, "Mother's full name, date and place of birth, education and social background."

"Madeleine Groff Zollern. March 24, 1964; New Hope, Bucks County, Pennsylvania. She was never a debutante. Penn State grad, anthropology major. Married Dalton Eckersley in the spring of 1986." Groff smiled. "And I was born in 1987. Fast work but, *Lastima!*, no siblings."

"What was her social life like? Was she in the Register?"

"I don't know," he said, looking genuinely puzzled. "Maybe. The American Social Register isn't important when your family's in the old *Almanach de Gotha*. Groff was an Americanized version of Graf. It's a title... 'count,' and Zollern is an old German name. Her mother's maiden name was Orsini. Big in blood, small-to-medium in money. They hated that pretentious title crap. My father told everyone that I was named for the Graf Spee, a German battleship. He always admired Von Langsdorff, who captained the ship. Of course, Langsdorff was a genuine hero, a man with honor. Maybe that's why he admired him - having none of his own, you understand. What else do you want to know about my mother?"

"First, the Trasks.. What are their first names?"

"Clive Trask. His wife's Teresa. They've lived in the carriage house for 40 years."

"I talked to the artist who did the green feather portrait, one Ernesto Duran. He told me that your mom said the painting was for a man she adored. It was done as some kind of 'fun thing.' She gave him no other details. He did tell me that he started it in the beginning of February but then she cancelled her appointment until the end of March because, 'she was healing from an injury.' Did you ever hear about an injury?"

"No. But it might have been from a surgical procedure."

"Yes, I thought so, too. What about these other Aztec things? They've got to be important since they're so out of place in here. They really clash with the room's decor."

"Ah... the woman's angle. The figurine is so weird. It's a man who's wearing the skin of another man. The other thing looks like a solid piece, but it's actually a box and a lid. It was full of Jamaican 'bud.' Quality shit. I don't understand what she was doing with the stuff. I've never known her to use any kind of drugs... *nada*."

Beryl lifted the lid. Except for a few shreds of marijuana, the container was empty. "So that's what you've been doing all summer. And you say it was full? Did you use some of it for bartering?"

Groff laughed. "Are you suggesting that I 'paid' the pizza guy to come back after work with a couple of girls?"

"Please tell me that you didn't entertain anyone in that pigpen downstairs."

"I didn't. He has a camper. Great for small, intimate *soirees*. He parked in front of the portico... after midnight when the spies were asleep."

"And nobody had to go to the bathroom?"

"I made sure there was a little one inside the camper. Good hygiene is very important to me."

Beryl laughed and shook her head. "Let's get back to the case." She picked up the figurine. "I recognize it. I can't remember its name, but I think it's called the 'Flayed God' - some kind of symbol of renewal, like spring, or a snake that sheds its skin. The piece looks old, but I can't tell if it's a copy or the real thing. If it's genuine, without the proper provenance we can get into trouble. Let's find out who it is." She took out her iPhone and searched "flayed god" and found the name. "Xipe Totec. He's an aspect of the great god Tezcatlipoca, 'the obsidian god.' That may explain the necklace she wore. Let's look at the other piece."

The container's large lid was of a human head that faced forward and wore circular earrings and another type of feathered headdress.

Beryl searched for "Aztec boxes" and found nothing. "Maybe it's not Aztec." She took photographs of the pieces with her iPhone, and looked up the university's archeology department. She called and the department secretary directed her call to Dr. Joseph Vasquez, a specialist in pre-columbian ceramics.

Groff knelt beside Beryl and put his ear close to the phone to listen. Dr. Vasquez was happy, he said, to help her identify any questionable piece. He wanted her to bring it in.

"Ah," she said, "I'm not able to do that. I'm an investigator looking into a suspicious death. These objects, a container of some sort and a small statue, were found in the victim's bedroom. May I email you photographs?"

Vasquez saw the photograph for less than two seconds. "This is a copy of a Zapotec funerary urn. The original is in Mexico's National Museum."

"And the effigy of Xipe Totec? Can you give me a reason why a well-to-do modern woman would keep such a figurine in her bedroom? What spiritual relevance would it have?"

"Symbolically? A modern woman? In a bedroom it might signify love's eternal rebirth. That's just a guess."

"The Flayed God seems grotesque for such a romantic purpose," Beryl said. "Human sacrifice and all that."

"You have to put it in a cultural context. Christ crucified is considered grotesque by some people. He is often spoken of as a 'sacrifice.' Getting shot in the heart doesn't sound like anything but a cause of death. Yet, an arrow piercing the heart is the great Valentine's Day sigil."

"What I'd like to learn is what that effigy connotes at a deeper level that might accord with the lady's purpose in keeping it near her bed."

"If you are interested in a spiritual connection to the piece - as a Catholic might have a statue of a saint or the Virgin - then I'd suggest to you that you call back on Saturday at 3 p.m. and ask to speak to Arturo Rosales. He's a graduate student who specializes in the spiritual connection individuals make with the various members of the Aztec pantheon. Most people look at the gods and the religious practices of the Aztecs and dismiss them as barbaric. This young man can tell you in specific terms why a worshipper would be devoted to any god. He'll be in here for only a short time, so call at three o'clock precisely. Tell him I suggested that you talk to him."

"At least," she said to Groff, "we have a basic idea of what they are. Now all we need to know is why your mom has such pieces and why the urn was full of marijuana. What about her alcohol intake? I noticed a dozen boxes of empty wine bottles out in the trash."

"She didn't drink much, a glass occasionally. But that was the wine she liked. Argentine Cabernet Sauvignon."

"What about your father?"

"He hated this house. When he was home he sometimes stayed in my grandfather's townhouse, but mostly he stayed up at the hunting lodge. And he didn't drink wine. He drank single malt scotch."

"Then let's get some of those bottles. She had a lover. He was associated with Aztec things. And he no doubt smoked the dope and drank the wine up here in her bedroom. Can you handle that?"

"It occurred to me back when she was so upbeat. It also occurred to me that she might be with him now... or that he might have killed her... assuming that she's dead."

"Let's not create too many possibilities," she said, following him down the stairs.

A few of the boxes retained the wine-shop's label: Warren Liquors in Malvern. She copied down the name and address. "How much of this wine did you drink?"

"One case. That's all."

"I'll need samples of your mom's prints, yours, your father's and the caretakers' to use for elimination."

Clive Trask came to the gate and standing less than fifty feet behind it, took note of the activity and hurried back to the carriage house. Beryl handed her car keys to Groff. "Bring the Bronco down here so we can load a few cases."

She counted the boxes. "Twelve cases less the one Groff drank. That's eleven with twelve bottles to a box. 11 x 12 equals 132 bottles. Argentine *Achaval Ferrer* Cabernet Sauvignon 2006."

Groff pulled up and parked. She helped him to load two cases into the Bronco. "The two of them drank 132 bottles of wine. He must have spent a lot of time here."

Groff shook his head. "I don't know what the hell went on in the house. Sooner or later you're gonna have to talk to the Trasks. But you'll need my grandfather's approval before they'll even say 'good morning' to you."

They drove back to the house and went upstairs to the bedroom. Beryl looked at the portrait. "My partner, George, met her once. Years ago."

"I want you to tell me about him... but only if he's normal. I'm guessing that he's my father's age. But I don't want to hear about any more middle-aged weirdos."

"Ah, George is the opposite of weird. Ten years ago he was quite a guy. Looks, brains, charm, great hair. He wasn't rich like the Master of The Hollyoak, but he had his own sailboat, he skied, and he was great on the dance floor. On the gun range he was fantastic. Beautiful wife and two beautiful kids. And then he walked into an ambush. Ah, you'll meet him yourself tomorrow. He'll come here to pick up the fingerprint exemplars."

"Tell me more. I want to hear about him. Look. I have 'housemaid's knee' and 'dishpan hands,' and the least you can do is indulge me."

"I'm working. I have a missing person or a suspicious death case. Somebody you know. Behave."

"Then just tell me how you came to be a P.I. Please."

"In Zen there are two schools, Gradual Enlightenment and Sudden Enlightenment. Northern and Southern. I'm in the Southern school. The important things in life come suddenly. Within a moment all that came before reaches a limit and a new timeline begins.

"George got shot and became disabled. The police asked him to consult on a few cases so he decided to open his own agency and asked me to join him. That was eight years ago."

"Are the two of you 'an item'?"

"No. I met him while he was undergoing twenty-two surgical procedures. I was working part time as a nurse's aid while I went to college. His wounds were so painful that he was kept in a constant morphine haze. Right brachial plexus and left knee. His wife got tired of visiting a semi-conscious man. She divorced him and married a man with money. She took the kids and the dog. He got everything else including her orchid collection which she paid a plant nursery to care for until he could accept them. Two years later, when he got them, the original hundred plants had grown to three hundred sixty-seven."

"Why did he wait two years?" Groff asked.

"He had to go to a special rehab facility near L.A. for the second year. Physical therapy and morphine addiction. He wrote regularly to me. I'm still the only person who can read his writing. Ok. I've got work to do. Meanwhile, I'd like you to sit down and write out everything you can remember about your mom's last year of life. What she wore. How she looked. What she talked about. If you can remember a name, fine. If not, don't call around or start digging to get it. Just leave it blank and move on."

Beryl got up and started to walk to the door. "And be careful how you use that phone. It's not a toy."

At midnight the phone rang, awakening her. Groff was apologetic for disturbing her but thought she might want to know what had just happened.

"I was standing upstairs in my mother's room. The window was still open and it was cold so I had a hoodie on. I see a small car pull into the driveway. It turns off its lights but I can see it continue up to the house. I figure it's a girl from my Pizza connection. So I go and brush my teeth. As I start to come downstairs I can hear somebody trying the front door. I tell myself that it's good I cleaned the joint. I see that there's a note that's been pushed under the door. I go pick it up and hear the car drive off. The envelope says, 'To M.' I take the note out and it says, 'M, Please call me. Please...' And it's signed, 'R'"

"Do not touch the envelope or note any more than you already have. If there's a clean dry place to lay them down near where you're standing, just lay them down. George will collect them tomorrow. This could be your wine drinker. If it is, it tells us that he thinks she's still alive. A comparison of the prints will tell us if he's the same man."

"I put them on a table here in the living room. I'll latch the casement windows now. I'm sorry I disturbed you."

"You did the right thing. That's why I got you the cellphone. Ok. Get some sleep."

WEDNESDAY, OCTOBER 7, 2009

Groff Eckersley sat on the portico steps reading as he waited for George to arrive. At 10:45 a.m. he looked up to see the dark blue pickup truck turn into the driveway and proceed towards the house. Groff stood up and waved.

George parked and stood for a moment admiring the building's exterior. "Pretty impressive for a bachelor pad," he called.

"You should see the toys in the basement," he said slyly.

"Ya mean you have a bowling alley and a skating rink down there?"

Both men were laughing as they shook hands. Groff made a sweeping gesture of welcome. "The famous George. Come on in. I don't know how Beryl is as a P.I. but as your P.R. agent, she's got the job nailed."

"I have to pay her double," George grinned. "You got the exemplars and the note?"

"Right in here."

George entered the foyer and looked around. "I see the portrait of your father," he said, "but when I met him he was Major Eckersley."

Determined not to be sarcastic, Groff muttered, "Yes, this was painted in 2004." He clenched his teeth to prevent himself from saying *before he got his ass shot off.* "'He cuts a fine figure,' as my grandfather would say." He led George into the living room. "You can't sit. The stuff's still wet from my cleaning binge. I'll get the items you wanted. The note is on the end table."

George took two plastic bags from his pocket and, using forceps, bagged the note and the envelope. Minus the garbage, the room was exactly as Beryl had described it. He took a fingerprint ink pad and placed it on the table.

Groff returned with a half dozen clear plastic bags that contained Madeleine's prayer book; salt and pepper shakers that had been on the breakfast tray and a few other items the caretakers had touched; his father's day book and several letters he had written. As Groff inked his finger pads and rolled his prints onto the card, he said, "The wine was purchased in unopened cases, so you won't find any wine shop employees' prints on the bottles... but maybe some workers in Argentina."

George handed him a wet wiping tissue. "Do your left hand, too. You never can tell."

"For when a hacked off arm comes floating up in the Delaware?"

"That's the reason." George look at his watch. "I called your grandfather's office earlier. His secretary questioned me and then told me to call back at eleven o'clock. It's eleven now. Let's see if the great man is willing to give us an appointment." While Groff looked on apprehensively, George called Eckersley, Elliott, Jamison, and Fine's office. Lionel Eckersley's secretary asked if he and Beryl could come to their offices the following afternoon, Thursday, October 8th, at two o'clock. George assured her that he and Beryl would be there.

Groff went to one of the open casement windows and looked out. "Clive," he called, "when you're finished copying down the license plate number, ask Teresa to bring me and my guest a pot of tea and some decent pastries."

George went to the window to see Clive Trask with his pen and notebook in hand. George laughed. "That's creepy. I ought to take a shot at him."

"You are a god. Do it!"

George grinned and turned back into the room. "I saw the portrait of your mom in that green thing. She looked a little thinner than I remembered her. But she's still one beautiful woman."

"Come on upstairs. I'll show you the really nice one."

"I've been warned not to do a Dana Andrews number on her."

"Will you please tell me what that means. What is a Dana Andrews number?" Groff went up the stairs with George slowly following.

"There was a famous movie called *Laura*. She is supposed to be murdered and a police detective played by an actor named Dana Andrews goes to her apartment and walks around looking at her things... especially her portrait... and smelling her perfume... and he falls in love with her just by look–" They had entered Madeleine's bedroom and George saw the portrait over the bed. "Yes," he whispered, "a man could fall in love with the portrait of a beautiful woman." He looked around the room. "It's beautiful. Show me her things... her closet and bathroom."

Groff led him into her closet. "This is it."

George looked at the shoes that were lined up on the floor under a row of dressing gowns. "She wore shoes with feathers on them?"

"They're not *shoes*. They're bedroom slippers."

"If they're bedroom slippers, how come they have mud stains on them?"

Groff sank to his knees and picked up the slippers. "Jesus!" he said. "I never noticed this. They do have mud stains on them! Where the hell could she have worn them?"

"Bring that white pair out there to the window... and can you open the window?"

Groff brought the white slippers and opened two of the oriel's casement windows. In the clear daylight the mud stains looked dark and oily. "A garage?" George asked.

"No... and our mud around here is redder. This has a carbon look to it. An outdoor fire pit?"

"Feathered slippers for a barbeque? Well... we'll just remember it. It may fit into another part of the puzzle we're putting together."

"I can't help you with anything. I feel so goddamned helpless. I sat here half the night trying to remember details of my mother's last year of life. I didn't realize how little I knew." He showed George several loose-leaf sheets. "I'm so sorry. This is all I've been able to come up with."

"Hey! Don't get upset about it. If I know Beryl it was a 'Purchased Devil' exercise. And it couldn't have been for nothing. You probably remembered some important details."

"What's a Purchased Devil?"

George groaned. "Oh, shit. I just let the cat out of the bag. It's an old Zen story. I'll tell you some other time. Just don't rat me out with Beryl. Let's keep looking through your mom's things."

George moved through the room, opening drawers and stooping down to look at their underside to see if something had been taped there. He checked her medicine cabinet. "Everything is indicative of nothing special," he said. "Did you look through every shoe in every shoe box?"

"Yes. And every pocket in every garment. Nothing. *Nada.* I sat in this house with nothing else to do but search. I went up to the attic and down to the basement. She left no trace of herself behind... except those mud stains."

"Keep it accurate. She left no trace that *you* were able to find. Other people went through this house before you got home." George got up to leave. "I've got work to do running these tests."

"What's a Purchased Devil? Don't leave without telling me. Please. We can go downstairs and have tea."

George followed him downstairs to the kitchen. "I'll pass on the tea," he said, sitting down. "A man was going through the marketplace when he saw a sign that advertised a devil for sale. He asked the merchant why anyone would want to buy a devil. And the merchant tells him it's a really good deal. This devil will do all the housework. Every morning before its owner goes to work he has to tell the devil what to do for the *entire time he's away,* and when he gets home, everything will be done. The guy buys the devil and all goes well. But one day it's his birthday and the people in his office take him out for dinner and drinks and he winds up sleeping at a girl's place, and in the morning he goes right to work from her house. And when he finally gets home that day he finds the devil roasting the neighbor's kid over the fire."

Groff began to laugh. "Are you trying to tell me that she was keeping me out of trouble?"

"That's right. Did it work? The Zen answer is that he should have told the devil that after he completed his chores, he was to climb up and down a tree in the garden and not to stop until he got home. That's another way of indicating the breathing exercise, 'watching the breath.'

In your case she probably meant it as a variation of 'Idle hands are the devil's workshop.'" He added, "But she's still gonna grade that paper. So keep pulling those details out of your memory."

Warren's Liquors in Malvern was stocking up for the Thanksgiving Day and Christmas holidays. Beryl talked to the owner who had been "extremely sorry," he said, "to learn of Mrs. Eckersley's death. She was such a good customer." He was happy to help in any way he could, time permitting.

"All I want to know," she said, "is about the wine you delivered to her home."

"Oh," he answered. "We didn't deliver it. She always picked up the cases here. She has a dark green Jaguar. My clerk always put the wine in the trunk of her car."

"Can you tell me the date of her last transaction?"

"No problem," he said, flipping through the pages of an old-fashioned hand-written ledger. "She always bought Argentine Cabernet Sauvignon. And she bought a lot of it." He found the page. "Here it is. 2006. *Achaval Ferrer.* I sold her the first case she actually ordered and picked up on December 23rd, 2008, and the last case on May 19th, 2009. Twelve cases total."

"How did she pay?" Beryl asked.

"In cash," he said. "She always paid in cash."

Beryl stopped at a bakery and bought two boxes of pastries; one for Groff and one for the kitchen meeting held after Buddhist services at the temple.

She returned to The Hollyoak to give Groff the pastry and the information she had gained from the wine seller.

They sat in the kitchen. "I liked George," Groff said. "He's my kind of guy. Finish telling me about him. What happened when he got home after being away for a long time?"

"He had the water, gas, and electricity turned on, and I took him to buy a car with an automatic gear shift. He had to get an automatic because of his left knee injury."

"He drove manuals?"

"Yes. A Porsche."

"I *love* this guy! When he saw Clive copying down his license number, he said, 'I ought to take a shot at him.' I nearly asked him to marry me."

"How big a dowry would I have to come up with?"

Groff laughed. "Tell me more about what happened."

"I had my degree but I needed a job that would allow me to be at home when my son got home from school. There were not many such jobs around. I helped George set up 367 orchid plants. We had to move furniture into the garage, buy tables and shelves and orchid food and take the drapes off the windows."

"You like him. I can tell. When you talk about him you look the same way my mother looks when she talks about me. Proud and caring. Is there just the two of you?"

"No, we have a third operative. My Zen priest and karate master. I call him Sensei. George calls him Percy. You'll like him, too."

"What's he like?"

"Wonderful personality. Great karate teacher. Truly spiritual Zen Buddhist priest. He's in his forties, same as George and I. He's also single."

"You're all my mother's age."

"Yes, we're the generation that followed The Greatest Generation." She stood up. "I have to leave," she said, finishing her tea, "I have to attend services at the temple. I'm the official bell ringer so I can't be late."

"Stay and grade my Purchased Devil paper."

"What? George told you about that?"

"Yes. He is a forthright individual."

"Then let him grade it. But keep trying to remember things and write them down. *Adios. Hasta la vista.*"

..

Beryl drove to her office-apartment and changed into the garments she usually wore to temple services. George remained in the office while a friend of his on the force ran prints through the Integrated Automated Fingerprint Identification System (IAFIS).

As she sat in the Zendo, she noticed that the temple incense, which never before failed to draw problems out of her mind and let them float away with the smoke, was ineffective.

Ordinarily she had no difficulty getting into a peaceful Zen state, but on this Wednesday evening, as she sat on her *zafu* and chanted, she could not find her way out of the Eckersley fog that was becoming more dense by the hour. She was not focused on her chime-sounding duties and the cues, printed as little circles in the chant's text, went unnoticed. Sensei had to look at her and nod expectantly before she rang the chime.

After services, as they drank tea in his little utility kitchen, he noted, "You were distracted."

"Tell me what you think," she said. "This case is so peculiar. It's like we've plopped down into the middle of a dysfunctional family's squabbling. You know, the usual accusations of drugs, murder, spying, insanity, adultery, theft, and unless I miss my guess, incest."

She brought Sensei up to date with the case's development and asked for his opinion. "Let's see," he reasoned, "Groff went to Ireland in December; and she came home and bought her first case of Argentine wine. I think you need to look at what she did in December. And we may know more when I pick up a copy of the death certificate tomorrow morning."

"So far there's no paper trail, and I still don't know if the contract we have is valid. We probably shouldn't get any more involved than we already are without his grandfather's approval. We see him tomorrow at 2 p.m."

"You were in her home... her bedroom. If she bled to death, there may be blood in the bed or bathroom, or on the rugs."

"I saw no evidence of blood - but then I wasn't looking for it when I was there. She had had a man up there in the bedroom - and marijuana - and some truly weird Aztec artifacts. And that strange portrait of Madeleine in Moctezuma's feather headdress."

THURSDAY, OCTOBER 8, 2009

By Thursday morning George had determined that only one set of prints was on the bottles and that it did not belong to any of the exemplars Groff had collected. It also matched the prints he took from the note. He had a friend at the Department run them through IAFIS and they did not belong to anyone who had a criminal record. The envelope had been glued using saliva. He took a sample and submitted it to an independent lab for DNA testing. With normal service, he'd get the results within a week.

Sensei came to the office to hand-deliver a copy of Madeleine Eckersley's death certificate. It had been signed by the county medical examiner and indicated that Dr. Aubrey Euell, her gynecologist, was in attendance at her death. The cause of death was exsanguination resulting from the hemorrhage of a cancerous cervical lesion. She had died in the emergency room of Eggleston General Hospital on May 22nd. He checked with the hospital and learned that Madeleine Eckersley's body had been picked up by the Vaughn Crematory Service in Berks County. "And they," Sensei said as he concluded his account of the search, "assured me that she had been cremated and her remains placed in a #85-A Brass Urn. The crematory service and the urn, the #85-A Brass model, were paid for by Mr. Lionel Eckersley. He also signed for the receipt of her ashes on June 3rd."

George studied the certificate. "What's odd is that there were only two people in her life: her son and her lover. There was nobody else. Yet, neither of them was aware that she was fatally ill, and neither of them knew of her death even close to the time she died. It took Groff weeks to find out, and the man she evidently loved *still* thinks she's alive. This is one wacko case! How can it be that the two closest people in your life know nothing of your death or know so little that they doubt you're dead? She died in May and it's October and they still can't accept it."

Lionel Eckersley sat at his mahogany desk fortress waiting as his secretary seated Beryl and George in the Wassily chairs that faced him. Several times he slowly turned over the business card she had given him. His face was expressionless, his silence awkward.

George waited long enough. "If we could have a moment of your time..."

Eckersley looked up. "Yes, of course. I am wondering how and even why my grandson has engaged you."

George had no reluctance to show his annoyance. "Our client fears that you may have compromised his right to sign an agency contract with us. We can't proceed without a standard contract. Could you tell us if his signature on this document executes the contract." He gestured to Beryl and she placed the document on Eckersley's desk.

"What are you investigating?" Eckersley asked.

"Normally that would be confidential," Beryl said, "but since you're the trustee of his estate, we'll try to be cooperative, although, frankly, I find it surprising that you would wonder why your grandson was seeking help. There's the circumstances of his mother's death; the disappearance of certain valuable pieces of diamond jewelry and an undetermined amount of bearer bonds;" she shrugged her shoulders, "his lack of funds which he believes you have deliberately blocked; and a few other incomprehensible situations."

"First, Ms. Tilson, Madeleine Eckersley died of natural causes. Cancer. What do you propose to investigate about a death from cancer? Second, certified and thoroughly bonded specialists are conducting an account of my daughter-in-law's assets and liabilities in connection with her estate. She had international interests. The inventory of furnishings and other valuables at The Hollyoak was taken immediately after her death. It is true that among her personal effects bonds and certain pieces of jewelry were not included. I cannot say 'missing' because I do not know that they were there to begin with. However, we are still investigating the possibility that she kept them in a safe deposit vault in Switzerland or in any of the other countries she visited during the last ten years of her life. Her passport bore many stamps. As executor, I have written literally hundreds of letters attempting to locate any remaining property. Groff will have to be patient."

George broke in. "What about insurance policies, trust funds, or other funds that could and should have been transferred to him immediately?"

Eckersley's attitude changed. For a long minute he said nothing. Then he pointed to a gathering of framed photographs on either side of his desk and on several bookshelves on the side of the room. "This is a gallery of ghosts, Mr. Wagner. My wife Alicia, Groff, and I are the only living persons among all these faces. My wife had two miscarriages before our son Dalton was born. He was our only child. My parents and my wife's parents are, of course, deceased. My two brothers and sister died without issue. One died of meningitis during his first year of college. The other two were lost at sea during a storm off Cape Hatteras. My wife is an only child, as was Madeleine. Groff has no cousins. My wife and I have no nieces or nephews."

He laughed sardonically. "I imagine it is rather like China after several generations of 'one child only' families. Before long the words 'brother', 'sister', 'aunt', 'uncle', and 'cousin' fall out of the language. Nobody has any. For us, what remains is limited, biologically. My wife and I are able to use only one of these blood designations. We have a grandson. And he has only two of these names. My wife, Alicia, is his only grandmother. I am his only grandfather. He has no one else but us, as we have no one else but him." He grew stern. "Do you think for one moment I would harm him in any way? Do you think I am in any way pleased that he despises me?"

He expected sympathy. Beryl gave him none. "He doesn't even know you," she scoffed. "How many times has he seen you and your wife in the last ten years? What he feels for you is not contempt. He is confused. You don't tell him that his mother is sick or even inform him that she has just died. And then when you do tell him, you initiate actions that will commit him to an asylum. And because he doesn't feel particularly insane in his grief and comes home to be with *his* only relatives, you give him three hots and a cot and lock him up... like any inmate in a prison or asylum." Beryl's voice had steadily risen. "He didn't even have the chance to see his mother's body in her last moment on earth. You threw *her* in a furnace and *him* in an asylum. Now you keep him penniless 'for his own good.' Tell me, Mr. Eckersley, how or even why did you ever get the idea that your actions were in any way benign toward him?"

Eckersley glared at her and held the agency agreement tightly, his hand trembling. "You know one side of this dispute. His. And in your considered opinion, I suppose, living in the kind of filth you found him... that is the habitat of a sane person?"

"He's been living on a nice stash of marijuana that was being cached in that old, hallowed estate. He resents having to eat junk food. With all the money that's apparently coming to him, you could have hired a French chef for him. His own servants spy on the people who come and go and then report them to you. And he has no key to his own house."

"What do you mean 'a stash of marijuana that was in the house'? Any illegal substances that are there were brought there by him! The house was thoroughly inventoried before he returned!"

"Not that thoroughly. They missed a few kilos."

He laughed scornfully. "And where was this contraband allegedly hidden?"

"Inside a container, a copy of an Aztec funerary urn."

"Ah, yes. I saw that junk. A new religion! Proof of Madeleine's instability. Dear Lord! We saw those pieces and feared that they might indicate the presence of an inherited trait. And the inventory people didn't care to get close enough to those crude monstrosities to discover that one of them contained illegal drugs? I can't say that I blame them."

Beryl's eyes widened. "You forgive incompetent inventory clerks *who will be paid by the boy*, but you blame the boy for using what they missed? Yes, he smoked the marijuana that was in the house when he came home. And he also bartered with it. Bartered! Yes, Mr. Eckersley! You literally forced your grandson to deal drugs! And you didn't want to harm him?" She scoffed again. "I'd love to hear the D.E.A.'s assessment of that denial."

George patted Beryl's arm. "Easy," he said gently. "We don't want Mr. Eckersley to throw us out before we're finished."

Beryl shook off his hand. "The filth was a childish rebellion. He feared that the moment he took the trash out your servants would enter the house, at your instruction, and lock him out. And don't try to say his fear was irrational! We saw how they recorded our license numbers and monitored his movements. And you left him alone, a prisoner in that house, to grieve the loss of the only person on earth who loved him. Shame on you! *Shame on you!*"

Eckersley got up and walked to his window that overlooked the city. He said nothing for a few minutes while he plotted a new strategy.

He returned to his desk. "You don't understand," he said, wiping his eyes with his breast pocket handkerchief and trying to sound pitiable. "There is so much hostility in our little family. That my poor son should meet such a sordid end."

Beryl rolled her eyes. George quickly asked, "Why did Mrs. Eckersley decide to take Groff to Switzerland?"

Eckersley's shoulders slumped. "Madeleine paid the boy so much attention. Dalton was jealous. I suppose he felt rejected. Or he simply used rejection as an excuse to be intolerant of the boy's personality. He did treat the boy harshly at times."

George spoke gently. "Military men tend to be strict disciplinarians."

"Yes... He wanted to make a man - not out of an adolescent - but out of a child. On the other hand, Madeleine was far too protective. Her excessive attentions began to seem... well, pathologic. The relationship was not healthy."

Beryl did not intend to let the remark pass. "Are we supposed to read 'incestuous' into that? A mother protects her son from a bully because she's sexually involved with him?"

"I don't know how or why it started! It's what it became," he snapped. "His attachment to her is unnatural! It is physical as well as emotional.

Does Groff believe that she is dead? Or does he believe that she was or is pregnant with his child and is in confinement now, hidden away by us? Or does he believe that we forced her to have an abortion that proved fatal? We've heard these lunatic ravings from him."

George and Beryl stared at each other, not knowing how to respond to the old man's outburst. George spoke first: "I think we can assure you that if his mother was pregnant, it was not by Groff. If she died because of an abortion, it had nothing to do with him."

"I know what caused her death," Eckersley said abruptly. "She had cancer; but whether the disease was aggravated by a pregnancy, I don't know. 'But not by Groff'? Do you have someone else in mind?"

Clearly, Lionel did not know about the man who spent so much time in Madeleine's bedroom. "That is confidential," Beryl said. "Once again, does he have the right to sign our contract, and does he have the means to pay for our services?"

"Let us be clear. It was not by my design but by his mother's that he was admitted to an asylum. I enlarged upon the circumstance to mitigate the charges against him in Ireland. But I don't suppose he told you the truth about that sordid episode. A case could be made, however–"

George interrupted, "What is the disposition of his mother's financial records? The boy would like them returned."

"Unfortunately," Eckersley answered perfunctorily, "they are all in the hands of the accountants. She was not a careful record keeper, and the accountants have a long way to go to prepare for the transfer of assets. They hadn't even finished the documentation of my son's estate! In any event, he would have had to furnish the accountants with all her documents. There is nothing that can be done about that."

George countered, "But what is there to prevent him from gaining access to his own money… the insurance… the cash… the trust funds?"

Eckersley thought for a moment. "I appreciate that you are trying to champion his cause. Unfortunately, my grandson has other emotional problems you probably don't know anything about. There is nothing more that my dear wife and I want than to see him restored to wholeness. Regardless of what is past, he will have to be integrated into society. And then he will be a rich sane man, not a rich lunatic." He sighed deeply and dabbed his eyes.

He then began the subtle bribery attempt that Groff had anticipated. "It is obvious that you care, and I am grateful for that. I also hope that if your care translates into influence, you will use that influence to get him to cease making his outrageous accusations and to see a doctor... maybe once a week... someone professional. I won't tell you which doctor to choose. I'm sure you know many competent physicians. If you can get him to go to school and give some direction to his life, I will be eternally indebted to you. If you like, I will see to it that you are given a portion of my firm's investigative work. If you would rather have a lump sum of money, I'll give you that. You give me your promise that you will use your influence in this positive way, and I will give you whatever you want."

George spoke scornfully. "Is this a bribe of some kind? Money and business in exchange for not investigating the death of Madeleine Eckersley and for keeping the disposition of his estate in its current limbo? We know how that works out. He volunteers to see a shrink and the next thing he's inside a psychiatric hospital and can't get released. Money talks, Mr. Eckersley. And when you've got all of his under your control, its shouts can be heard from here to San Diego."

Eckersley furiously signed his name under Groff's and pushed the contract to the edge of the desk closest to Beryl. He opened a desk drawer and extracted a checkbook. "I'll write a check to you for twenty thousand dollars from Groff's account as your retainer. Have my grandson agree to behaving himself socially - and that includes keeping that house clean, and to seeing a physician regularly, and to getting an education..." He paused to continue writing and signing a check. "And have *him* call me and tell *me that*, himself, and I will restore his credit cards and bank accounts... whatever he wants and as much as he wants. Then you can bill him directly." He slid the check across the desk.

"No," Beryl said. "He's our client and we'll not make any side deals with you. I don't understand your goals. I talked to him about the house, and he cleaned it. There's no more trash downstairs... but I'm sure the Trasks have already told you that. As far as his education is concerned, *you* are the reason he couldn't continue his studies. He has his bachelor's degree; but you have his car locked up. How did you expect him to get to the university? Walk? What did you expect him to pay tuition with? He is deeply distressed about his mother's death and you've not given him any details about it. He needs to know, to understand, to have his mind set at rest."

Eckersley's mouth dropped open and he stared at her dumbly. "What are you talking about?"

"He has engaged us to investigate his mother's death," Beryl replied firmly, "and that is precisely what we are going to do."

"I don't give a damn if you investigate her till doomsday! You may be amused by what you find. But what do you mean...'continue his studies'? 'Bachelor's degree'? He doesn't even have a high school diploma!"

Groff's account of the Prep school plans were verified the moment Eckersley mentioned 'education.' Groff had called it a joke, and, indeed, the old man knew nothing at all about his grandson's academic life. She quietly said, "Groff finished high school years ago, Mr. Eckersley. Oxford accepted him in 2002. He had to travel back and forth constantly for his tutorials, but his mother paid for everything - tuition, residential fees, transportation costs. Fortunately, early on, Groff was mentored by a patient who occupied a nearby cottage on the sanatorium grounds. He had taught at Oxford and took a liking to Groff. The boy is brilliant, and the quality of his work at Oxford was such that Exeter College granted him a bachelor's degree this year."

Eckersley scoffed. "You are a gullible woman!"

"Verify it. We did."

He summoned his secretary on the intercom. "Check the list of bachelor's degrees recently awarded by Oxford University's Exeter College. Tell me if you find the name of Groff Eckersley on it." He turned to Beryl. "It is so easy to be taken in by the boy. He has his father's charm."

Nobody moved. Beryl kept wondering what Groff would say if he heard himself described as "having his father's charm."

The secretary finally buzzed. "Do you want me to forward the whole list to your computer? There's a photograph, too."

"Send it!" Eckersley opened a small computer on his desk. He stared at the information and seemed offended. "Nobody told me! Why am I finding out about this only now?"

"I don't know," Beryl sighed. "He's not my only living relative and I knew about it after knowing him... what? a total of thirty minutes? Maybe if you ever visited him you might have seen him with a calculus text. That might have given you a clue."

Eckersley stood up and nervously wiped his lapels, sleeves, hair and the top of his desk. He was giddy. "Wonderful. Wonderful." He began to talk to himself. "And if he needs help with an admission... he's got it. Ivy League... any school whatever. How could this have happened? I had no idea. No idea. A degree from Oxford! My God! His grandmother will be delighted." He turned to Beryl, "What about Yale Law?"

"He's a little too old for you to tell him what he should be when he grows up." Beryl picked up the check and the agency document. "We'll talk to him and have him call you. Incidentally, is his mother's car insured?"

The old man's excitement grew more intense. He clapped his hands together and announced, "As soon as he calls me, I'll have the title transferred to him and restore the insurance. If you would help him with the license problem, I'd be further indebted." He opened a drawer and removed a Jaguar keypod. He tested the spring action and, seeing that it functioned properly, handed it to George. "You'll see to it that he doesn't operate the car on a public thoroughfare... please... until he gets his driver's license."

George accepted the key. "We won't give him possession of the key until we clear it with you. There's something else you could do. Tell your caretakers and Dr. Euell and maybe even your wife that we'd like to interview them. And tell the Trasks to give us his keys."

"Of course. But what is there to investigate?" He began to pace. "Oxford. Oxford. Exeter. My God."

Beryl turned to leave and then stopped. "One more thing. Did you happen to see the corpse of Madeleine Eckersley?"

Eckersley looked up quizzically. "The corpse? No. She was practically dead on arrival at the hospital. Aubrey Euell was in attendance. He saw it. She was cremated. There was no ceremony. What was the point? Madeleine had no friends whatsoever on this side of the Atlantic."

George repeated, "Call Euell and the Trasks and tell them we will be interviewing them!" He took Beryl's elbow and walked out of the office.

George thought about food. "Let's buy a couple of pizzas and take them out to Groff's for dinner.

"George," Beryl said incredulously, "he's being fast-fooded to death and you want to take him more food in boxes?"

"Ok. Call the kid on his new cellphone and tell him we'll pick him up and take him out to dinner."

Beryl called. "George is trying to get out of eating health food. He wants to invite you to go out for steaks."

"Thanks, but I want to hear what my grandfather said. Can't you and George come over here tonight? I'm getting claustrophobic."

George said, "Tell him we'll pick up salads-to-go and be right over."

"Make mine Caesar's with anchovies," Groff yelled loud enough for George to hear.

Beryl called Sensei. "We got the contract. If you want to call around about the wine, go right ahead."

They ate at the kitchen table. Groff was agitated. "What all did my grandfather tell you?"

George replied gently. "We were mostly there to get the contract affirmed."

Groff nodded, but he turned his head. His question had not been answered.

George continued. "He thought you were the only male in Madeleine's life. We told him he was wrong, but we refused to elaborate."

"And the death certificate?" Groff asked.

"Dr. Aubrey Euell was in attendance. He was your mother's ob-gyn doctor."

"Yes. Yes. I know who Euell is. He delivered me. He's a society doctor. He'd lie and they'd swear to it."

George ignored the remarks. "The cause of death was exsanguination. She had cervical cancer. The tumor evidently ruptured in her abdomen. She bled to death. She was transported by ambulance to Eggleston Hospital in Berks County where she was pronounced dead at 2300 hours, May 22st. The county medical examiner signed off on it."

Groff gasped. "Eggleston? That's a maternity hospital! I remember as a kid we used to laugh about a lying-in hospital. We didn't know what it was. Are you trying to tell me that in an emergency situation an ambulance took her from Chester County all the way up to Berks County to a maternity hospital? Did you ask him if he saw her body?"

"I asked. He did not see her body. Who knows why they took her to Eggleston? It was a long holiday weekend. Memorial Day was on May 25th. Local hospitals may have been jammed. Nobody called 9-1-1 for some reason. It's a good point. I'll ask Dr. Euell about the choice of hospital when I see him tomorrow. You have to call your grandfather so he knows first hand that you're alive and well and sane."

Beryl wanted to interview the Trasks. She could hear Groff still cursing society doctors as she unbolted the kitchen door and left to walk back to the carriage house.

Lionel had already called them. Stiff but cooperative, they didn't like Groff and regarded Beryl as the friend of an enemy and therefore no friend of theirs.

Teresa Trask was frail for a housekeeper. Beryl estimated that she couldn't have weighed more than a hundred pounds. "I'd like to know about the night Mrs. Eckersley died," Beryl said, looking directly at her. She did not want Clive to enter the conversation.

Teresa looked at her husband. He nodded positively. She sighed. "Madam was sick all day Friday. Her back hurt. She wasn't hungry. I don't think she wanted to be bothered with people. She told me to call the chambermaid and tell her to start her holiday early. Madam said she wouldn't be needing her until after the Memorial Day weekend. Clive and I were the only ones home with her.

"I checked her after lunch when I went up to get her tray. She had taken the last of her aspirin and wanted more, so I asked my husband to go to the drugstore. We had aspirin in our medicine cabinet, but it was the kind that contained caffeine. I stayed with her for nearly an hour until Clive got back from the store. She was watching television. We had a portable television moved into her bedroom. I turned it off when I came back at five-thirty or six to see if she wanted some supper and found her asleep."

"Did she have anything to drink in the afternoon?"

"Just a pot of camomile tea that she drank with the aspirin. There was nothing wrong with the tea. We drink it ourselves."

"I'm sure it was fine. When did you notice she was comatose?"

"About eight o'clock I came up to see how she was doing. She seemed to be sleeping, so I didn't disturb her. Then I went back again an hour or so later and she looked strange. She felt a little cool to the touch. I went into the hall closet to get the down comforter, but it wasn't there so I just got another blanket for her. As I was straightening her sheet and blankets, I saw the blood. I screamed and called my husband to come and help, and then right away, before he even got to us, I called Mrs. Eckersley. I didn't know what to do. There was so much blood."

Clive put his arm around her. "Then the ambulance men came and took her away," he said. "That's all we know."

"What happened to the bottle of aspirin?"

"I looked for it," Teresa said, "but the men must have taken it with them."

"That's standard procedure," Clive insisted. "It helps the physician understand if what she's taken is part of the problem. They asked me if the bottle had been full. I said it was. They didn't take the time then to count the pills. We heard later that there were nine missing."

"Nine? In one afternoon? She must not have been thinking clearly."

"I know," Clive agreed. "And she may have had more earlier that day."

"Tell me about her social life before she got sick. Did she have many guests?" Beryl asked.

"Madeleine Eckersley?"

"Yes, of course."

"No. None that we ever saw." Clive looked at his wife.

Beryl shrugged. "You wouldn't necessarily have to see the guests to know they had been there. What about dirty glasses, ashtrays, trash in the cans, soiled bed linens, leftover food?"

"The chambermaid would have cleaned up, and she never said anything," Clive insisted. "If Mrs. Eckersley was home, she would have a late continental breakfast. The chambermaid got here at ten in the morning. She bought croissants at the bakery on her way. She did light cleaning and some laundry, and there at the house she made breakfast tea which she served usually by eleven."

"What about lunch?"

"When Mrs. Eckersley got home in December, we never knew what to expect. Sometimes she didn't seem to have come home at night. She went out a lot. After Colonel Eckersley died, she had to attend to so many details. She sometimes went up to the hunting lodge on weekends."

"Did she have any visitors? Evening visitors?"

"Yes," she said, defying her husband's stare. "I'm sure there was someone. I never saw him face-to-face and neither did Clive. But someone did come. I saw a man once carry a case of wine down through the cellar doors; and Clive had to sweep up the ashes in her bedroom fireplace around lunch time and lay a new fire which she wouldn't light until dinnertime. The chambermaid would know."

"And how can I reach the chambermaid?"

"She was only with us for about six months. She was let go in June," Clive said. "She started in December and the accountants sent her a W2 which came back. When we tried to locate her, we found that she left no forwarding address."

"Did you tell Mr. Lionel Eckersley about the man you saw?"

"No. I assumed it was a delivery man... well, I could always say I thought it was a delivery man. I didn't think I should gossip. She was such a wonderful lady."

"Who serviced her car?" Beryl asked.

Clive answered. "I did, at the Texaco station near the highway."

"Is there anything else you can tell me about the house? I expect you know that it's been cleaned. All that trash is gone now. How was it before Groff returned?"

"After Madam's death, the house was cleaned professionally," Teresa said. "We personally cleaned Madam's bedroom. There was long hair in the shower drain. It wasn't Madam's. Then young Groff came home."

Beryl sighed. "Is the garage locked? And what happened to the Colonel's car? I'm told Mrs. Eckersley's Jaguar is in the garage. Is that the only car in it? And do you have a set of house keys?"

"Yes. The Colonel's car was signed over to the Lodge caretaker, an old bearded fellow there named Brunton who takes care of the place. He lives in the apartment over the garage all year." Clive opened a drawer and took out a remote garage opener and a set of house keys. "This opens the garage here. Mr. Lionel told me to give you whatever you wanted."

"How far away is the hunting lodge?" Beryl asked. "Is it hard to get to?"

"About seventy-five miles. You go straight up Highway 476 to Emmaus. But just before you get to Emmaus, you exit at Greystone Road, go west, and a few miles back you'll see a sign that says *Hollyoak Lodge*. An unpaved road takes you from the highway straight up to the lodge. It's steep and muddy in the rain. You'll need chains if there's snow."

Suddenly Teresa Trask blurted out, "I want you to know that I never would have given her aspirin if I knew she was bleeding." Her chin and lower lip quivered.

"I know you wouldn't," Beryl said softly. "You did what any caring person would do." She stood up. "That's it. Thanks for all your help. You've been very kind."

Groff and George were still sitting in the kitchen when Beryl returned through the back door.

"What did you learn?" Groff asked.

"George saw mud stains on your mom's shoes. Teresa Trask says she went up to the hunting lodge. Boudoir slippers in a hunting lodge says 'rendezvous.' Is the lodge in coal country?"

"Yes."

"Then that's the reason for the carbon type soil."

"Who the hell is this guy?" Groff shouted. "This is so crazy! Why don't I know anything about him?"

"Give us time," Beryl said. "We'll find out. Just do not interfere. Do you understand?"

"Yes, I understand. But I'm not calling my grandfather. I'm not talking to anybody until I get some answers."

"You have to call your grandfather," George insisted.

"What I have to do is think," he answered.

"About what?" Beryl asked.

"I don't even know what school I want to go to."

"What do you want to study?" George asked.

"I don't know."

George pushed. "Why don't you talk it over with your grandfather?"

"No. Nein. Niet. Negomundo."

Beryl ended the discussion. "We've got the garage opener and the keys to your mother's car. While it's still light, let's go see what we can learn from whatever is left inside it."

The garage door folded up. George whisled as a forest-green Jaguar came into view. "Nice," he said, "British racing green."

"This is the first time I've seen it," Groff said. Dejected, he looked at George. "The key?"

George tried to lighten the mood. He affected a sinister expression, stared into Groff's eyes, and took the Jaguar key pod from his pocket. As he pressed it, the ignition key sprang out like a little switchblade knife, and he began to sing, "*Und der Haifisch, der hat Zahne, Und die tragt er im Gesicht.*"

Groff burst into laughter. "I gotta marry this guy. I gotta keep him near me. This is too fucking rich. *Mac the Knife.* Sing the rest of it. Go ahead."

George laughed. "I only know the next two lines. *Und MacHeath, der hat ein Messer, Doch das Messer sieht man nicht.*"

The car doors had unlocked at the click. While they were laughing, Beryl got into the driver's seat and checked to see that a woman her approximate size was the last to drive it. The mirrors and seat were properly placed. She got out and George motioned to Groff to get into the car.

They were still laughing as they sat in the front seats. "Look," George said confidentially, "There are two cats on a Jag. The chrome one on the bonnet... the hood... is called the Leaper. And these on the wheel, shift, and dashboard are called the Growler. Did you know that?"

"No," said Groff. "We had a Mercedes in Switzerland. Leaper and Growler. Another secret my mother kept from me."

George got out. "Wanna take this down?" he called to Beryl and began to read the information on the oil change sticker. "She had her oil changed at a Texaco station in Chester County on February 20th. There were 22,601 miles on the odometer at that time. And when it was parked here, it records 23,713. Where," he asked, "did she drive for eleven hundred miles?"

It was a rhetorical question. Nobody knew or could guess.

"When do I get to drive it?" Groff asked.

"When you have a grownup talk with your grandfather." Beryl took the key, locked the car, and dropped the key into her purse. "Call the Department of Motor Vehicles and find out what you need to do to operate a car legally. We'll get to the car soon enough. Rehearse your grownup talk."

There was nothing else of interest in the car. They returned to the house and went directly to Madeleine's bedroom. Beryl gave Groff the keys that the Trasks had given her.

Groff opened the closet and turned on the light. "Did you want to see the muddy slippers?" He lifted one of the dressing gowns off the bar. "What do you call these things?"

"Peignoir sets... complete with matching boudoir slippers."

"She never wore stuff like that in Switzerland."

"Teresa said that when she came up to check on her, she felt cool to the touch. She went to put a down comforter on her, but it was missing from the hall closet. Have you come across it yet?"

"No. It's still missing. Maybe she took it up to the Lodge."

George and Groff sat on the two pale green silk chairs in the oriel. George was staring up at Madeleine's portrait. "So much controversy about such a beautiful person."

Groff nodded. "I'm not the one who suggested that my mother could be pregnant. They... her in-laws and her physician started those rumors. Look around. You'll find tampons but no prenatal vitamins or stuff for morning sickness. Prescriptions for sulfa drugs and antibiotics, mostly filled in Europe. There's nothing in her medicine chest that has anything to do with her sex life. No strawberry flavored vaginal jelly. No vibrators. Pregnant women gain weight. My mother lost weight. I can believe she had a lover. But to paraphrase Jonathan Swift, 'My mother was beyond child-bearing age.' Why do people make up this crap?"

George answered. "People don't like blank spaces. They try to fill them. They get suspicious when they don't know something they think they should know. Why has the information been kept from them? It must be something terrible.

"So they talk about pregnancies and abortions and missing jewelry. We told him about your Oxford degree. *Your mother should have told him about it.* Your mom was a human being and so is your grandfather. Talk to each other! If you and your grandfather leap to fantastic conclusions, it's because no sensible ones are ever discussed.

"Call him! And if you're worried about the diamonds, forget it. They'll turn up. If not, you'll survive. You can buy more." George got up and started down the stairs.

Beryl followed. Half way down, she called back to Groff, "If you call your grandfather tonight, we'll come back tomorrow and have lunch at a restaurant. Then we'll take you to the DMV for your license."

"Wait!" he called. "Take me with you now. I promise I'll call my grandfather from your house." He ran down the steps after her. "I don't want to be here alone in case another missive comes under the door."

George was standing impatiently in the foyer. "Confront the guy! Save yourself our fee!"

"With what? I don't have a weapon. And suppose he asks someone else to put the note under the door. Or he lies to me. Where am I then?"

"Call your grandfather!" George shouted.

"I can't!" Groff shouted back at him. As Beryl turned to look at him, he sat down on the steps and whined, "I don't know what to say to him!"

George and Beryl exchanged a look of resignation. George opened the front door. "Then come on. Turn out the lights and lock the doors."

They drove back to the office in silence.

They parked in the rear of the building. Before George opened the passenger's door, he looked back at Groff. "I've got a bedroom you can use, if you want to stay at my house."

Groff didn't know what to say. He looked at Beryl, and she answered for him. "For tonight he can sleep here in Jack's room. He'll fit into his clothes."

George got out of the car. "Make sure he sees the Japanese meditation room."

Groff called, "No! Wait! If we follow you home can I see the 367 orchid plants?"

George looked at Beryl and grinned. "You told him about the orchids?"

"It seemed important at the time," she said. "Ok. It's early enough to give the kid a quick tour... if you're willing."

"All right," George said. "Get in the pickup. You can ride with me and Beryl will follow us."

It was late enough for the traffic to have thinned. In twenty minutes they arrived at George's house.

Groff got out of the pickup and looked around as though he had been deposited on another planet. It had been months since he had seen a house other than The Hollyoak up close. Inside the house, he laughed at all the orchids placed on tables and shelves in what had been the living room, dining room, and den. George played into his mood by pointing out the personalities of the plants and the relationships he had formed with them.

"This one's my wife. She needs to be pampered every day. If I want her to bloom, I have to touch her and tell her how pretty she is, or I get nada. I had to marry her." He lowered his voice. "That's why all the way over there... is my harem. Those girls will bloom... anytime... under any conditions. But I have to be careful so that she," he pointed to his "wife" plant, "doesn't see me spending too much time over there." He moved on. "This one is my boss. I can actually hear her bitch and moan when I'm an hour late watering her. And this one is my mother-in-law. When it's time to give them orchid food, she nags me. I'm serious. I get nightmares in which she keeps reminding me that I'm overdue - as usual - and stingy - as usual - with putting food on the table."

"Do you have a brother-in-law?" Groff asked.

"Yes. Yes, I do. A row of them." George showed him a table with plants that were not blooming. "No matter how much you do for them, they just won't produce."

Before the subject of kids could come up, Beryl ended the tour.

Once again they parked at the rear of the office. "If we go in at ground level," she explained, "we enter the utility kitchen and then can walk straight through to the front of the office. Inside, there's a stairway that leads up to the second floor - right into my office-slash-bedroom. And," she indicated an exterior flight of stairs, "if we climb these steps, we arrive at my kitchen door." She went to the stairs.

"Lay on, MacDuff," Groff said, following her.

Inside the kitchen, she turned on the lights. Groff looked around. "It's nice," he said, "but it doesn't look Japanese."

"All right," she said, "I'll give you the guided tour. This floor of the building was designed to house the owners of the first floor business. It contained the kitchen, a bathroom, and four other rooms to be used to suit the purposes of the occupants. If we follow the hallway that runs along the side of the rooms up to - but not including - the front room, we find, here on my left, a bathroom. They like to keep all the water pipes together... so a partition separates the kitchen from the bathroom."

She began to speak in the peculiar way of tour guides. "Moving right along, we find my son Jack's bedroom." She flicked on the lights. "TV, computer, CDs. Books. Bed. Drawers. Closet. Junk. I hope these accommodations are satisfactory. The telephone is at your disposal and may be used to call your grandfather."

"It looks like my room in the cottage."

"Good. And now we come to the utility room." She flicked on the light. "Ironing board. Cleaning supplies. Mop. Bucket. Storage bins. It's full of junk and more junk. Don't die in here. It would be weeks before we found you. The room is divided into two... the other half is a big clothes closet for me." She turned off the light and continued to walk forward.

"This is the second room, which has the entrance doorway at the top of the stairs that come up from the office. As you can see it is a multi-purpose room and functions as my bedroom, private office, Tv room and Buddhist library. There's nothing particularly Zen about it. A bamboo shade covers the view of our lush tropical parking lot. For easy access, the office land-line has an extension phone that rings there beside my bed. Now you have to take your shoes off."

The wall at the far end of the room was a complete line of shoji screens and sliding doors. She flicked on a switch. "With a slight movement of my index finger I start a symphony of soul sounds." The recording of a single Shakuhachi flute began to play softly.

"Nice," Groff said, taking off his sneakers. "And you work downstairs. Cool."

"For me," Beryl explained, "it's more than a convenient address. My mother always said that when you open the front door of your house, the house has to say 'Peace.' If it didn't say that, you should move, get a divorce, dump your roommate, move to a more affordable place... do whatever is necessary to hear that word when you turn the key. Nothing is more important in your life than the sound of peace when you turn your house key. I hear 'Peace' loud and clear when I open my apartment door."

She opened the shoji screens. "I use this front room, which has a large bay window, as my meditation room." She turned on the recessed lighting and the room glowed in the elegant simplicity of Japanese Zen design. Groff stood in the entranceway and said, "Ahh!" with surprise.

Beryl lit some incense and, continuing her tour guide intonations, she pointed out the room's features. "The rice paper, in the panels and the window coverings, is set in walnut mullions. The paper filters the light and removes the sight of our unfortunately dilapidated neighborhood. Recessed yellow lighting behind them gives the feeling of late afternoon. The tatami platform flooring requires the removal of shoes.

"In the bay we see and hear a fountain that circulates water that trickles down over rocks to fill a pool in which real lotus flowers grow. Real goldfish live in the pool. It required imaginative plumbing and continuous maintenance, but I think we'll all agree that the trouble is worth the unassuming companionship.

"And there you see my altar with a Buddha statue, a sand-filled incense holder, and a porcelain bowl for an *ikebana* floral arrangement. On that low walnut table I keep a single bowl containing an orchid plant - a *cattleya* who took holy orders after being worked too hard in George's harem. There's a small drawer in the table. Open it and take out the pair of keys... one is to the kitchen door and the other opens the door that opens into my bedroom from the office stairway."

Groff opened the drawer and casually put the keys in his pocket. "Thank you, Ma'am," he said. "Would you like me to make a security deposit?"

Beryl stifled the urge to laugh at his suggestive remark. She pointed to a scroll on the wall. "The scroll says in very fine Japanese calligraphy, 'Happiness is knowing when you've got enough.'"

"I agree. And I really like this place. I like this room more than The Hollyoak's entirety."

"More than your mother's bedroom?"

"A few days ago I would have said, 'No.' - but that was before 'the wine-guzzler' spoiled it all."

Beryl took him back to her son's room and told him to use whatever clothing he needed. "Sleep as late as you like," she said. "I'll be back to get you for lunch tomorrow. But use that phone before it gets too late." She closed his bedroom door.

She showered, brushed her teeth, blow-dried her hair, and put on her pajamas. Then, exhausted, she flopped onto her bed and sank into sleep.

Suddenly she was awakened by Groff, who was stooping on the floor beside her bed. "Beryl," he whispered, "my Grandmom wants us to have breakfast with them before you see Dr. Euell. What should I tell her?"

Beryl opened her eyes for a moment and said, "Yes."

FRIDAY OCTOBER 9, 2009

Alicia Eckersley's hands fluttered all over the breakfast table, making sure all the flatware and dishes were positioned within a micrometer's specs as Lionel, Groff, and Beryl looked at each other with amusement. "I called our florist last night," she said in a quivering voice, "right at his home just to make sure he got the centerpiece of chrysanthemums here on time."

"At midnight, Grandmom? You actually called him at midnight?" Groff turned his face away so that she wouldn't see him grinning.

Lionel Eckersley looked up at the sky. "Lord, keep the juice cold and the eggs warm. I want to eat and go back to sleep." He turned to Beryl. "I haven't had three hours of sleep since Groff called."

The breakfast meeting was more agreeable than they had expected it to be. However, any introduced topic quickly morphed into a discussion of Groff's future. Lionel pointed out all of the advantages and none of the disadvantages of nearly every law school in the country.

"I'm not going to be false with you. I researched your academic experience at Oxford. Have you considered Harvard or Yale?"

Groff shook his head. "I've had enough cold weather to last me through five lifetimes."

Lionel visibly brightened. "Well then, Duke or Virginia?"

Groff seemed irritated. "What do you have against the U of P?"

Lionel stammered, "Nothing. That's where I went! That would be wonderful... beyond wonderful. Marvelous. I didn't want you to think I was trying to influence you."

Beryl noticed the time and also that Madeleine's name had not been mentioned once. "Well," she said, standing up, "I have to keep my appointment with Dr. Euell."

Lionel summoned his car. "My driver will take you and wait, if that's agreeable. Groff and I can discuss," he paused to consider his next remark, "whatever he would like to discuss, until you get back." He turned to his wife, "Alicia, would you call Aubrey and tell him that Beryl will be arriving shortly."

Groff whispered, "A limo? Getting used to the good life, are we?"

Beryl looked at him. "What am I supposed to say? No, please let me walk two blocks to the parking lot and then drive six blocks and spend an hour trying to find a parking space that's within a mile of the medical building." She thanked Lionel and Alicia and went to the door. The limo was already at the curb.

As she exited the elevator on the third floor of the medical building, she could hear women laughing in the only office that had an open door. As soon as she entered the room the laughing stopped. The three well-dressed women in the waiting room looked up at her with a slightly indignant expression that suggested they had caught her eavesdropping.

Beryl knew what the magic words were, so she said them in a sweet clear voice as she handed the receptionist her card: "The Eckersleys have made an appointment for me to discuss their daughter-in-law's case with Dr. Euell."

Immediately the chattering started again and their attitude toward her changed. Now they wanted to engage her in conversation to find out why she was there.

The receptionist took her card back into the inner offices. The doctor's nurse immediately came out of an examining room. She extended her hand, which Beryl shook. "Ms. Tilson?" she asked, "I'm Isabel McAndrew, Dr. Euell's nurse. We're running a bit late. Would the delay inconvenience you?"

"Not at all," Beryl said. "And I promise to be brief."

In a deliberately loud "sing-song" voice - more for the seated women than for Beryl - the nurse said, "Today is Fri--half-a-day-Day, Ladies. So let's *all* try to be brief."

One of the women countered, "When has it ever been less than Fri--two-thirds-a-day-Day?" Everyone laughed.

One of the ladies extended her hand to Beryl. "Come and sit down here. I'm Claire, and this is Miranda." Beryl nodded and shook fingers and repeated her own name. "And this is Gloria." The introductions were finished. The interrogation could begin.

Claire immediately said, "I haven't seen Alicia Eckersley in months. How is she?"

Beryl smiled. "Fine; and still an impeccable hostess. The world will end if the eggs are cold and the juice is warm." Everyone found that suitably amusing.

Gloria asked, "Did you have breakfast with her?"

Beryl said that in fact she had just left 'Alicia and Lionel.'

Miranda inquired about Lionel.

"Hmmm," Beryl said. "Let's see if I can find the proper cliché. He's sharp as a tack and has a mind like a steel trap."

"That's Lionel!" two of them said simultaneously. This response engendered such risibility that that Miranda was inspired to launch a gossip missile: Lionel, she confided, was also as stubborn as a mule since it took Alicia many months to get him to be more receptive to Daniel Moor's astrology - which was what they had been talking about, she said, when Beryl arrived. Apparently, someone named Carly once took Alicia's advice and went to see an astrologer named Daniel Moor.

Miranda explained for Beryl's edification, "Carly was having marital problems. Her husband was cheating on her with his secretary - and she asked for Moor's advice. He gave her a reading and assured her the stars indicated that a watery vacation - which clearly indicated a cruise - would facilitate 'high romance.' Then, wouldn't you know it, she talked her husband into going on a Caribbean cruise and he got e-coli from something he ate. He was hospitalized in Aruba for a month. She stayed with him, of course, alone in her hotel room with room service, and she was the type who needed comfort food - always fighting fat. She swilled down these tropical smoothies and scarfed down Dutch ice cream by the quart. When they finally got home, the 'season' had started. He had lost twenty pounds and she had found them. He was as thin and trim as a GQ model. None of her clothes fit her. She looked like an overstuffed sofa. She got herself a new kind of 'personal trainer' and no longer speaks to Alicia."

Nurse McAndrew, rifling through a file cabinet, interjected, "But have you seen her lately? She looks fabulous. She's lost forty pounds. She looks years younger. Daniel Moor is a quack. She was smart to dump him."

The women hadn't seen Carly, but one of them had heard the same thing. But who was the new "personal trainer"?

The nurse didn't know his name. "But I know he's not an astrologer," she said. "And he doesn't do calisthenics - at least not the kind you talk about in polite conversations."

Everyone again laughed and Claire wondered if this was the Indian shaman or guru Madeleine Eckersley had seen.

The conversation ceased to be pointless chatter. "Oh," Beryl said, "Madeleine saw a shaman? That's exciting. Amerindian or India Indian?"

Nobody knew. Gloria said, "Madeleine was still seeing Daniel Moor to get her readings. She went with Alicia Eckersley. But somebody did tell me that she was seeing another health guru. Maybe he had more new and exciting things to play with than Daniel Moor had." Everyone laughed. "I mean," she clarified humorously, "with all that astrological junk he keeps in his consultation room!"

"Girls!" said the nurse in mock disapproval. "Behave yourselves!" Then she turned to Beryl, "Who knows why they went to an astrologer? Maybe it gave them something nice to do together, something they could talk and laugh about. But he was still a quack."

Miranda agreed with Gloria. "No, Madeleine stopped seeing Moor because she found somebody else. I heard that Alicia was furious with her."

Claire said, "Well, Alicia was right. Whoever he was, he didn't do Madeleine any good, now did he?"

Gloria came to the unknown Indian's defense. "Madeleine was set in her ways. Look at how long she stayed in Europe. No wonder Dalton was so frustrated. She probably didn't follow her guru's advice. She was very independent."

Claire sulked. "I detest these diet pills I'm on. I think I'll call Carly and get the name of that shaman she used - the one who got her into shape."

"Good luck with that," called the nurse, shutting the file drawer. "I've been so tired lately. I've no energy at all, and I'm not sleeping the way I used to. I literally begged her to give me--" she lowered her voice, "his name. Not that I'm faulting traditional medicine, mind you. But Carly just said, 'Darling, even if I were free to give you his number, you couldn't afford him.'"

Claire replied, "I can weasel it out of her. But Isabel, you sound like you're having menopausal symptoms. Talk to Aubrey."

Just as the nurse went into the inner office, Miranda had a revelation. "Maybe this is why Eleanor Teasdale suddenly looks so vibrant! She was going through the change. She looked awful and was moody all the time. Then, Poof! She's wearing her skirts way above the knee. My sister asked her if she was taking hormone pills and she said something like, 'That is so old hat. I found a better treatment.' Then she practically skipped away."

As the patient in the inner office came out and made her next appointment with the receptionist, Dr. Euell entered the waiting room and shook Beryl's hand, asking her to come back into his office. He was not a large man. She noticed that she stood eye-to-eye with him and also that his hands were soft and delicate.

Euell sat at his desk, drumming it with a pen. "I've assured the family that Madeleine's death was the result of natural causes. Notice, I didn't say it was unavoidable. Her last Pap smear came back indicating atypical cells which should be immediately retested. We sent her an automatic request to contact us to make an appointment for retesting. She didn't respond. We sent a second request. Again, she didn't respond. I wasn't surprised because she was so rarely home."

"When was this?"

He opened a folder. "I saw her on December 22nd. The lab sent the report back - it's dated December 30th, but we may not have gotten it until the January 4th. Our first notice was sent January 5th. The second notice was sent February 5th. Then Alicia Eckersley told me that Madeleine had a new physician."

"Do you recall when she told you that?"

"I didn't make a note. And it wasn't during an office visit. As I recall, I saw her and Lionel at a friend's anniversary party. That was around Valentine's Day. Nevertheless, she was sent a third request to come in for retesting in March. We usually don't 'hound' patients. After three requests it is assumed that they have exercised their right to see someone else or to be left alone. And that is where things stood until, in May, I was called late at night to attend her."

"Can you tell me about that night? I'm interested in the choice of hospital. Wasn't Eggleston a maternity hospital. Eggleston Lying-In?"

"It once was. The hospital was founded in 1946 to accommodate the post-war baby boom. In those days, a woman spent five days in the hospital after giving birth. But then the babies stopped coming and the post-natal hospital stay was shortened to a couple of days. So the hospital became a more general health facility and changed its name to Eggleston General. There are no accommodations for transplants or other complicated procedures. Still, it's well staffed and has a good reputation.

"Alicia Eckersley called me after the housekeeper called her. I live in northern Montgomery County. For me to connect with Madeleine as quickly as possible, I selected Eggleston in Berks County which was midway between The Hollyoak and my home. I called a private ambulance service - one that was close to The Hollyoak. They picked her up and I drove directly to Eggleston. We arrived simultaneously. Perfect timing.

"I tried a few heroic measures to no avail. She was moribund when she was brought in. Deep shock. She had cervical cancer, a lesion that involved certain pelvic blood vessels. She had taken aspirin, which inhibited her blood's clotting mechanisms. Her abdomen was distended with blood and she had also bled in her bed. To the untrained, it probably suggested a miscarriage. I suppose that is how that rumor that she was pregnant got started. I trust you heard that rumor."

"So she definitely was not pregnant."

"Absolutely not." He stood up.

Beryl also stood."Did you ever try to explain any of this to Groff?"

"I've tried, but Groff is delusional. Has he told you that he suspects that his mother is still alive?"

Beryl wanted to ask how he managed to communicate with Groff, but thought it would be foolish to ask. "Yes, I've heard that. And she was cremated?"

"Yes. As I recall, the hospital placed a call to Groff's sanatorium in Switzerland. He was not in residence at the time. They turned to her next nearest of kin who was, of course, Lionel Eckersley. He saw no reason to put his wife through another funeral ordeal. Madeleine was friendly, but she did not socialize. She spent time with Alicia Eckersley when she was in town. But other than that, there was no reason to have a funeral service. I think a memorial service was considered for when Groff returned. But you'll have to ask them about that."

"Do you happen to know where her ashes are?"

"As a matter of fact, I do. They're in the Eckersley mausoleum. He smiled slightly. "I find it strange that you didn't know that."

"Oddly enough... so do I."

"Groff never asks normal questions. He concocts these theories and then makes charges accordingly. His mother and father had not divorced. She was Dalton's widow. Ultimately, her ashes were sent back to the Eckersleys.

"Miss Tilson," he said checking her card, "before you conclude your investigation you will discover that the Eckersley family is a rather complicated one."

On her way to the elevator, Beryl called the driver. By the time she exited the building, the car was pulling up to the curb. She asked if he knew where Daniel Moor's residence was located. He did and offered to call ahead if she wanted to visit him. "Yes," Beryl said, "I'd appreciate that." Before the car pulled away from the curb, Moor had happily agreed to see her immediately or at any time that was convenient for her.

Daniel Moor's astrology "laboratory" - as he called it - occupied the top floor of a corner three-storey house on Locust Street near the Delaware River. The door bore the legend, "Moor's Temple of the Stars, by the Stars, and for the Stars." Beryl laughed, wondering how Alicia Eckersley could be taken in by something as foolish as this. She rang the bell. The buzzer sounded, unlocking the door to the entrance room.

Moor was dressed like Merlin, but without a conical hat. In a purple caftan he moved through the room with studied concern as if the astronomical paraphernalia - the antique astrolabe, the geared model of the solar system, the zodiac belt around an earth globe - were conveying vital information to him that he had to verify in old Latin books and charts that lay upon tables for all to see and be suitably mystified about. Only the presence of a client, whose needs were obviously greater than the fate of the universe, could disrupt his work.

Beryl stood in the room's vestibule and watched him as he turned a page with one hand and held his other hand up, indicating that she should wait until the page disclosed its secret to him. Then he tore himself away from the page that had bound him and said, "Oh, this can wait until later. A human being needs to communicate with the stars, and I must not forget how I am honored to be an official translator. Please forgive an old scholar's obsession with his books and instruments. Come in and sit down."

As he referred to himself as "an old scholar," he gracefully waved his hand towards a wall that contained framed certificates of accomplishments... academic diplomas, awards, and memberships in medical and financial investment societies. Beryl's attention focussed on a medieval chart which showed how the zodiacal signs influenced various parts of the human anatomy.

"How can I help you?" he asked.

Beryl handed him her business card and sat in the consultation chair. "I'm investigating the death of Madeleine Eckersley. I understand she was a client of yours."

"Yes, for a short time. She visited me with her mother-in-law, Alicia Eckersley, a great lady of our time. When her chauffeur just called, I rushed to finish my calculations immediately. Each day brings new challenges."

"When did you see Madeleine Eckersley last??"

He removed a file from a cabinet and put it on his desk. As he searched the documents inside, Beryl could see several 5" x 7" index cards that had been stapled to the inside of the folder. She could clearly see dates and names and Madeleine Eckersley's relationship to the persons named. These were exactly the kind of "memory cards" salesmen and phone sex operators used to make the caller feel that he is well remembered. He selected a document. "This is the last horoscope I prepared for Mrs. Madeleine Eckersley. She came with Alicia in January."

"Did she ask you any specific questions?"

"As you can see it is a charting, specific to her of the day-by-day indications of celestial influence, of calamities which may be avoided, of felicities which may be accommodated. That is all it is." He held it out for her to see. "But is that not enough?" She noted that he had written a forecast to and including the month of September.

"Do the stars indicate the felicities and calamities of investment portfolios?" she asked.

Moor returned the horoscope to the file. "I am a Virgo, a humble perfectionist with a need to serve and a penchant for discriminating analysis. The stars guided me to receiving a master's degree in economics." He pointed to several of the latin diplomas on the wall. "They were given to me with the spelling 'Moore' - for my astrology work I use the spelling 'Moor.' It suggests the mysterious moors of England... Druids... Stonehenge... ancient wisdom." He feigned embarrassment. "I am shameless," he giggled. "My academic credentials are quite in order and when I give financial advice based upon an interpretation of the stars, I assure you the advice is as good or better than that given by any broker you can name. Alicia listened. She is a Capricorn. Madeleine was an Aries. She didn't."

"I'm not trying to be offensive in any way, but why wouldn't you have used your celestial insights to enrich yourself?"

"The reason for that is my life's 'storm before the calm.' I once had a partner in a brokerage firm. He duped me and our clients. He made off with the money and left me with the debts, fines, loss of license, and the humiliations. I wanted to repay everyone, but I couldn't because I couldn't work. I prayed nightly for answers. I never got any answers from traditional religion. One night I dreamed that I should consult my horoscope. It said I would find answers in the Zodiac. I had a newspaper and for the first time in my life I read my horoscope. It said, 'Look to the stars when trying to help others.' I didn't understand astrology, but I was desperate. And so I studied. The next thing I knew, people were coming to me for advice. It took me ten years, but I repaid everyone."

"Did you ever give Madeleine advice about her health?"

"The stars control our health, naturally. She asked me about everything: life and the way the heavens influence our lives, including matters of health. We also discussed Planets, Signs, Houses, Aspects. I merely interpret, compute, and convey. The science of astrological prediction is difficult to comprehend."

"I noticed on her horoscope you had predictions for her up to September. She died in May."

"Hah!!" he shouted. "No one considers the value of negative advice. If I tell you the stars warn against travel in December and you heed that advice and spend a quiet month at home, you don't say, 'Thank God I didn't go to Key West.' But if you do go ahead and are involved in a boating accident, then, *then* you say, 'I should have listened to Moor.' Well, she should have heeded my warnings!"

"What did you warn her against?"

His entire demeanor changed. He stiffened with anger. "To beware of Scorpions!"

"What does a Scorpion have to do with her health?"

"There is a Scorpio in Dr. Euell's office. Go find that Scorpio and you'll find the person who pushed Madeleine off the Path of Faith!"

Beryl rolled her eyes. "Does the Scorpio have a name?"

"Isabel McAndrew, that slanderous witch of a nurse! She used to come to me. I even gave her a discount. I gave her good advice about where to invest her nest egg. She didn't heed my advice and the stock took off. So she resented me and slandered me. I've lost valuable clients because she steered them to someone else, some mysterious guru. She exaggerates his accomplishments just as she denigrates mine. I have a master's degree in economics and he is a voodoo shaman! Now, if there is nothing else, I must prepare for my next client."

Once again Beryl called the chauffeur and returned to the Eckersley's Rittenhouse Square brownstone. Lunch would be served outdoors, in the back yard which Alicia called their "urban patio."

Alicia laughed about Moor's purple caftan and his master's degree. "Lionel had his credentials investigated. He didn't get past his first year at Temple University. During his summer vacation he was arrested for trying to sell artifacts he had stolen from several private collectors. He had seriously injured a security guard during his last burglary attempt and spent his next nine years in prison. He studied economics and astrology in prison."

"So how did he develop his technique?" Beryl asked. "Practicing on the other inmates?"

"Yes," she laughed. "And from what Lionel heard, many of the tips he gave to the prisoners that they passed on to their families let them get out of jail as rich men. They wanted to continue to get his advice when he was paroled, but the terms of his parole forbade contact with them or their agents. He made a few investments for himself that, as they say, tanked." She lowered her voice as though she were speaking to a fellow conspirator. "That's what they call a stock that fails. They say, 'It tanked.' And I'm sure he didn't need the stars to tell him that he did better in advising others than in making choices for himself. On balance, I've come out ahead by following his advice. It's not as good as my cook's method of closing her eyes and sticking a pin in the stock pages of the newspaper, but it is more sociable. What is there to talk about with pin-sticking? There are no details!"

"Why does he hate Dr. Euell's nurse?"

Lionel broke in. "Because when she heard the society women talking about him, she wanted to share the experience, but he was out of her league financially. They could afford to laugh about those 'details,' but she couldn't afford Moor's fees. He gets a retainer! Can you imagine that? Like an attorney? Aubrey Euell told me. His wife is a client. Can you imagine an intelligent woman keeping an astrologer on retainer?"

Alicia interrupted him. "Don't start, Lionel. Why must you always--"

Groff put an end to the discussion. "Let's not start a war." He turned to Beryl. "What else did you learn from Euell and Moor?"

"He said your mother was definitely not pregnant. She bled to death and no doubt her distended abdomen and the vaginal bleeding might have made some uninformed people think she had a miscarriage. She had a cervical cell test - a Pap test - in December, and the lab wanted to retest her. He says his office notified her three times to come in for retesting, but she never did. He claims that your grandmother," she nodded to Alicia. "told him that Madeleine told her that she had another doctor. He therefore ceased pressing her. More importantly, there is a new source of gossip in town... somebody who has more magic than the stars, an Indian of some kind."

Groff's eyes widened as he stared at her.

"I also heard that your mother's ashes are in the Eckersley Mausoleum," she said.

Groff looked at Beryl as though she had just slapped his face. Lionel saw his expression and said, "I'll take you there at any time. Just tell me when you're ready."

Beryl quickly changed the subject back to the Indian. "I understand that someone named Carly goes to him... and someone else named Eleanor Teasdale possibly goes, too. Did Madeleine ever mention an Indian doctor?"

Lionel asked, "A doctor from India... or a doctor who was an American Indian?"

"I asked that, too. Nobody knew which one he is."

Alicia said, "I went to school with Eleanor Teasdale's mother. She'll tell me everything she knows. The poor woman loves to gossip."

Groff said, "What about my mother? Did she ever mention seeing an Indian shaman or medicine man of any kind?"

"Not to us," Alicia said. "But then Madeleine could be rather secretive."

Beryl changed the topic. "There's something I'd like to know. I'm interested in Madeleine's Christmas 2008 activities. What happened with Groff and the girl in Ireland, and Madeleine's decision to let Mr. Eckersley go there to resolve the problems? What was that all about? I really do need details."

"You could have asked me when we were alone." Groff was irritated.

"I'm asking now because your grandfather knows more about it than you may know, at least about certain aspects of it."

Groff tried to act in a casual manner. He put his hands behind his head and tilted his chair back. "What aspects? It's not that complicated. I was grieving over the death of my good friend and mentor. My mom tried to cheer me up. Her relatives invited us to go pyramid-traipsing before Christmas. When the Michaelmas term ended I met my mom in Cairo. My mom's relatives are on the conservative side, so she asked me to cut my hair. I refused. There were several fancy dress balls and at one of them I met an Irish girl named Meghan. I dated her, leaving Momma to entertain her relatives. I had Meghan up in our suite a few times and during one of those times when my mom was there and she insisted again that I get my hair cut, I demonstrated my hair-torture trick. I would get my mom down on the bed or the floor and sort of sit on her and flip my long hair over my head and let it hang down and tickle her face with it. Meghan took pictures with her cellphone. We were all laughing.

"On the day we were scheduled to fly back to Zurich, my mother stopped at the hotel desk to get her jewelry box out of the safe. She brought it up to our suite. I saw the diamonds, myself. Meghan was with me. She saw them, too. My mother went down to the gift shop for something and while she was gone I stupidly went to the bathroom. I was in there less than thirty seconds when Meghan yelled that she forgot that she had a hairdresser's appointment and would try to get back before we left for the airport.

"My mother came back to the room and we finished getting ready to leave and then she saw that a necklace, bracelet, and ring were gone. I tried to reach Meghan, but she had checked out. Momma hired an Egyptian detective who traced her flight to Dublin and also got her true home address. I felt responsible so I flew to Dublin. My mom flew home to the States. I broke into Meghan's apartment and found the necklace and bracelet. I put each piece in a bubble envelope and mailed it to my mom, regular mail, no insurance.. as just a regular piece of mail among all the Christmas gift boxes. I went back to Meghan's apartment and waited. When she came home she was wearing the ring, which I pulled off her finger and forced onto mine. As I started to leave she laughed and showed me the photographs. She was getting ready to blackmail my mom and me!

"The pictures showed me on top of my mother with me getting ready to do that hair thing. I only glanced at them but they appeared to me to be photoshopped. It looked like we were in what is politely called 'a compromising position.' She said that if I didn't give her back the ring, she'd make them public, blah blah. She didn't know that I already had the other pieces. I said, 'You ain't getting this ring, you thief.' Then a couple of her 'brothers' beat the shit out of me. They couldn't get the ring off my finger because it had gotten swollen during the fight. Neighbors came to the door or they might have cut my finger off. Meghan claimed I had attacked her and I was blamed for starting the fight - which I found out when I regained consciousness. The doctors got the ring off and gave it to me. I wrapped it in cotton and bubble wrap and put it in a manila envelope and mailed it right from the hospital to my mother at The Hollyoak. In a note I said that the fight to get the ring back put me in the hospital and that technically I was under arrest. I printed, 'Send help!'"

Lionel looked confused. "She told me that you were in the hospital as a result of a fistfight and needed legal help. I immediately went to Ireland. But she never mentioned the stolen jewelry. She was wearing the ring."

Alicia broke in. "Dalton bought her that ring."

Lionel shook his head. "I was interested only in the case against you," he said to Groff. "I had an old friend intervene with the authorities. He explained the circumstances of your mental health. They verified your address at the hospital in Zurich and were willing to dismiss the criminal charges, but the girl claimed that you had hurt her during the fight and she wanted to be compensated. I interviewed Meghan. Her story was that you had given her an engagement ring and the two of you were to be married. Someone sent her indecent photographs of you and your mother. She was so shocked that she immediately returned to Ireland, broken-hearted. She showed me the photographs. I could sympathize with the girl."

Groff glared at his grandfather. "And here, all this time, I thought you were a man without pity."

Lionel did not respond. Alicia asked if anyone wanted more tea and when no one did, Beryl asked the old lawyer to continue the story. He directed his remarks to Groff. "You weren't coherent. This Meghan... she hadn't attempted to contact you, so there was no attempt to extort money from you. You pursued her from Cairo. Your mother wasn't there. She wasn't likely to mention the stolen jewelry to me. I didn't know what to think. Meghan insisted that you claimed that she had stolen your mother's ring to cover your attempts to obtain the obscene photographs from her. To show her innocence in the matter, she was happy to let you keep the ring. Incidentally, her emotional distress was very expensive. I wanted to get you out of there as quickly as possible."

Groff said, "I didn't know you saw and believed the fake photos."

Alicia gasped. "Nobody told me anything!"

Beryl was astonished. "You are the single most uncommunicative family on the planet."

Lionel laughed nervously. "Strange, isn't it? Especially for a family of lawyers and gossipers."

Groff pushed his chair back, stood up and turned his back to the table. A sadness came over him and he began staring into an empty sky as if he were searching for answers. "I need to take a long autumn drive down country roads," he said. "I'd walk, but I'm not rich enough to be alone on foot, especially not on country roads."

The remark was cryptic. Lionel asked, "What does that mean?"

Groff slowly replied, "It's about a haiku verse I read in a Zen book last night. An impoverished Zen monk named Issa suffered many hardships but he still found a wealth of beauty everywhere he looked as he walked from place to place. He wrote his last will and testament in a haiku: *I here bequeathe in perpetuity, to wit: to this bird, this fence.*"

Beryl stood up and saw that tears had lined Groff's cheeks. She put her hand on his arm. "Let's go," she said. "I have to get back to my office."

Hurrying to get there before closing, George and Sensei took Groff to the Department of Motor Vehicles to get his driver's license. George called Lionel Eckersley. The Jaguar was registered in Groff's name and was fully insured. They could pick it up at The Hollyoak at any time. They drove directly to the garage.

"Do you want to go back to the temple?" Sensei asked Groff. "If so, I'll ride with you."

Groff looked relieved and grateful. "Sure. Thanks." George followed in his pickup.

Beryl, exhausted from the non-stop events of the day, made tea, kicked off her shoes, and sat in a recliner she kept in her bedroom/office. She intended to get to bed early.

At eight o'clock, Alicia Eckersley called to say that she had gotten through to the Guru. "I've made an appointment for you on Tuesday morning and I'll see to it that you get the thousand-dollar 'retainer' donation and another thousand in case you need extra advice."

"Whoa! That was fast."

"I promised Eleanor that Lionel would give her son a recommendation to be Judge Rankin's law clerk.

"I bet Lionel loved that!"

"Lionel is the one who suggested it! The trouble, Eleanor had told her mother, was in getting the appointment. So I called and introduced myself to the fellow who answered the phone. I said I was Madeleine Eckersley's mother-in-law. I didn't even know if he knew who Madeleine was, but I promised Eleanor's mother I would not mention Eleanor's name. I needed an 'in' and figured if he didn't know who Madeleine was, we were barking up the wrong Guru. I said I didn't wish to discuss anything over the phone but he could call me back if he wished. I gave him my number and told him that I wanted an appointment for my niece, Laura Orsini. I said she was rich and naive, but her love life was a quagmire. She needed advice... that is to say, you need advice because you're Laura Orsini."

"I'll try to do the family proud," Beryl said. "So how do I get there?"

"He's going to call me back with the particulars."

Alicia called an hour later. "The fellow who worked for 'Master' confirmed the 10 o'clock Tuesday appointment and gave me directions to "the temple" - which used to be a residence called *Haddon Manor*. Monday, he reminded me, was Columbus Day and was therefore 'out of the question.' Maybe they're Italians. He also specified that on no account should I call their number Friday evening through to Monday night. Ordinarily, he explained, the 'no-phone zone' would extend from Friday evening through Sunday night. And aside from my niece Laura, no one was to be told about the appointment."

Alicia remembered the old Haddon estate. "It's an old house in Montgomery County. It lost its value when a new interstate highway chopped off a big part of its land and most of the access to it. The only way in, according to the master's assistant, is to go out Highway 15 past Green Lawn Memorial Park to Elmport Road and make a right, then go down Elmport for about a mile - you'll pass a Shell station - and then you'll see an arrow sign that indicates Haddon Manor's private road. Take that road and drive straight back to the house and make a sharp turn onto the driveway." She hoped she got the directions right.

"Orsini is Madeleine's mother's name. How am I related to you?" Beryl asked.

"Laura, my dear, Madeleine is a distant relative of yours, a second cousin, I think. Your second cousin married my son, Dalton. Now, as an Orsini, you'll need to drive up in a fashionable car. Take the Jaguar. You can say you're using it while you're in town. And I want Groff to take my credit cards and get you some suitable clothing, something appropriate."

"I'll get something nice."

"Get shoes and bag and anything else you need. A suit would be best. Another thing, do not use a cell phone or any traceable instrument when calling them. The assistant emphasized this."

"Got it. But what is my problem?"

"You can make up a story about a fiance who suddenly died or," she paused to say something in her own Alicia Eckersley way, "whatever tragedy you're comfortable with." She paused again. "Come here for brunch tomorrow and I'll see to it you get the credit cards and money you need. Oh! You are to call the fee 'a cash donation' for his religious organization."

Beryl said that she understood.

"What's the latest?" Groff asked.

Beryl told him about the meeting with Madeleine's guru and the brunch with his grandmother and the shopping spree. "I'm to take your Jaguar Tuesday when I go."

"I'm coming with you."

"No you're not. If you bring it up again, I'll drop the case. Go watch TV in Jack's room. I want to get ready for bed. I'll see you in the morning."

She went into the bathroom and stepped into the shower. While her hair was full of shampoo and her eyes were closed, the shower door opened and Groff slid in beside her.

"I'm here to wash your back," he said. "And there isn't enough space for you to use any Ka-ra-te moves on me. As payment for your cooperation, you can wash my hair."

"Get out! Get out now!"

"No," he said simply. He put a bottle of shampoo in her hand. "You do have cream rinse?" he said as he pushed his head under the shower head.

She wiped her eyes and pushed him away from the stream of water so that she could finish her own hair. Then she took a deep breath. She shampooed his hair, rinsed it, applied cream rinse, and while he applied body wash to his own body and sang *Volaré* in Italian, she opened the shower stall. "Don't ever do this again," she hissed at him as she closed the door.

As she dried off and listened to him sing, she could not stop smiling. It really was impossible to stay mad at him.

SATURDAY, OCTOBER 10, 2009

With Groff making all the selections, they bought a navy blue cashmere suit, a shoulder bag, shoes, and a blouse. When they returned to Rittenhouse Square, Alicia gave Beryl some jewelry to wear: a gold circular brooch for the suit, a gold bracelet and signet ring.

"I hope I don't have to make a return trip," Beryl joked.

"Ultimately," said Groff, "you're spending my money... so you can go back as often as you like."

"Oh," said Alicia seriously, "he intends that you be a 'kept' detective. I don't know if I approve of that."

Beryl sighed. "Your grandson belongs in a maximum security facility."

They talked about family relationships and why "Laura Orsini" was in town. It was necessary to get their stories straight.

Groff opened a bag and handed Beryl a gift: a small bottle of Chanel No. 5. He whispered in her ear, "I want you to smell good for the wine-guzzler."

Beryl looked at her watch. It was two o'clock. The Aztec expert was going to be available for consultation at three. She had hoped that by Saturday the need for more insight into the presence of the pieces in Madeleine's bedroom would have diminished. It had not. In fact, it had intensified. She gathered her purse and packages and made the obligatory remarks of appreciation and regret. It was time, she said, for her to return home. Groff said simply, "Let me come with you. I don't want to go back to the big house."

She sighed. "Then make yourself useful and carry some of these things."

She piled the packages on the kitchen table and asked Groff to go back to Jack's room to watch television while she made a few phone calls. He went without question, and she called the number Dr. Vasquez had given her.

Arturo Rosales poured himself a cup of coffee and sat down to "chat about the Aztec pantheon." Doctor Vasquez had shown him the photographs Beryl had taken.

"I'm interested only in the small statue of the god Xipe Totec," she said. "What was he the god of? I mean in the sense that Athena was the goddess of wisdom and Vulcan was the god of the forge. The books say, 'renewal,' like spring, but that's so broad it tells us nothing."

"At the outset, let me correct you. This piece does not depict a god, but rather a priest of the god, who is conducting a ritual. And Xipe was an aspect of an "uber-god" so to speak, the great god Tezcatlipoca, the god of the obsidian mirror in which one's sins could be seen. Xipe Totec was the great god's 'agriculture and war' aspect. There were, of course, other gods of war and agriculture."

Obsidian and mirrored sins were already pieces of the puzzle. "For what specific reason would a person venerate an image of a priest conducting one of Xipe's rituals?"

"You mean, in pre-Columbian times?"

"No, in any time. I have a client whose mother kept a statue of Xipe Totec's priest in her bedroom. I need to know what it could possibly have meant to her."

"In modern times, tourists often buy copies of pre-columbian artworks. Perhaps they display them; but it wouldn't be, for example, with the same intention that they'd display the statue of a Christian saint."

"Why wouldn't it be?" she asked innocuously.

"Well, let me restate that. It's unlikely that a Christian would violate the restrictions placed upon his acceptance of Christianity's creed by worshipping an alien god. That's the first Commandment."

"Let's say that the person does not subscribe to another creed. Why then would he or she venerate a statue of Xipe Totec's priest?"

Rosales laughed pleasantly. "I'm trying to visualize this. Let's say we're in a remote area of Mexico and we find a little village and in several huts in that village there are statues like this one. This doesn't mean that people actually worship the god. Worship involves ritual, participation, a liturgy. In one of the rites of this particular god, a human being's skin is worn. No matter how remote that village is, the people are not likely to gain access to somebody's flayed skin."

"How did they gain access to the skin six hundred years ago?"

Again he laughed good-naturedly. "That depended on whether wearing the skin was a sacred ritual or just a spectacle of sorts. Solemn human sacrifice was not the spectacle of gladiators in the Coliseum. People tend to regard the Aztec's sacrifice of a line of captives as though it were a spiritual event, a high-Mass kind of religious observance. That's absurd. The Coliseum was not a church. And no matter how drenched with blood the temple steps became, there was nothing spiritual about it.

"Gladiators fought to the death. Let's compare their combat to a Mayan ball game. When it was merely a spectacle of sport, the losing captain would often be killed. That would be akin to a gladiatorial contest. In Xipe Totec's case, nearly all of the skins that were worn were those of the casualties of war. An ordinary person would put one on in a kind of 'boogie-man' thing. Forget these. And forget the gladiators.

"The effigy of a priest wearing a flayed skin speaks to a solemn ritual. When the Mayan ball game was played on a special religious occasion, the captain of the winning team would be sacrificed. When you truly believe that by shedding your blood the whole nation will be saved, then great honor is accorded your heroism. The icon that your client's mother had would not be of some gladiatorial secular offering. The priest would be wearing the skin of someone who gave his life for love of others, so that the crops would grow and people would be safe from invasion. He would receive great honor."

The talk of a voluntary "loving" sacrifice and all the blood in Madeleine's bed had a disquieting effect on Beryl. She felt a ripple of fear disturbing what had been the calm surface of an academic discussion. "I get it," she said although she did not get it at all. "But surely, not all the sacrificial victims were volunteers. If, on a certain date when a ritual was scheduled, nobody volunteered, would the selected person receive the honors even though he went kicking and screaming to his 'great reward'?"

"That's like asking whether a guy who is drafted into the army is automatically excluded from receiving any medals for his bravery or other military service.

"When people thoroughly believe in something, they will sacrifice their lives for it. Belief trumps just about everything else in human experience. Christian missionaries attempted to thwart people's belief in the tree-god by chopping down the tree. But hundreds of years later, we still knock on wood."

"What did they believe in when it came to this god?" she asked. "I still don't have a clue."

"Xipe Totec was a particularly important god. The image is growth: gain without loss. Agriculture and War. In a civilization that has no refrigeration or transportation, you ate what you grew on your land. If your crops failed, you starved. A man does not lie around and do nothing while his children starve to death. If there is no other way, he'll attack a man who has food and take it. On the other hand, when he is the one who has food, he needs to be able to fight to keep it from being stolen. It's true in love also. You are blessed with finding a lover, but you often have to struggle to maintain that love, to keep yourself worthy and to keep an intruder from stealing the loved one."

"I'm sorry. I just don't get it. The effigy is so grotesque for such benign purposes. There were so many of these little statues produced. The internet is filled with examples. They must have been household items. There were corn gods and war gods and love gods. Why this image? Why today, here, in a lady's bedroom?"

Rosales sighed. "The messages associated with the god are timeless. All right. I do know people who find consolation in these old gods. They don't advertise it, but they are serious believers. I knew a very old lady who lived in a remote part of Mexico, Copper Canyon, to be specific. The kids in my family would spend summers in the house she lived in. She had a statue of Xipe. If we made fun of somebody because of how he looked or how he was dressed, she'd point to the statue and ask, 'Which is the man and which is the skin, the wrapping?' Then she'd threaten us. 'Xipe is watching you and if your soul is so lazy that it won't look for the true man who is underneath the surface of the man that you're mocking, Xipe will come in the night and turn you into pulque.' That's an alcoholic drink. 'And then he'll swallow you.' When we'd tell our parents what she had said, they'd say, 'She speaks an old language of the inditas.' That's what they called indigenous people. Inditas. We were supposed to believe that she was trying to say Jesus but in her Indian language it sounded like Xipe. Maybe that's why she used different names to refer to him. Most of the time she called him 'Youalahuan,' The Night Drinker.'"

Beryl's jaw dropped. "Ah, The Night Drinker. That's interesting. And the lesson was told in a charming way. I agree. I've not heard it put that way in any Christian story."

"Yes, it is. And the goddess associated with him is Xilonen-Chicomecoatl. A corn goddess with seven snakes. Here, again, you see the gain and retain motif. Remove the husk, retain the corn cob. Remove the snake-skin, retain the bigger snake.

"But getting back to Xipe, when somebody died, for example, a woman's husband, the old lady would say, 'The skin on Xipe is like the widow's weeds, the veil of sorrow. You see that skin now and it looks fresh and strong. But in a little time, that skin will decay and fall away. If that woman believes that everything that she can see wears out and changes, she'll understand that her grief will also wear out and fall away. And maybe she'll learn that the only thing that has value is the one thing she cannot see, the spirit inside, the soul.'"

"Really," Beryl said sincerely, "that's a nice way to teach a universal truth. Wasn't the skin regarded in any grizzly way?"

"The skin seems universally to be a billboard of sorts. Tattoos and scarification. And when something is 'under your skin' it has passed the point of being superficially considered. It has great power once it gets under the skin. It takes on a spiritual quality. And the grizzly aspect fades. Years ago it was common to see a person carry the foot of a rabbit in his pocket for good luck. But nowadays you don't find anyone walking around with an animal's foot in his pocket. You will find in a prosperous man's den stuffed skins of trophy animals hanging on the wall. Fur coats for glamour are now passé, but we still routinely wear the skins of animals... leather coats... shoes. The people didn't wear human skin as a garment, but they did wear it as some special victory statement, like a human head on a pike, a triumph over starvation or an enemy's intrusion."

"I read that he was also the god of gold."

"Yes. Gold is special in the material world. It has that immutable quality. Gold is like the eternal spirit that forever renews itself. Gold doesn't change though it can be shaped in myriad ways."

"Your guess, then, as to why she had such an effigy?"

"The reminder to see beneath surfaces; the realization that in our material world all things change; that the spirit is golden no matter how it is shaped; that spring will follow winter; and that when you have been given a blessing, you need to preserve it."

Beryl thanked him. "Someday we may shed our complicated philosophies and return to the basics, the simple life, the life worth living."

"Save a place for me," he said.

She called Groff Eckersley. "Listen up, Grasshopper. I found out more about that funny Aztec statue."

Half-way through the account of her conversation he said he didn't want to hear more. He found nothing charming in the teaching lessons. Beryl supposed that he did not want to hear anything good about the man who came in the night.

SUNDAY, OCTOBER 11, 2009

Sunday morning, as they ate breakfast in Beryl's kitchen, she asked Groff if he could think of a good way to get fingerprints from "the wine guzzler." "We don't know how many people we're dealing with. I want to be sure we get the correct one. Give me some ideas," she said. "What can I use?"

Groff thought for a moment. "In my mom's bedside table is a box of rare domino tiles. They're ivory and onyx. When Teresa cleaned the room after my mother died, she washed them. My mom loved to play dominoes. Chances are she played with him. So why don't you take one of them and hand it to him as an indication that you are for real. He'll take it and leave his prints on it."

It was a good idea. "And naturally he'll return it to me since it belongs to a valuable set. Let's take a ride out there to get it." She went to the sink and began to wash the breakfast dishes.

Groff went into Jack's bedroom and came out with a bag of dirty clothing. "Do you want the Trasks to launder the stuff of Jack's I've been wearing?"

"No. Leave it in there. I'll do it."

"I trust you're not the kind of laundress who examines soiled briefs for signs of... unusual wear."

She looked heavenward and laughed. "Lord," she whispered. "What else will I be required to do?"

"You haven't begun to exhaust the list of your duties," Groff said, pushing her toward the kitchen door.

She hesitated, and for a moment she considered warning him about the risks inherent in saying something in jest. Although she knew he was not serious and could therefore regard his teasing lines as funny, other people were all too eager to quote his words *verbatim* - but devoid of their charm.

Then, just as quickly as she had thought about warning him, she decided against inhibiting his manner of speaking. No doubt he had survived emotionally because he was able to create humor out of miserable situations. "Please submit the list to my office," she said to him as she started down the stairs.

"Ok," he answered. "I'll tell George you suggested that he keep it in the bathroom... along with other inspirational material."

MONDAY, OCTOBER 12, 2009

While Beryl spent the Columbus Day holiday paying "holiday rates" to the hairdresser to get her hair colored and styled and her nails manicured, George, Sensei, and Groff washed and waxed the Jaguar.

Groff, everyone was relieved to see, required no instruction in operating the car. He did not, however know his way around Philadelphia's streets, especially in the old colonial neighborhoods. And he was not the best parallel parker.

"Nobody can teach you how to do that," George confided. "It is one of those things that must be learned by practice."

Since the stores were open, Sensei and George took Groff to buy jeans, shirts, underwear, and a variety of toiletries, which he brought back to the Temple.

Groff would be staying with Sensei on Monday night.

TUESDAY, OCTOBER 13, 2009

At 9 a.m., Beryl, made up and dressed in what Groff called "Republican Chic," walked to the Zen Temple and for a few minutes sat with Sensei in the downstairs utility kitchen. He gave her the Jaguar's key and the proofs of registration and insurance.

She did not see Groff until she was adjusting the car seat. He stood at the top of the back stairs and smiled, making a thumb's-up sign which he then turned into a finger-gun that he fired at her. She laughed, waved, and started the engine. She did not bring her gun. She had only her mostly empty new purse and a domino in her jacket's breast pocket.

George followed the Jaguar in his pickup truck.

When they reached the Shell station, George parked as Beryl turned off and continued to follow the route for another half mile until Haddon Manor came in sight.

From a distance the house looked stately and well-kept, but as the distance shortened, the more obvious the signs of decay became. The paint on the woodwork and the portico's columns was peeling. The curtains in the upper storeys were tattered. The windows in the first floor seemed to have been covered with tar paper. The landscaping had reverted to weeds.

At the front door, she saw that the old door knocker had been removed, and on the wall an electric door bell had recently been installed. She rang the bell. A moment later the door was opened by a dwarf in a Mexican white farmer's shirt and pants and a little red poncho. "Come in! Come in! Miss Orsini! I'm Pablito, Master's assistant." He did not speak with a Spanish accent.

"So nice to meet you, Pablito. You, I imagine, are the very kind person my aunt spoke to on the phone last Friday," Beryl said sweetly.

"Sí, sí. I'm the one who spoke to her. She made the appointment for you. Come in and sit down. The Master is still performing his ablutions. I'm afraid you'll have to wait, but I will do my best to make you comfortable." He gestured toward a pair of sliding doors at the side of the foyer. As he spread them open, Beryl could see the interior of a dark room lit by a single candle that stood on a small table in front of a sofa. Beside the candle were a silver samovar and a porcelain cup and saucer.

Pablito indicated that she should sit down. As she did, he tilted the samovar and poured a cup of herbal tea for her. As Beryl's eyes grew accustomed to the darkness, she could see that shiny draperies - possibly a brown silk shantung - covered the tar paper on the windows. Pablito said, "The ceremony requires that you consume this tea. Also, Senorita, the donation, if you please."

"Here it is," Beryl said, reaching into her purse and extracting an envelope that contained ten one-hundred dollar bills.

Saying "Gracias," Pablito accepted the envelope. Now I will teach you the words that you must say each time you take a sip. You must whisper aloud, 'With each sip I drink the cleansing love of God.' When you are finished your tea, the ceremony can begin."

He retreated to the sliding doors. "I'll look in on you in a few minutes," he said.

At first, Beryl made no attempt to drink the tea. Then she noticed that a mirror had been built into the room's rear wall. She supposed that she was being watched. She picked up the cup and sipped the strangely bitter tea. Staying in character, she continued to take small sips of what she was certain was drugged tea. Pablito re-appeared. "I'm happy to see that you enjoy our special brew."

"Wonderful," she cooed.

She repeated, "With each sip I drink the cleansing love of God," and took a large swallow.

"Yes," said Pablito. "That's it exactly." This time, as he slid open the doors, a woman of his same size entered. "This lady," said Pablito, "is my wife, Doña Maria. She will entertain you." Dressed in a *huipil* and long flounced skirt, Doña Maria pushed a tea cart, lit by a single candle, to a corner of the room where a large kettle drum was standing.

Her cart was filled with bowls and small musical instruments. She spread a cloth on the floor and positioned the candle at the side of it. One by one she placed the various instruments in a wide circle. The light flickered strangely, creating auras around the woman and the instruments. Beryl could tell that the tea was affecting her. She saw translucent bowls and what looked like a silver systrum. And there were chimes and gongs and a kind of drum. Then she noticed that straps hung from the ceiling. On the straps were bells, like the bells on a sleigh... silver bells of different sizes. In one hand the woman held a flute on which she played a single note, and in the other, a gourd rattle which she rhythmically shook. Beryl wondered how one person could possibly play all those instruments; and then she saw the woman reach toward a CD player and press the "play" lever. Immediately a haunting flute melody filled the room.

The woman now picked up a rasp and played it, keeping the beat of the slow and plaintive flute. Beryl said, "With each sip I drink the cleansing love of God," and took another large sip.

She could see the woman's bare foot slide out from under her skirt. The sleigh-bell strap ended in a loop, and she slipped her foot through the loop and began to tug on it rhythmically. As the bells jingled, her hands began to circle the rims of the largest bowls, creating the deep hum of harmonic motion that reverberated around the room. The sound of two dissonant notes continued on without stopping. Doña Maria picked up a gourd and began to shake it.

"With each sip I drink the cleansing love of God," Beryl said again, drinking more of the tea.

The recorded music continued to play its accompaniment to Dona Maria's shaking gourd, and while the low sounds of the large bowls echoed throughout the room, she began to rub the rim of a smaller bowl, letting a new penetrating hum join the music and the reverberations.

Soon Beryl heard the systrum tinkle rhythmically. Then she heard chimes, sounding like glass wind bells, mingle with the systrum. She repeated the mantra and drank more tea, finishing the cup.

The doors opened. Pablito came in, swinging a censer which contained charcoal briquettes that had been impregnated with gunpowder. He stopped at Doña Maria's table and put a spoonful of powdered incense on the burning briquettes. Tiny sparks leapt through the smoke as the scent of sandalwood filled the air.

The bells, she noticed, were getting louder, and the rasp seemed to tantalize the drum. The music grew bolder, deeper in tone, its commanding rhythm vibrating with a tactile effect. Under all came the deep hum of the translucent bowls. The sounds grew louder, becoming almost unbearable, until the cacophony ended with the heart-stopping peals of the kettle drum.

The sounds slowly faded, and then a gong signaled an end. Pablito said, "The master is ready." He raised a lit candle and said, "Please follow me."

Beryl followed him into the foyer and saw that two lines of tiny lights marked the pathway down a hall that led towards the rear of the house.

They entered a room and immediately a tiny, tinkling chime teased the air. The room was filled with the smell of copal incense. Pablito pointed to a velvet covered *prie dieu* that was placed before a high altar. "You are the supplicant," he said, "therefore you must go to the *prie dieu* and kneel. The High Priest of the God Tezcatlipoca will be with you shortly." He bowed and went behind the altar. He climbed a few steps, and dipped his candle into a wide but shallow bowl of alcohol. As the blue flames lapped the edges of the bowl, he descended the steps and left the room by a rear door, gently closing it as he left.

Beryl went slowly toward the *prie dieu* and knelt down, resting her arms upon the upper cushion. The bells grew louder, their pitch deeper, their cadence more urgent. More instruments joined their sounds to those of the bells. The harmonic vibrations began to resonate more forcefully. The room, without Pablito's candle, was darker. The alcohol flames were evanescent, like the dancing lights of the aurora borealis.

Beryl noticed that the bowl was slowly being pushed toward the edge of the altar closest to her.

As she watched the bowl and listened to the bells, she noticed a strange fluttering of something rising from behind the altar. Soon she could distinguish the plumes of a white peacock's spectacular tail.

The rippling chimes, bells, and drum throbbed with increasing intensity as the tips of the white plumes rose higher and higher, forming a graceful arch of feathers that framed a golden eye-mask. The arch continued to rise and expand until the god-priest's face and neck appeared. And then, adorned only with obsidian and jade jewelry, his muscular shoulders, arms and chest rose until his upper body was completely visible. Then, in a gentle baritone, the god-priest spoke: "Tell me, beloved, what is troubling your heart?"

Beryl took a deep breath and was suddenly sober enough to say, "Whoa! Dude! Whoa!" Her response was not what the god-priest expected. His mouth opened.

Beryl shook her head, trying to free herself from the giddy high of the hallucinogenic tea. She felt warm both in temperature and in a slightly erotic way. In the midst of all this she thought about the effect any sweat would have on her cashmere suit.

"Jesus!" she said, "Let - me - get - a - grip!" She couldn't rub her eyes because she was wearing mascara. This frustrated her. She violently rubbed her hands together and stood up, stamping her feet. "God damn!" she said stupidly. "Wow! No wonder Madeleine was bowled over. This ain't no cheap con, Dude! This is first-rate!" Her words seemed to stretch out and drag in the air.

"What are you talking about?" asked Tezcatlipoca's priest. His voice had a distant quality to it, as if the echo were heard, but not the original sound. The vision and the voice fascinated her. She looked around marveling at everything. And then she remembered the domino.

Holding onto the altar's edge, she reached into her breast pocket and pulled out the ivory domino by its edges and slid it across the altar towards him.

He picked it up and asked, "Where did you get this?"

Beryl detected fear in his voice. She answered, "From Madeleine's bedside table."

"*Where is she?*" he demanded.

She decided that she didn't know how to answer. She put her hand out for him to return the domino. He placed it in her hand and she carefully dropped it into her pocket. She took a deep breath and exhaled.

"*Where is Madeleine?*" he repeated.

"Madeleine is believed to be dead," she said simply. "I'm investigating."

"Dead? What do you mean, 'Madeleine is believed to be dead'?" He pulled off his mask and headdress and tossed them on the altar. "Pablito!" he shouted. "Make some coffee! Sober her up!"

A door behind him opened and Pablito appeared. "I just made a fresh pot!" he said indignantly.

The god-priest reached down and picked up crutches. Gruffly he said to Beryl, "Come around back here! You need some coffee." Again he shouted, "Open the kitchen door and let some air in here!" He hoisted himself onto the crutches and swung himself into the kitchen ahead of her. He went to a table in the middle of the room, dropped into a chair, and motioned for her to sit opposite him.

Panting as he spoke, he asked, "What do you mean, 'Madeleine is dead'?" Then he pulled a paper napkin from a dispenser and began to bite it.

Beryl looked around the room. On a shelf she saw an effigy of Xipe Totec's priest that was identical to the one Madeleine had in her bedroom. A votive candle was on one side of it and a vase of fresh roses was on the other. There was a small 'food offering' dish in front of the statue. In Zen temples a similar dish was placed before an icon of the Buddha or a bodhisattva to hold a tiny sample of the meal, offered as a sacrifice. This one contained what appeared to be an oxidized piece of apple. "You kept one of these in Madeleine's bedroom," she said. "But there wasn't any food offering dish."

"Where is Madeleine!" he shouted. "Sit down here! What do you mean, 'Madeleine is dead.'?"

Beryl sat at the table. "Well… Groff's not sure she's dead, but everybody else is. Her death certificate says that she had cervical cancer. She bled to death at home in bed. Just before Memorial Day which fell on May 25th this year. She died May 22nd." Her attention was drawn to a wine bottle that sat at the table's center. It had been used as a candle holder, and tallow from different colored candles had dripped down, nearly covering the label. She could still read that the wine it once contained was Cabernet Sauvignon from the Argentine. She began to pick at the hardened tallow drippings. "Friday night."

All of the man's muscles became flaccid, incapable of supporting him. He leaned over the table until his face nearly touched it. "I had a feeling. I knew it," he whispered. "I knew something was wrong. She got tired too easily. She had pains. Infections."

"Tell me about them," Beryl said, trying to sound normal.

"In Emmaus we were shopping for groceries. She got those pains. I wanted to take her to the hospital. She wouldn't go. The cashier said there was a doctor around the corner. He had office hours. I made her see him. Oh, my God. She can't be dead. No…. not this. She can't be dead." He began to sob in great gulping spasms.

Beryl blinked and continued to try to act normal. "What did the doctor say?"

When he stopped convulsing in sobs, he no longer could connect her question to anything he had said. "What? What did you ask?"

"What did the doctor say when you took her to him… in Emmaus?"

"He said he thought she could be pregnant in her tube. He told me it could be fatal. He said I should take her to the emergency room in a hospital in Allentown. She said I should know she wasn't pregnant and she would see a doctor down here. But something was wrong. I begged her to go."

"Did she say why she wouldn't see a doctor up there?"

Pablito served Beryl a cup of coffee. "Drink this," he said. "It'll clear your head." She put her fingertip into the coffee to see how hot it was. It was only warm. She drank half of the cup and repeated the question. "Did she say why she wouldn't see a doctor up there?"

He shuddered and hiccoughed and began to fill his chest with great chunks of air until he burst out crying again. When he finally gained control of himself, he answered, "She wasn't worried that it was anything serious because after it first started she saw a specialist, and if there was something wrong with her he would have said so." Then he began to make strange grunting sounds. "I had a feeling. She would have contacted me. Madeleine..." He covered his face with his hands and began to sob again. Doña Maria unclasped the necklace he wore and covered his back with a denim shirt.

The air was cold, the coffee, strong and bitter. Beryl could feel her perspiration chill on her face and neck. "This is October. She died in May. How is it that you don't know that?" she asked.

"I didn't know where she was," he pleaded. "I drove past The Hollyoak so many times, but the lights in her bedroom were always out. I thought maybe she was getting treatment somewhere, maybe in Europe. She might have been with Groff. She didn't answer her house phone and her cell was disconnected. I didn't know what to think. I went up to the lodge, but Brunton said he hadn't seen her. Why are you involved with this?"

"Groff hired me to determine whether or not she was dead, and if so, how she died. Did you go to the lodge often?"

"She took me there after Dalton was killed. She had to get some of his things and talk to Brunton. I liked it so much we found ways to go back." He wiped his eyes with the napkin. "Why does Groff want you to find out about her death?" A look of suspicion froze his expression. "Does he think somebody killed her?"

"He doesn't know what to think. For the last few months of her life she didn't communicate with him very much. The family isn't exactly communicative." She began to feel queasy and didn't want to drink any more coffee, but she did because it was helping to clear her mind.

Pablito interrupted. "Master, what you're talking about is confidential. It shouldn't be discussed."

"I need to know exactly what happened," Beryl said. "You visited her at The Hollyoak?"

"Yes, during the week at night. It was a big house. No people in it... just us."

"When did you first meet Madeleine?" Beryl asked, noticing that she had begun to feel nauseous and was swallowing copious amounts of saliva as if to dilute venom in her stomach.

"December. Last December was the first time she came here. She was so beautiful. I couldn't even remember my pitch. I watched her through the two-way mirror. She was sick and couldn't drink the tea. Pablo didn't want to let her come back to the altar room. But I couldn't let her go. She came back and I didn't have the costume on. I knew it would be a strain for her to kneel at the prie dieu so I took her into my bedroom and put her on my bed and I sat in a chair beside her and we talked." Beryl indicated that she understood and he continued. "I told Madeleine about Tezcatlipoca, the Mexican High God. We laughed about it. Pablito was going nuts because I was spilling so much. She was so easy to talk to." Now he lapsed into memories of Madeleine and fell into a stubborn silence.

He sighed and shuddered. "Something inside me snapped. I swear, it took one instant, and I was in love. I never in my life loved a woman... not like that." He began to cry violently, gasping for breath. He had emptied the napkin dispenser. Pablito brought him a box of tissues. Finally he wiped his eyes and blew his nose. "Dead?" Again he sobbed and shook.

Beryl realized that she did not know his name, "Just what is your real name?" she asked.

Pablito reached up and tried to keep him from speaking. He snarled at Beryl, "He's in no condition to talk to anyone right now, Laura Orsini, or whatever your name is. Just leave your phone number and when Master's composed he'll call you."

Master had other ideas. He swatted the dwarf's hand away from his face. Then he grabbed Pablito's collar and poncho and lifted him off the floor. "And you should have told me she was coming!" He shoved the dwarf hard and sent him sprawling onto the floor.

"Why?" Pablito whined. "She's nothin' special!"

The master-priest's demeanor changed. He was now a man who had been fatally wounded. He tried to compose himself. When he spoke it was in a monotone, completely without emotion. "Orsini was her mother's name. I know that. He didn't know that. After the first visit, I never called Madeleine by her name." He put his face into his hands and pressed his eyes. After another couple of minutes, he shuddered and looked up.

"My name's Revere Sanchey Porter. That's a funny name, huh? You want to know how I got it? I was left at the door of an American couple's trailer in Belize. They were Texans. They once lived in a commune in Sanchey, France. They dreamed about going back to it. The word for dream in French is 'reve.' That's how they made up my name."

"I didn't have a birth certificate. Somebody said an Australian guy in the Peten had "huipil fever" which means he had Indian girl friends. I guess my mother was one of them. Who knows?" He paused. "Who knows anything?" He covered his face and began to whisper Madeleine's name in great gulping shudders.

"Did the American couple take you in?"

"Yes. Do I sound like a foreigner?" He hiccoughed and wiped his eyes. "They were good people. She home-schooled me. They had a little boat. Small-time drug smugglers into Galveston. I'd watch the truck and trailer. One day they didn't come back. I waited and a few months later a hurricane destroyed the trailer and the truck, too. A man gave me a ride up to Nautla, Mexico.

"I got a job shooting sharks. That's when I had my accident and lost my foot to a shark bite. My ankle wouldn't heal. A lady from San Antonio - her last name was Porter - bought me some antibiotics and I was cured. We needed each other. She needed sex and I needed a future. She got me into Texas with a fake birth certificate. No problem. I was a tall kid. I not only spoke English, I spoke it with a Texas accent. The summer I finished high school, she was killed in some kind of family fight. I was on my own. I worked at a ranch until I met Pablito and got started in this con."

He wiped his eyes again and blew his nose. "She loved me. We were going to be married in June when Groff was finished school. He was supposed to come to the wedding, in Emmaus. We were going to live in the lodge. It was Spring. Instead of putting my winter stuff away down here, I took it all to the lodge so I could get away quick if I had to. All my personal papers are there, too. We wouldn't leave any forwarding addresses. Just us and our privacy. " He began to sob, again. "Are you sure she's dead and not just in a hospital someplace... maybe in a coma or something? I thought she had another doctor... maybe he put her in the hospital someplace. I kept driving past Hollyoak late at night, looking for her bedroom light to be on. That was my signal to come up. She'd leave the front door unlocked. The other night I saw the lights on up there. I thought I saw her at the window. I went crazy... happy. But the door was locked. I left a note."

"Groff got the note. Do you know the name of the doctor she was supposed to see?"

"No. I made an appointment with a doctor in Norristown. I got his name from the phone book. But she had to cancel it. Later I heard there was another doctor, but I don't know who it was. Somebody said that she heard Madeleine was getting treatment in South America or Europe. I didn't believe it. All I could do was wait."

"Do you think she could have gone to the doctor in Allentown?" Beryl spoke slowly, still feeling as though every word she spoke had to be dragged through time and her stomach. She began to feel the urge to vomit. "Did she ever tell you where she put some jewelry?"

"We have a safe deposit box in a bank in Allentown. There's a bunch of bonds in there, too." He groaned. "Where is she buried?"

"She was cremated. Her ashes are in the Eckersley family mausoleum."

"Ashes in a jar?" he said. "That's what's left of my Madeleine?"

Doña Maria forced her way into the conversation. "Can't you see he's in no condition to talk? It's time for you to leave. Please! Just leave!"

Beryl had reached the end of her ability to restrain the urge to vomit. She stood up. "Well, if you want your papers... I planned to go up to the lodge in a day or so. Where did you put them?"

"In the kitchen hutch cabinet, middle drawer." He put his head down on the table and began to sob so hard he was choking. He finally stopped and said, "I was going to teach her how to cook on a wood stove." His voice suddenly became a kind of squeak. "I was going to teach her how to fish." And the tears and sobs started again.

Beryl's stomach churned. She had to leave immediately. "I'll have Alicia Eckersley call you," she said, "as soon as I retrieve your documents."

"Just tell her not to call us on Friday afternoons or on the weekends," Pablito said as he held the kitchen door open for her.

Beryl reached the Jaguar and clicked the lock open. Before she could open the door, she turned her head and threw up a stream of bitter coffee, herbal tea, and yellow bile onto the dirt. After she made sure she hadn't gotten any vomit on her suit, she got into the car.

George was waiting at the station, expecting her to stop, but she motioned to him to follow. Her head had begun to throb.

Beryl staggered into the rear of the Zen temple, with George following close behind. Groff and Sensei stood up and came over to her.

"What's wrong?" Groff asked. "Are you hurt?"

She retched. "I'm sick to my stomach and my head is killing me," she said, gasping. Sensei opened a patio lounge chair and lowered her onto it. Again she retched. Groff found an old empty flower pot. He put some paper towels in the bottom and put it on the floor beside her. Immediately she bent over and threw up some bitter yellow bile.

Sensei got a towel and put it under the faucet. He wrung it out and tried to put it on her forehead.

"No. No." she said, pushing his hands away. "It'll drip on my silk blouse."

Groff saw a *gi* hanging on the back of a door. "Can she wear that?" He asked.

Sensei got the *gi* and handed it to him. Groff unbuttoned her suit jacket and handed it to George. "Could you hang this up," he said simply. Then he reached around her and unbuttoned the silk blouse at the back of her neck. Slowly and carefully he eased the blouse up. As he began to pull it over her head, he said to the others, "Turn around." Beryl almost laughed. He handed the blouse to George and said, "This, too." He reached around her again and with one quick slide maneuver, unhooked her bra and pulled it off. He slipped her left arm into the *gi*, pulled her forward, and put her right arm into the garment. "Lean back," he said as he looped the belt around her and tied it in front. She leaned back and he unzipped her suit skirt and gently grabbed her underpants, panty hose, half slip and skirt, and began to pull them down. "Lift your hips a little," he said. She did. He put her shoes on the floor, finished removing the garments, and put on the *gi* pants. Finally he took off the earrings, bracelets and signet ring and dropped them into her purse.

"Now," he said to Sensei, "you can put the cold cloth on her head."

George put all of the smaller articles in a shopping bag.

Beryl retched again and spit up more bile. Groff announced, "She needs promethazine suppositories."

Sensei said, "I don't have suppositories of any kind."

George, however, had been prescribed the medication when he had been in drug rehab. He periodically renewed the supply. "I don't know what the name is, but I keep a special kind in the refrigerator. Do you want me to go get them?"

Groff said, "Sure. It's too late to get a doctor now." He knelt down beside Beryl and asked, "Do you want to stay here or go home?"

"Home."

Groff picked her up, carried her out to the Jaguar, lowered her into the passenger seat, and secured the seat belt. As he got behind the wheel and adjusted the seat, he leaned over and whispered in her ear, "I can tell you're not used to hashish. I must have a talk with Jack."

Half an hour later, as she lay on her own bed, George arrived with a container of suppositories. He looked at Groff. "You are not going to insert these, so get that thought out of your mind."

Groff said, "You've got a bum right hand. You think you can do it better?"

Sensei broke in. "There's nothing wrong with my right hand. Give them to me."

Beryl said, "For God's sake, give me the suppositories! First take one out of the container." It took them ten minutes to get a suppository out of its stiff plastic covering. They couldn't find a scissors and had to get a kitchen knife to cut the plastic that was designed simply to peel apart.

Beryl told them all to go into Jack's room. She inserted the suppository, and a few moments later she was sound asleep.

Sensei had just gone to prepare for services at the temple when she awakened at five o'clock. She told George and Groff everything that happened after she arrived at Haddon Manor.

"So he needs drugs to get them in the mood," George said.

"No, he's a sexy guy... handsome and muscular. And he's kind of sweet."

"Oh, Jesus," Groff snapped. "You're still high."

"Madeleine went for him and she was sober. I'm just saying that I understand her response to him."

"What did he look like?" Groff asked.

"His hair was dark and long. He wore it in a braid in the back. His skin was like caucasian - with a tan. His eyes were hazel and he had very long eye lashes... very expressive eyes and nice hands. And you know the way a person on crutches can develop a really muscular torso... well, he had one."

"Why was he on crutches?"

"He's missing his left foot. He had a run-in with a shark when he was a teenager."

"How did they make contact with Madeleine initially?" George asked.

"I didn't get the chance to ask... but it can't be a mystery. Those rich women have nothing to do but gossip, and a muscular Aztec shaman is something they can talk about anytime, anyplace."

"Evidently he was a "full service" medicine man," Groff said, "a guy who can cure a cold, recommend a stock, cast a horoscope, and fuck sacramentally. I wonder how much he pulled in a week."

George tried to estimate his net income. "He's got overhead. The house. Gas. Electric. Water. The staff. Food. Argentine wine," he paused for humorous emphasis, "condoms, lubricants, Viagra." Everybody laughed. "Hey," he said, "it all adds up. How many clients could he see in a day?"

"I don't know," Beryl said. "A dozen?" Both of the men laughed.

"What's so funny?" she asked.

Groff tossed a towel at her. "There's a big difference between men and women. '*Mistah Kurtz. He dead.*'" It was an old line from Conrad's *Heart of Darkness* and though it had nothing to do with the conversation, it seemed appropriate. George and Groff found it funny.

Beryl changed the subject. "He wasn't available on weekends. That's another thing I just remembered. Nobody's allowed to call on weekends. Yet he said he was with Madeleine up at the lodge for a few weekends."

"When?" Groff asked. "Before or after my father was killed?"

"After, obviously," she said. "He had even started to take his personal stuff up there... winter clothes, documents. And he was emphatic about it. He and your mom were going to get married and live at the lodge. This news was her big Memorial Day surprise for you. A June wedding. He insists that she loved him, and he did spend a lot of time with her. He wasn't faking his grief. He really loved her."

Groff did not take these comments well. "Yeah, he really loved her! He's told that her life is in danger because she could be pregnant with his kid and he doesn't drop everything to take care of her. No. He's got that plumed snake of his to worry about. He does serious fucking... the kind that pays well. No wonder she didn't take him home for Sunday dinner. Things were bad enough for her when it was only me who was slammin' her." He made his voice sound comically maudlin. "Madeleine and her Eurotrash morals! No wonder poor Dalton was tempted by that teenaged skank one lonely night at the lodge."

"Can we dispense with the drama? I've got a headache and I don't want to hear your useless bitching. She gave your grandmother the distinct impression that she did have another physician. He doesn't know squat. But," Beryl said slowly, "something still doesn't add up.

"She was sick in December before she met Sanchey. That's why she went to Euell in the first place. She did tell your grandmother in February that she had a new physician. If Euell was so damned concerned about her questionable 'atypical cells report' that he claims he sent out three separate requests for her to come in for re-testing - and he sent out a request even after he's told she has another doctor - why doesn't he react with more concern. He knows all the talk in his office. His patients are full of gossip about a medicine-man of some kind, someone who could not possibly be qualified to treat a cancerous condition. He just blows it off. That does not make sense. These people were more than physician and patients. Their families had been friends for generations."

George looked at the problem from another point of view. "Suppose that in January or February Madeleine had some surgery by some other doctor. The Eckersleys didn't know about Sanchey's existence. They only knew about Groff. If they got wind of the 'female problem' they might have thought she actually was pregnant. The photographs Lionel saw in Ireland would have convinced them that Groff was the father and in these days of DNA that would have been an undeniably scandalous occurrence. So this might account for their attitude, for the hostility, anyway. Everybody's lying or repeating a lie. For all we know they all might have thought that she had a botched abortion. The cellular changes Euell's lab saw might have been consistent with pregnancy.

"Look, she was in her forties. Her own health was already bothering her. *Let's not forget she was still married to Dalton Eckersley.* These rumors would be creating one scandalous mess involving this Sanchey guy. She couldn't have known in advance that Dalton would be shot in the ass and she'd be free to marry again. Who knows what she did or said to head-off a scandal?"

George and Groff thought that this was a reasonable scenario. Beryl objected. "Who cares what they thought? The fact is that she was sick in December and she wasn't pregnant and she wasn't alarmed about her condition. Something doesn't jibe. Somebody was treating her medically and she was relying on this medical advice. She was not a stupid woman!"

Groff went to the refrigerator and got a bottle of water. "She went to see a fake medicine man. She couldn't have been in a very smart state of mind."

"She went to see a yogi who knew something important about you, a guy who had a great psychic track record. Jesus! Call *The Guinness Book*! Somebody went to see a yogi."

George tried to return to a sensible discussion. "We know that if she did have an abortion it would have been performed secretly."

Groff had a theory. "Sure. And by some butcher Euell recommended. The Pap test may have been a cover. Euell could have given her a pregnancy test right there in the office and just bullshitted a story about the Pap test. Euell owns the goddamned lab that did the test. What do we know?"

"She wasn't pregnant!" Beryl shouted.

"Fine! So he saw that she had a serious condition and he did my father a favor by ignoring it. Nothing would have pleased the bastard more than to see her rot away. Yes, Euell and my father were tight. They grew up together. They went hunting together up at the lodge. They were born in the same goddamned month!"

Beryl was tired of all the pointless discussion. "She had another doctor. She had cancer. Euell sent her requests to come in for re-testing. He didn't recommend another doctor but she found one. She wouldn't knowingly have gone to see some unqualified quack. Let's just find out who this doctor was and put an end to all this insane speculation."

Groff grew quiet. "I want to know who he is. He needs to be stopped."

Beryl tried to reassure him. "If I'm up to it tomorrow, I'll talk to Euell again."

Groff stood up. "Time to go. I hung your suit and blouse in the closet. Your shoes and purse are in there, too. And your underwear and stockings are on the ironing board. I was going to take your panties home... as a trophy... but I put them back." He turned to Beryl, "Will you be wanting the Jag tomorrow, dear?"

"No," she said. "The kitty is all yours. What do you have lined up for tomorrow?"

"The locksmiths will be coming, and I'm getting all my electronic stuff installed. Tv. Internet. Satellites. Wi-fi. iPhone. Land line. Laptop. iPad. I don't have anyone to contact; but if I did, I'd be able to reach out and touch them in a thousand ways."

"Stay away from social media sites," George said. "You're too rich and inexperienced."

"Yes, Dad. Oh, and Mommy, I forgot to tell you that Sensei gassed up the Bronco. The keys are on your ironing board."

"Promise me that you won't go out to Haddon Manor," Beryl said firmly.

"For now, let's all just settle-in for the night," George said. "I'll go home and tend my hungry plant family."

As they left Beryl could feel herself sliding back into sleep.

WEDNESDAY, OCTOBER 14, 2009

Alicia Eckersley called at 9 a.m. to get the details. While they talked, Beryl made tea and sat at her kitchen table and slowly began to feel more human.

"I know Daffy is going to call me, asking for details," Alicia said. "What should I tell her?"

"Daffy?"

"Eleanor Teasdale's mother is called Daffy. I cannot for the life of me remember what that name stands for. Her maiden name was Druck. Naturally, we called her Daffy. I don't know... maybe it was Delores."

Beryl refused to allow herself to laugh. "Just tell her I thanked you profusely and that I was delighted with his help and didn't give you any details. By the way, do you happen to remember the name of the doctor Madeleine said she was seeing? Aubrey Euell says you mentioned to him that she said she was seeing someone new."

Alicia hesitated. "I had seen her a week or so before that night I saw him. I asked her how she was feeling and she said fine and that she had a new doctor. That's all. She never told me his name. And then when I saw Aubrey I said to him that Madeleine said she had a new doctor. He didn't even ask me who it was. Can you imagine that?"

"I need to learn his name."

"If you want to find out anything," Alicia advised, "your best bet is to find someone who gossips and then make up some theory and you'll be surprised how much that person will reveal in order to disprove your theory. They always want to replace your inaccurate gossip with their own, except that often their own is based on something factual whereas your gossip was just made up. Of course, I'm not an expert on gossiping, but I find that that approach works best for me."

Beryl shook her head. "I will certainly follow your suggestion. I'll go to Aubrey Euell's office. His waiting room is a font of gossip and much of it flows in Madeleine's direction."

"Just be careful about what you make up because whatever you say will be repeated as authentic gossip."

"I understand... and thank you for the warning." Alicia, Beryl decided, always made things clearer.

THURSDAY, OCTOBER 15, 2009

Beryl, afraid that if she called for an appointment she'd be turned down, walked into Euell's office unannounced. As she approached, she could hear women talking in his waiting room. Once more, as she entered the room, all the talking stopped, and the women looked at her. Fortunately, Isabel McAndrew was at the filing cabinet in the receptionist's area.

"Hello there," she said, bending over to look at the appointment schedule. "But this time nobody's expecting you. And you, no doubt, will want to be squeezed in."

"Can you do it?" Beryl pleaded.

Isabel lowered her voice. "Two of them have to be taken in order - they are mother and daughter! But I can get you in before the third. Just act natural... as if you aren't going to take up a lot of time."

"In fact, I'm not. I just have a couple of questions about Madeleine Eckersley. So, how have you been?"

"Same-o. Same-o. My life doesn't change much. But I understand you visited that lunatic astrologer, Daniel Moor."

"News travels fast around here," Beryl said. "I saw him less than a week ago."

She grinned. "I'm sure he told you that I'm the love of his life."

"Why does he dislike you so much?"

"Hate is a better word. Now, why does he hate me so much? That's easy." She looked around. "We can't talk out here." She led Beryl back to an empty examining room. "He hates me because I tell anyone who will listen what a fake he is. He claims I'm ruining his business. I hope it's true."

"What happened between you two?" Beryl asked.

"He told one of Dr. Euell's patients that if she knew of a woman in white she should tell her that the stars predicted great romantic adventures for this woman. So naturally she thought of me in my uniform and encouraged me to see him. It was so kind of her to think of me. I borrowed on my credit card to get the thousand dollars his first interview cost. He said my romantic destiny would be realized where the ocean met the land on all sides. That was obviously an island. And, the island had a woman's name.

"Like a fool I took my two weeks' vacation in Martha's Vineyard. Between travel, hotel, and the new clothes I bought, I was really in debt. I didn't meet anybody, not a single soul. The weather turned cold and I couldn't even go to the beach. If my destiny was eating canned soup for six months and paying late fees and interest on my credit card debt, then I met my destiny, all right. I asked Dr. Euell for a loan." She made an exaggerated expression of pity, "but he said he didn't want to set a precedent. If it were for something serious, now, that would be different." She sighed. "As if drowning in debt wasn't serious. Doctors are notoriously cheap employers. Loretta, the receptionist, and I could make three times as much working in a hospital or a five-and-dime."

"I know. I used to work in a hospital. Why don't you leave?"

"I don't know. This was my first and only job. I've never worked for anybody else. You get hooked by sentiment. When you're single, he becomes the only man in your life. The patients become your only family. You see them regularly. They have babies, then their babies have babies. You know how it is. I've never married. Maybe if I had I wouldn't have stayed here. Are you married?"

"Widowed. One son who goes to Arizona State."

"You don't look old enough."

"It helps if you marry at eighteen. But let's not talk about me. What prompted you to see Daniel Moor in the first place?"

"It's not that I took him seriously, it was just that everybody talked about him. Like a kid, I wanted to see for myself. The patients believed in him and they did report beneficial results. I know it's stupid, but what does intelligence have to do with belief in the supernatural? Sometimes

I think the smarter you are, the easier you're taken in. I've learned my lesson. In a way, it was a good thing. It brought me back to my religion, in a big way. I'm seriously considering entering a convent. A Catholic order in Michigan. Roman Catholic, of course."

Beryl felt sorry for her. She could see grey roots coming in under her dyed hair. "No more Daniel Moors in your life?"

"No. Jesus Christ will more than suffice. No more false prophets promising the moon."

"And what about this other guru the patients were discussing the other day?"

"He's not a false prophet type. He's some kind of self-help guru. Despite all the money these women have, they still have their weaknesses. Alcohol, drugs, smoking, gambling, all kinds of immoral behavior. He helps them change their lives. He tells them to become vegetarians and to do yoga. I could tell them that for free. But they think that what is free is worthless."

"Did Madeleine Eckersley see him?"

"Maybe for yoga and stuff, but she also had to be seeing another doctor. She told Alicia she was. She wasn't like the other patients."

"Why not?"

"Because they all came back. Dr. Euell's still their doctor. Their health guru didn't turn them away from traditional medicine. But Madeleine didn't come back."

"I wonder why she didn't call him the night she died."

Isabel shrugged her shoulders. "Maybe he wasn't local."

"So there were two new men in her life, a medical man and a medicine-man! It makes sense that the physician wasn't local or was just far enough away to be useless in an emergency."

"You mean... like in Atlantic City?"

"Why Atlantic City? Did she go there?"

"I don't know if she did, specifically, but many of the gals do. If they have problems they say that they'll wait until they get home and see Dr. Euell. But if it's an emergency, he's too far away to call."

"I was thinking more of Lehigh County, where their hunting lodge is."

"That's where her husband went." She giggled. "You know how when you have magnets, the opposite poles attract and the same poles repel? If one of them was in Lehigh County you could take a globe of the world and push a needle through it to its opposite point, and that's where you should look for the other."

"But the repulsion dies when one of them dies. Dalton was dead. She had to go up there to attend to things. The Eckersleys had a circle of friends there. Surely they would have come to her aid particularly because of the way he died. Even Dr. Euell spent time up there with Dalton. He was in that circle of friends... and physicians tend to associate socially with other physicians. Maybe he can think of a doctor up there she might have seen."

The nurse shook her head. "I don't know... If you're someplace away from home and you have a problem and see a doctor there about it, you don't come home and say, 'I got myself a new physician.'"

"You might if you were switching 'home base.' She might have selected someone in their social circle, so to speak. I'm looking for anything that could lead me to him."

"You know, there was talk around here that she was going to start living with her health guru... that Indian guy the women talk about. I thought that was ridiculous gossip. Madeleine was a bit of an iconoclast but she wouldn't just shack-up with some swami, and certainly not in the place where Dalton was murdered. Besides, Groff's a big boy and big boys get married. What family would want Madeleine's wacky sex life hanging on the family tree? It would have been scandalous."

"Not if she married the man. It would be eccentric but not scandalous."

"Married? But that would mean, as they say on those TV lawyers' programs, 'entitled to a share of the marital assets.' I'd like to be a fly on the wall when the Eckersleys find out that an Indian medicine-man is the master of The Hollyoak!"

"By now Lionel would have known if she had gotten married. Nobody's come forward with a marriage certificate. But she did start to move things up there... clothing, personal papers. She intended to start a new life up there, so she very well might have acquired a new gynecologist. It didn't have to be an emergency situation. A new bride getting herself checked out - that sort of thing."

"Maybe the man doesn't know she's dead. These gurus usually have ashrams back in India and they go back periodically. Maybe it's just an immigration thing. Visa expired. If he wasn't a citizen of the U.S. then sometimes it's easier to get married outside the country. It would take him a while to get a visa so she could have come back without him and he still might show up with a marriage certificate. Then he would be Master of The Hollyoak! Oh, that would start a revolution!"

"No. She hadn't gone anywhere. And Groff was supposed to attend the ceremony but she died a few weeks before it was to take place. Besides, he inherited the estate."

"As far as we've heard around here, that estate has not yet been settled. Maybe this man is some kind of master magician and just when everybody thinks his hat is empty, *Shazam!* he produces a marriage certificate and claims his share of her property."

"That would be quite a trick! But the boyfriend's not my problem. My job is to locate this doctor. If in anticipation of her marriage she used her new married name, and she had a medical problem, the new doctor might have requested X-rays or lab reports. They often do. Like in a mammogram when a new radiologist wants to see all your previous films. The request might have been handled routinely. I know that that's a long shot, but short of it, I'll have to go up there this weekend and see if I can find a prescription bottle or some indication written on a calendar or in an appointment book."

"This is like the movies, isn't it?" Isabel said. "Finding clues. A pill bottle's label can tell you who, where, when, and what."

Dr. Euell entered the room. Annoyed, he said to Isabel, "I thought you were in the ladies' room. There are patients waiting! We're running late!" He looked at Beryl. "Not again! What is it this time?"

"There's evidence that Madeleine Eckersley planned to move to the Lodge up in Lehigh County. I was wondering if you knew of any gynecologist that she might have met socially or been referred to up in that area. Or possibly, if a physician, known or unknown, ever requested any of Madeleine's old records. She might have used another surname, and the request might have been filed..." her voice dropped, burdened with implausibility.

"I have hundreds of patients, but I assure you I know of only one Madeleine who could possibly be the Madeleine you're interested in. I would not have forgotten where I put any information about her."

"I'm just trying to find if any other doctor was involved with her case."

"I've told you that she said she had another physician, but I don't know whether that meant she was going to see one or had already seen one. What difference does it make? I've tried to be cooperative; but now I really must insist that you end this harassment. If I see you here again, I'll complain to Lionel Eckersley. You can show yourself out."

FRIDAY, OCTOBER 16, 2009

Friday's weather forecast for Lehigh County was for snow, a heavy wet snow, the first of the season. The temperature was dropping fast.

Alicia Eckersley said that she would call Brunton on his cell phone - the house line at the Lodge had been disconnected - to tell him to be sure to be there "to greet the visitors."

George's pickup truck had four-wheel drive, but without chains he feared getting stuck on a mountain road if the road became icy. Also, the "cold snap" had come so suddenly that he had not had the opportunity to winterize the cooling system. By the time the truck was serviced and they located chains that would fit his extra-wide wheels, it was mid-afternoon before they began the drive.

Halfway up to Emmaus, the wiper blades began to push accumulating snowflakes into slushy rills on the windshield. They drove on until they came to the base of the Lodge's hill. It had just stopped snowing, and it was still daylight. They could see the Lodge's clearing at the top of the dirt road that snaked up the thousand feet of elevation to it. "Between those switchbacks and the snow we'd never make it without chains," George said. "Pull onto the road and we'll at least be off the highway when we try to figure out how to do this." Neither of them knew how to put chains on.

Beryl drove onto the base of the snow-blanketed road. There was no level area and the grade not only made it impossible to install the chains on two wheels at a time, it also made it extremely difficult to install even one. It took more than a half hour to get one chain on properly. An overhead light came on. George looked up at it. "This is a private light," he said. "Maybe Brunton can see us acting like clowns down here."

110

It began to snow again. The overhead light provided enough light for them to see the wheels and the chains, but did little to improve their efficiency. George's right hand did not lend itself to finessing the task, and Beryl's fingers inside her wet driving gloves quickly became numb with cold. By the time they got all four chains secured more than an hour had passed, and daylight was long over. George got into the driver's seat. When they finally started up the hill, visibility was down to five feet.

Immediately, at the first turn, the road narrowed. Tall weeds that lined its edges bent under snow loads, making the path seem even narrower. George's right arm ached. Even with power steering, it was difficult for him to hold the wheel tight through the hairpin turns. Beryl could see him wince as they proceeded. There was no place that they could stop and change places, and he drove on without complaining.

At the top they could see how the Lodge had been notched out of the hillside. The headlights illuminated the row of four garages on the left, the carriage house directly in front of them, the two storey Lodge on their right and a ledge that served as a driveway to the rear of the Lodge. The center area was small but landscaped with shrubs and wagon wheels and other decorative items. "You're gonna have to drive down. I'll turn around and point the nose down so you won't have to worry about getting stuck, seein's how you're so great at driving backwards and parking," he teased. The truck's headlights made a sweep of the center 'courtyard.' "Where the hell is Brunton?" George asked.

They got out of the pickup and walked to the steps that led up to the front porch. The house was completely dark. "I thought he was expecting us," Beryl groused. George knocked on the door and waited only half a minute before he turned the knob. The door opened, revealing nothing but darkness inside.

The moonlight's sheen on the snow put whatever light there was behind them. "Wait a minute," Beryl said. "You still got two flashlights in the glove compartment? All I've got is a penlight in my bag."

"They're there. Go ahead and get 'em." George pushed the door open.

Beryl retraced her steps, got the flashlights, and tested them. She ran back to the house. "They're at full strength."

George directed a beam of light around the buildings. "They've got an electrical connection and a phone line. The wires come in laterally, maybe from another lodge. If Brunton's not up here, who is? Somebody had to turn that light on for us down there. You carryin'?"

She patted the slot in her shoulder bag. "Yes... I've got the Beretta. Ok. Let's see what's going on here that the door was left open."

The first room was large and dominated by a stone fireplace. The floors were varnished planks; the furniture, a rustic kind of 'Old West," complete with a bear skin rug. The door to a coat closet was louvered to let air in to help dry wet garments. The couch and chairs were leather and the end tables held oil lamps. "So this is Dalton's 'man cave.'" Beryl quipped. She shouted, "Anybody home?" There was no answer. They walked farther into the room, stopping at a staircase.

"You check the upstairs," George said. "I'll take the kitchen."

As George walked to the kitchen, Beryl climbed the stairs. From the hallway at the top, her light shone on several open bedroom doors. She stepped into the doorway of the nearest one. Everything seemed in order. She saw a down comforter on the bed and wondered if it was the missing one from The Hollyoak. She turned her light back into the hall. Suddenly she heard a terrified shout from George. She stiffened. She heard a chair scrape and the thud of a body hitting the floor. She bounded down the stairs trying to hold the flashlight in her left hand to see where she was going as she pulled her right hand glove off with her teeth. She needed to get her gun out of the slot in her shoulder bag.

As she ran toward the kitchen, the light beam in front of her stopped at the swinging door that was now ajar. Not stopping to determine what it was that held the door open, she pushed and stumbled headfirst into the room, tripping over George's body. She fell forward, landing on his back. Her arm struck his flashlight. It rolled in an arc on the floor, coming to rest against a chair leg. Its beam shone directly into her face. She raised her head, momentarily blinded by its glare. George was face down and she could not tell if he was wounded or dazed. Clutching her gun and flashlight, she got onto her knees and pointed her gun at the circle of light her flashlight made as she drew its beam around the room.

Seeing no one, she laid the Beretta and the flashlight on George's back and tried to examine his head in his flashlight's glare.

"George," she shouted. "*George!*" She bent forward and touched his head trying to see if there was a wound under his hair. Her fingers touched warm pulsing blood. She whimpered and recoiled and scrambled to reach inside her shoulderbag to get her cellphone. She heard a noise coming from behind the swinging door. Someone was in the room with her. The beam from George's flashlight still shone squarely in her face. She shielded her eyes and looked back at the door. "Brunton?" she yelled. Her left hand groped George's back trying to find her gun. "We're not burglars! Alicia was supposed to call you! I need to call 9-1-1." Suddenly the door pushed against George's body and she saw the glint of metal raise up and then swing down at her. The pronged end of a barbecue spit struck her wrist and hand, hurling her phone across the room, skidding into the darkness of an open door. Her hand was seared in pain. She raised it to her mouth and whimpered as the cellphone bounced down wooden steps. She jumped back into a squatting position, still groping for her gun. Again the door moved and again she saw the glint of metal as the barbecue spit rose up from behind the door's edge. Frantically she tried to crawl under the kitchen table. Again the barbecue spit struck her shoulder. The blow glanced off her shoulder pad and hit the chair. Beryl lunged forward until she was completely under the table.

A noise came from the corner of the room on the other side of George. Her flashlight, still lying on George back, was now pointed directly at her. Her phone was in the cellar and her gun, no doubt, was on the far side of George's body, the side where her attacker or one of her attackers stood. She did not know how many people were in the room with her. She had nothing but her purse and an injured right hand. George's flashlight was within reach and she slowly extended her hand until her fingers circled it.

She blinked against the beam of her own flashlight and discerned the outline of a figure stepping over George's body. Not until the figure moved far enough away from the light so that she could turn her head and shield her eyes from the glare, could she see anything at all with the flashlight that she unsteadily held in her left hand. The beam fell upon four feet... four sets of blood caked toes. She squinted and strained to see that there were only two legs, and that two of the feet were only dragging on the floor as they hung by a flap of skin, skin that was the garment the legs were wearing. She gasped in terror and confusion and then slowly moved the beam up the one pair of legs. A man's genitals swung from beneath folds of skin and strands of blood caked fat. She knew what she would soon see, but she could not resist letting the beam rise higher until it illuminated the hideous grey bearded skin that covered a face whose living eyes stared down at her from the eye sockets' cut-out holes. A vacuum of horror sucked air into Beryl's lungs with a strangling rasp. Standing in front of her was the grotesque figure of a priest of Xipe Totec, the Flayed God. She could not breathe and stared dumbly at it. Brunton's hands had been cut off at the wrist and hung from skin flaps, while the hands of the man who had flayed him protruded from the wrists' skin directly into thick latex gloves. Blood had matted and stiffened his hair and beard enabling them to be pulled into points, like a macabre crown that circled the face. A safety pin held together the distorted lips. Beryl stared up at the recessed living eyes, and then her gasp reversed itself into a shuddering shriek. The grizzly figure began to chuckle in soft guttural sounds and once again the metal bar came down, striking the table that protected her, splintering its edge.

The figure took a few steps and stopped in front of her. Frantically, Beryl unzipped her shoulder bag and searched for something she could use as a weapon. Her fingers touched a small eye-glass repair tube that contained tiny screws and a three inch long screwdriver. She flicked the lid off the tube and the screwdriver slid out into her hand. Her fingers curled around the tiny weapon. A latex gloved hand now grasped the edge of the table and Beryl knew that her shield would soon be lifted off her.

She covered her right hand with her left and raised her arms as far as she could and then plunged the sharp point into the naked arch of the figure's left foot. She heard a deep grunting sound as the figure hopped back onto its right foot. Beryl lunged out from under the table, trying to tackle the figure, but the barbecue spit swung laterally at her, striking her ear and cheek. She scurried backwards to the safety of the table. She had to think. George's flashlight was now out of reach, but it was shining away from her, its beam directed near the figure. As the figure nimbly went from a sitting to a stooping position, Beryl could see the little screw driver stick out from its foot like a decorative cocktail pick.

Beryl was now in a squatting position, her hands stretched out in front of her, pressing down on the shoulder bag. It occurred to her that she was taking a football center's stance, with hands that clasped a leather shoulder bag instead of a football. She did not move.

Using the spit for support, the figure pushed itself up until it was standing. Beryl watched as it took several deliberate steps towards her. Football became the only logical model. For so long as the table was above her and the figure was in-close, she could tackle its legs without fear of the hammer-like spit. The moment a gloved hand grasped the edge of the table, Beryl lunged at the figure, tackling its legs. It staggered backward. Beryl continued to hug its legs as she pushed against them as hard as she could, digging in her feet, making the figure stagger back, tumbling backwards off balance. She saw the outline of the open basement doorway. She kept thrusting, pushing, and steering the figure toward the doorway until, with one violent shove, she toppled it over the threshold. In the same way her phone had bounced down the steps, the figure tumbled to the bottom of the stairs.

Beryl got up and slammed the door shut. There was no bolt she could use to secure it. The kitchen chairs were too high-backed to use as a buttress under the knob. She still did not know if there were others involved in the attack. She went immediately to George. His face was lying in a puddle of blood. Her shoulder bag's strap was adjustable. She unbuckled it, put the bag under his face, and pushed his shearling jacket up above his waist so that she could slip one of the bag's straps under his belt and re-buckle it into a secure loop that would hold the bag in place. When she pulled George across the floor the bag would protect his injured head.

She stood up, grabbed George's ankles and dragged him inch by inch towards the front door. There, she bent his arms, folding them in their heavy sleeves until they were under the bag, and pulled him over the doorstep.

Now she had him at the top step of the porch. She got his car keys from his pocket, ran to the pickup, lowered the tailgate, got into the driver's side, adjusted the seat so she could reach the pedals, and started the engine. The snow was falling in thick large flakes. She could see nothing except the red glow of the brake lights. She put the headlights on, and backed up, trying to bring the tail gate to the steps that led up to the porch. It required several attempts until she got the tail gate parallel and in line with the steps. She put the car in Park, put the emergency brake on, and got out to see how large the gap was between the tailgate and the porch floor. The separation was about three feet, and she whimpered, realizing that she could not possibly carry George from the porch to the truck bed.

She remembered the louvered door in the living room. She ran back into the lodge and pulled open the door, which was hung on two hinges. The hinge pins had wide flat nail-head tops. The top pin had not been pushed completely down into the hinge. She grabbed a brass candlestick and began to whack the pin's head, pushing it up and out. She did not have enough clearance to hammer out the bottom pin, so she pulled the top of the door down, torquing it, until it was close enough to the floor for her to jump on. After a few stomps, she had pulled the screws out of the jamb and the door was free. She dragged it to the porch and placed it beside George. Then she unbuckled her shoulder bag, lifted the back of his jacket until it covered the back of his head, and slowly rolled him over, face up, onto the door. There was only one way she could move the door closer to the tailgate, and that way was to grab the bottom louver, put her feet on a step, lean back and pull with all her might, grabbing and pulling each ascending louver until the door was half off the porch.

She turned around and got under the door, putting her back up against it; and then, like Atlas with the world on his shoulders, she lifted and pushed forward, again and again, until the door had edged onto the tailgate. She returned to the porch, sat down and pushed the top edge of the door with her feet until she got most of the door and George's body onto the truck bed and tailgate. The bed was too short. George's head and arms protruded from the edge of the open tailgate. She told herself that as long as she was going downhill, George would not fall out.

She jumped into the driver's seat and looked down to release the emergency brake. When she looked up again, Xipe Totec's face was next to hers at the driver's side window. She shrieked and watched the figure slowly twist; and then with a discus thrower's back swing, it flung the barbecue spit into the windshield. Beryl put the car into "drive" and floored the accelerator, trying to see through the web of cracks into the darkness. The driver's side of the windshield allowed for no visibility, and she had to sit on the right edge of her seat and stretch to see out of the right side of the windshield and operate the accelerator and the brake with her left foot. Many times on her way down she nearly went off the road. The windshield wiper blades, blocked on one side, would not operate on the other; and only extreme heat from the defroster kept the windshield clear enough for her to see where she was going. Only by proceeding slowly was she able to descend to the highway. Continually, she checked the rear view mirror and saw no sign that she was being followed.

At the bottom of the private road, she turned onto the highway and continued to drive towards town. Ahead she saw the lights of a gas station and convenience store. A police car was parked outside. She blew the truck's horn repeatedly and the officer emerged from the store. He glanced into the truck bed and shouted, "Follow me! The hospital's only two blocks away!" He got into his police cruiser and radioed the emergency room. As she followed him into the ER's receiving area, the medical staff was already waiting.

The officer stayed with Beryl in the waiting room and tried to get her statement. The moment she referred to the caretaker's skinning, he summoned homicide investigators.

A nurse hurried out of the ER and asked, "Is he the George Wagner that is listed in his wallet's identification? We need to give him blood."

"Yes. Yes," Beryl stammered. "He's a former cop." Without comment the nurse hurried back into the ER.

"My name's Tilson. I need my purse," she whined. "I need to call Sensei."

"Your purse is probably in the room with him and his jacket and stuff. I wouldn't bother them right now," he said, getting out his own cellphone and extending it to her. She tried to take it but her hands were stiff with dried blood. "Maybe you better tell me the number you want," he said. She couldn't remember the temple's phone number and in complete frustration, she burst out crying. "Tell me when you think of the name or number and I'll get it from information."

"Wong!" she yelled. "It's Percy Wong in Philadelphia... on Germantown Avenue!" The officer got the number from information who also put the call through. Groff answered. The officer handed her the phone. Her hands were caked with blood; she held them up dumbly. He put the phone to her face and she cried, "Sensei!"

"It's all right," the officer said. "Take the phone!"

Groff was on the line. She finally began to release the tension. She sobbed hysterically. The police officer took the phone. He told Groff that George Wagner was in the ER and that she was fine except for a possible broken bone in her hand or wrist... maybe both. "If they release her after they have a look at her, I'll take her to the Crestview Motel in Emmaus." Between shuddering sobs, Beryl told him to come up right away with Sensei. He relayed the message. Groff asked if she needed a lawyer. "He wants to know if you need a lawyer."

Beryl stopped crying. Her eyes widened. "What?" she asked.

"A lawyer," he repeated. "Do you need a lawyer?"

She stared at him and hissed, *"Tell that idiot to put Sensei on the phone!"*

Groff heard her. "Tell her we're on our way. I'll call my grandfather."

A police homicide investigator arrived. The officer who had stayed with her said, "This is Miss Tilson. Her identification papers are in her purse and that's inside the E.R."

The investigator patted her shoulder. "I'm Chief of Detectives Ron Mallory. I understand you witnessed a murder at the Eckersley's Lodge. Can I call anyone for you, Miss Tilson?"

"No," she said. "Groff's on his way."

Mallory turned to the officer. "Is this Groff her attorney?"

"No," he answered. "He asked her if she needed an attorney and then he said he'd call his grandfather."

"Miss Tilson," he said. "Have you asked for an attorney? Is that who you're waiting for?"

"No. I'm waiting for Groff... Eckersley... and my Sensei."

"Eckersley? Like Dalton and Lionel?"

"Lionel is Groff's grandfather."

"Is he your lawyer?"

"No, he's my client."

The two police officers looked at each other and shrugged. Mallory said, "Ok. Why don't we just get that hand of yours looked at and keep an eye on how your partner is doing. I know Lionel well. We can talk when he gets here. But without questioning you about what went on wherever you were, I need to know if there are any other persons who may be at risk there."

"No," she said. "Brunton up at the Eckersley Lodge has been killed. Whoever did it attacked George Wagner and me. We're private investigators. George is a retired investigator with the PPD. Disabled. Line of duty."

"Yes, I know. I saw his ID. Can you identify your attacker?"

"No. I can't tell you anything."

Mallory mistook her inability to describe her attacker as a reluctance to give information. "Can we not have a pissing contest here," he said, trying to be both firm and gentle. "Was it male or female, tall or short, white or black, young or old?"

Wearily she raised her head and looked directly into his eyes. "Brunton was skinned and the person who attacked us wore his skin. If it was a man, it was a short man. If it was a woman, it was a tall woman. I think its eyes are blue. I know it is insane."

"Jesus Christ!" Mallory whispered. "Holy Mother of God." He looked at the police officer. "Do we need a SWAT team?"

"No, Chief Mallory," Beryl said, mentally collapsing into a lucid resignation. "Whoever did it is likely to be long gone. It may have been a barbaric ritual or maybe there was method in the madness. I'm guessing that we interrupted some kind of attempt to retrieve evidence. But I don't know. If he's still there, he's got my fully loaded Beretta. So don't go up there without body armor."

Mallory left to consult his department.

An X-ray revealed that there were no broken bones in Beryl's wrist, hand, or arm. George, too, did not have a fractured skull, although the laceration was severe and would require "many stitches." When the doctor told her that a cosmetic surgeon had been called in to do "nearly invisible" scalp suturing, Beryl began to laugh nervously. "Thank God," she said. "He has gorgeous hair."

A doctor from the E.R. approached them. "We'll be admitting him. He lost a lot of blood. Head wounds are big bleeders. Are you a relative?"

"No, his partner. We're P.I.'s. I ought to tell you that he's a recovered morphine addict."

"I saw his scars. Gunshot wounds?"

"Yes. Ten years ago."

"Since you've not been injured, why don't you let the police officer take you to the Motel. I understand that your vehicle will be taken into custody. We'll know where to reach you if there's any change."

The officer asked, "She'll need to change those clothes... and we might need them for evidence... so do you have a pair of scrubs she could have?"

A nurse came towards them carrying a pair of blue scrubs and a clear plastic bag that contained Beryl's blood drenched purse.

At the Crestview Motel, the clerk checked her in with a minimum of questions. Beryl's hands were still caked with blood and the clerk did not particularly care to have her sign anything. The police officer assured the clerk that Beryl was working for the Eckersley family, and, aside from her name and address, that assurance was sufficient. "Do you have any luggage?" she asked.

"No," Beryl said simply.

The police officer took the scrub suit and bag. "If anybody asks, I'll be in the room with her. There's a lunatic on the loose. I'd keep that front door locked until you see and know who's there."

While the officer sat on a chair by the window, Beryl went into the bathroom, stripped off her clothing, and stood numbly under the shower. After five minutes of watching the water turn from pink to clear as it circled the drain, she picked up a bottle of shampoo and washed her hair.

When she opened the door, the police officer was gone and Ron Mallory was sitting in his place. "You need a comb?" he asked. "I got you one at the 7/11 and I also got you some snacks and a six pack of Dr. Pepper."

"I'll be sure to repay you for all of this. I'm starved." She took the comb and sat on the edge of the bed. "Have you checked on George?" she asked, nervously eating the candy and snacks.

"Before you came out of the bathroom I talked to the doctor. Wagner's in the I.C.U., but that's just to be on the safe side over night. Head wounds are tricky. Fortunately, he's got very comprehensive insurance. They're optimistic. It's not as bad as it looked."

"That was kind of you," she said, combing her hair. "Groff Eckersley ought to be here shortly. I don't know when Lionel will arrive."

"Do you feel like talking?"

"I don't know what to tell you. It was just a routine stop. We were hoping to find a clue that would lead us to the identity of Madeleine Eckersley's physician. We figured she had one up here; and until we could interview him or her and learn about her condition and treatment, we couldn't finish the case. She died in May. This is October."

"Who all knew that you'd be up here?"

"It wasn't a secret. Lots of people knew. There was no intention to prosecute the doctor. It wasn't a criminal matter. Her son Groff wanted details. He was in Europe when she died. It came as a shock and he wanted to know everything about her death. We knew she had spent time up here after Dalton's death and we knew she had seen one physician up here who recommended that she go to the hospital in Allentown. So, to tell you the absolute truth, we were hoping to find a prescription bottle in the Lodge's medicine chest. Maybe an appointment book... or doctor's bill... or one from a hospital. We sure as hell didn't expect to run into that monstrosity."

Mallory's cellphone rang. He mumbled something inaudible and finally said, "Secure the scene."

"So Lionel's coming up here tonight?" He grinned. "Haven't seen him in months. We go way back. Been friends for years. We were in the service together."

A car's headlights briefly flashed across the window. Someone knocked loudly on the door.

Ron Mallory called, "Who is it?" The reply was inaudible. He opened the door, but did not unlatch the chain. "I don't know either one of you." He turned to Beryl, "Miss Tilson, are these gentlemen friends of yours?"

Groff called, "It's 'Grasshopper The Idiot' and old Master Po. Let us in."

"It's ok," Beryl said. "That's Lionel's grandson."

They entered the room. Groff introduced Sensei. "We just checked with the hospital. George is holding his own. They're optimistic." He went to the bed and checked Beryl. Then he stretched out on her bed and picked up an empty cellophane bag. "You pig," he said. "Did you eat the whole bag of gummy bears?"

"It's my nerves," she said. "They were comfort food. Is Lionel on his way?"

"Yes... it's a bitch driving up here. Snow all the way. So I can't say when he'll arrive."

Ron Mallory stood up. "If you gentlemen give me your assurance that you won't leave Miss Tilson alone and unprotected, I'll go down to the desk and make some calls so she can talk to you in private. "

"Sensei's a better guard than I am," Groff said. "I'll go with you and get a room for him and me. If you want to be comfortable while you make your calls, you can use our room instead of the office."

Sensei sat on the the other bed in the room. "How bad is George?"

"He's unconscious. It's a bad head wound. Whoever attacked us killed Brunton and put his skin on, like that picture I took of the figurine."

Sensei got up and locked the door.

SATURDAY, OCTOBER 17, 2009

At 1 a.m. Lionel Eckersley arrived in his limo. He sat on the edge of Beryl's bed and exchanged pleasantries with Ron Mallory.

Lionel was gently professional. "Would all of you mind leaving me alone with Ms. Tilson? We shouldn't be but a few minutes." Groff, Sensei, and Ron Mallory went to the double room that Groff had rented.

As best she could, Beryl related the story to Lionel. He took Beryl's hand. "You survived this and it begins to appear that George will, too. As to the local police, let's not volunteer anything about Haddon Manor and the con game. I'm not telling you to lie... just not to disclose gratuitously any personal matters."

"I never mentioned any of that. I merely told the truth. We wanted to learn the identity of Madeleine's physician to satisfy Groff's need for details about her death."

"Let's get them back," he said, hitting the speed dial on his phone. Beryl could hear Groff's new ring tone, *God Save The Queen*, through the wall. Lionel said, "You can all come back now."

When they were all seated in Beryl's room, Ron Mallory said, "The scene's secure. Let's go up there and have a look. Lionel, it looks like we've had another homicide at your lodge. That place is gonna get a bad name."

Lionel was wearing a shoulder holster. He reached into his jacket, withdrew the gun, took a magazine from his pocket, and deftly inserted it into the weapon with a firm click.

Groff was startled. "My Gramps, a gunslinger?" he asked. He turned to Lionel and asked, "Do you know how to use that thing?"

Lionel returned the gun to his holster. "For God's sake, Groff. I fought in Vietnam. We used guns."

"*You* fought in Vietnam? Why don't I know about that?"

"There's a lot you don't know about. You don't know I have 'Fuck Ho Chi Minh' tattooed on my ass, either."

The detective pursed his lips and turned to Groff. "And from what I remember, your grandfather never missed what he aimed at."

"If it were big enough, Ron. If it were big enough."

Groff looked at Beryl. "Was that a Glock 9 mil he's packing? The world's gone mad."

"I know you've got a permit to carry," said the detective, "so let's roll."

"Wait!" Beryl called. "My Beretta's in the kitchen. If the Flayer didn't move it, it should still be there. It wasn't fired, so could you get it released to me? And my iPhone's down in the cellar."

"I'll see what I can do," Ron said. "Right now, it's still part of a crime scene. Get some rest and I'll get a statement from you in the morning."

In the morning, Lionel, Sensei, and Chief Ron Mallory went to the Lodge. Groff took Beryl shopping for clothing. She insisted that they go to Wal-Mart since, she joked, she wasn't dressed well enough to shop for clothes. Everything that she had worn the day before was filled with blood; and since she had wounded her assailant and also had had physical contact with him, there was a good chance that some of his blood was on her garments. She happily gave them everything she had worn.

They shopped and Groff claimed to be depressed because he couldn't dress her in "Republican Chic."

She smiled. "My beautiful cashmere suit. How I worried about vomiting on it. Little did I know."

She bathed again at the motel and put on fresh clothes. Sensei called Groff. "Brunton's corpse was in the kitchen of his apartment. His skin is nowhere around. The detective said that somebody with skill had done the flaying." Sensei quoted the detective, "'But hell, that could be anybody from the age of eight on up. We're all hunters.'"

Sensei continued. "The detective was certain that if the skin had been disposed of in the woods it would already have been eaten. Apparently they have many natural predators and packs of feral dogs that roam the woods. The bears have not yet hibernated and are voraciously eating anything they can get to sustain them through the winter. He said that he doubted that they would find any trace of the victim, and then Lionel said, 'You mean, other than his body.' It brought a light moment into an otherwise dark, foreboding scene."

"And no trace of the perpetrator?" Groff asked.

"None. If the killer got away by driving down the narrow drive, the police cars had obliterated his tracks. There were more flurries during the night. No signs of him at all."

Beryl interrupted. "Tell Sensei we'll meet him at the hospital or back here."

George had regained consciousness. Beryl spoke to the nurse in charge of the Intensive Care Unit. "He's been a very good patient," the nurse said. "Because of the morphine history, we've limited the drugs; but he's not complained at all. He had nightmares. I heard him say, 'Jesus Christ!' a few times in his sleep, but I don't think he was praying."

"I think that it was probably one of those dual-purpose exhortations. Part 'What the hell is this' and part 'God help me.'" She was permitted to go in while Groff waited in the hall.

At such times as this, they had a little test. One would ask, "Does it hurt?" and if the other was optimistic about recovering, the answer would be, "Only when I laugh." She pulled a chair up to his bed. "George... does it hurt?"

He answered, "What the hell do you mean? Does it hurt? Are you trying to make me laugh?"

Beryl began to laugh at him and at herself and for a moment the incident at the Lodge entered a dusty chronicle. "Give me your thoughts," she said. "After you went down, I tussled with the Flayed lunatic. He or she got away, but you know those little eye-glass repair kits you can buy for a dollar at a check out counter? I had one in my shoulder bag and I stabbed the little screw driver into its foot. I mean I buried that thing... through to its instep. It jumped. I doubt that it felt too much pain at the time... having just murdered Brunton... what with all that adrenalin going. By now the pain is there and a deep puncture wound in the arch is gonna cause a limp. "I want to ask Ted to video Aubrey Euell, and his nurse, Isabel McAndrew. It might be tough to catch them out in the open, but I think we should try to get them even before they go to work on Monday."

"I've been lying here asking myself who the lunatic was. I considered both of them because of the racket that was being run at Haddon Manor. Somebody was feeding the Oracle information. How big a guy was the astrologer?"

"Not big. He could have fit into the skin."

"Tell Ted to get him, too. He may have to call in a couple of associates. Weddings usually tie these guys up on weekends. It'll cost more, but money doesn't seem to be a problem with that family."

"I know. And I'm sure we'll be paying overtime. Have you given a statement to the Police?"

"Not yet."

"I think we're supposed to limit our accounts to just what went on here in Lehigh County. We went to look for evidence that would lead us to Madeleine's doctor. Groff just wanted to know more about her condition."

"In other words, Lionel Eckersley says, 'Don't talk about the con game.'"

"Right. For Groff's sake, I don't want to expand the scope up here at least until we can figure out who killed Brunton. But this is a police investigation. It's not a good time for either of us to be interviewed."

"I see your wrist is bandaged. Is it bad?"

"No. I got hit with that barbecue spit, too.

"Is that what the hell hit me? I thought maybe it was a poker."

"Can you think of anyone else beside the doctor, the nurse, and the astrologer?" Before George could answer, someone rapped on the glass door. Beryl looked up to see Lionel and Sensei. "The gang's all here. You want visitors?"

"I already saw Percy. I'm glad he's still here. Tell Groff to come in for a minute and that's all. I'm startin' to fade."

Beryl left and Groff entered. "Hi kid," George said.

"Do you have any objections to be airlifted to Philadelphia?" Groff asked.

"No. And I'm glad you're thinking along those lines. Somebody doesn't like me up here."

They walked to the hospital cafeteria. After they ordered lunch, Beryl went into the ladies room. Using the pay phone, she called Ted Fiorentino, a professional photographer who specialized in insurance disability-fraud cases. After a brief rundown of the case, she told him about the foot injury she was particularly anxious to document. Ted understood. "Ok, girl. I've got it covered," he said.

Groff took a no-nonsense attitude. "Since my credit cards haven't come through yet," he said to his grandfather, "you'll have to make arrangements to have George flown down to Philadelphia tomorrow - barring any complicating medical event. Have him put into the care of a neurologist. The hospital should be able to arrange the transportation. I intend to stay with Beryl. Sensei can spell me if I'm needed elsewhere; but whether she realizes it or not there's a killer out there who's looking for her."

"He or she is also just as likely to be looking for you," Beryl said. "We can stay up here until George is safely back in Philly and the doctor thinks I won't mentally disintegrate."

Lionel's cellphone rang. Ron Mallory wanted him to bring Beryl in to make a statement.

They all went to the station and with Lionel present, Beryl dictated the purpose in coming to the Lodge.

"You had said that probably the person who killed Brunton was there to get evidence. Evidence of what?"

"I don't know. We were looking for evidence about Mrs. Eckersley's physician - a prescription bottle or an appointment book entry; and I assumed the person who attacked us wanted to prevent us from getting that evidence."

"Do you know if she brought any friends up here... after Dalton's death, of course?"

"I think she did. But you must understand... I never met Mrs. Eckersley."

"What kind of god was this Flayed God?" he asked.

"I'm no expert, but I believe it's a god in the Aztec religious system."

"Did it have anything to do with Mrs. Eckersley? Did she belong to some kind of cult to your knowledge?"

"No. Not at all. She was a practicing Episcopalian as far as I know. A devout Christian. This doesn't mean that she limited her associations to Episcopalians. She was an anthropology major at Penn State and she had copies of pre-columbian artifacts in her possession at the time of her death. Alien civilizations were interests of hers, intellectual interests."

When she concluded her statement, Mallory said, "After we heard your comments last night, we checked the medicine cabinet, bedrooms, and kitchen. No prescription bottles whatsoever. Sorry."

"Did they have a calendar or chalk board... something that they might have written appointments on?"

"Nothing. Mr. Eckersley said that a table in the living room was used as a desk. We checked and it had been cleaned out. Brunton also kept a kind of day book... a 'things to do today' calendar, we took into evidence. If I find anything that looks like a doctor's name, I'll let you know. I can also keep my ears open. Mr. Eckersley has again assured me that Groff simply wants to learn about the medical condition his mother had. If anyone treated her locally, he'll come forward, I'm sure."

Lionel wanted to rent rooms at the motel for himself and his driver; but Groff insisted that he use the room that he and Sensei rented. They had slept the previous night in the second bed in Beryl's room. "Until the lunatic is caught, we'll be sleeping close by."

SUNDAY, OCTOBER 18, 2009

While Beryl, Sensei and Groff sat at George's bedside, the motel desk clerk called to tell Beryl that the repaired pickup truck had been delivered to the motel and that she had accepted delivery with the provision that it was "subject to the inspection of the owner," which she had written on the receipt. Beryl thanked her.

George's continuing improvement had gotten him removed from the I.C.U. and into a private room. Further studies indicated that he had not sustained additional injury. Nevertheless, the doctor suggested that they not "overburden" him with their company. "He's being taken to Philadelphia this afternoon... to Jefferson Hospital. I'd like him to save his strength for the trip."

They returned to the motel to get George's pickup and drive to the Lodge.

Lionel and Ron and the team of forensic technicians were busy at the site. Lionel called Beryl aside. "Were you looking for anything else beside prescription bottles?"

There seemed to be no point in trying to evade a direct answer. "Yes, Revere Sanchey, a friend of Mrs. Eckersley's, left his passport and other papers here and I told him I'd try to return them to him. They're in the hutch cabinet... the middle drawer."

"Wait until the crime scene is released," he advised. "They're thoroughly searching the place for evidence of the murder and the attack on you and George. Those papers probably will still be here later. Let's just go back to the motel and I'll take everyone to an early lunch. Chief Mallory will stay here overseeing the work."

At the restaurant Lionel announced that he didn't want to leave Alicia alone and that after they revisited the crime scene he would be heading back to Philadelphia. "Staying on here only attracts more attention to the incident and will tend to spread it to the lunacies at Haddon Manor. This Flayed God business is making me sick just talking about it." He sighed. "But it is a murder committed in Lehigh County, and I know for a fact that they have competent people working on the case."

Groff stared at him. "Oh, it's an 'intra-county' affair? I guess you've checked with Lehigh County's State Department… asked their consular officials to ascertain whether any foreigners from Philadelphia or Montgomery or Berks county entered the area."

"We can live without your sarcasm," Lionel said curtly.

Groff grinned. "You're trying to sever any connection to people outside this county. Except for the murder victim, that 'Flayed God business' doesn't involve anybody in Lehigh County. It involves friends, relatives, and associates of ours from several other counties." He scoffed. "How," he asked, "do you expect to prosecute a murder in the Eckersley Lodge that involves an Aztec god without alluding to Madeleine Eckersley's peculiar Aztec god boyfriend who would have been… Gee!.. the owner's stepfather?"

"You let the authorities and me worry about 'Crime and Punishment.' Let's try to narrow the periphery of the crime, not widen it."

Beryl reached across the table and touched Groff's hand. "George and I have been through so much these past two days. My nerves can only take so much. No arguing… please. Just do as you're asked so that we can get through this nightmare."

They returned to the hospital to wish George a good trip back to Philadelphia. Standing in the doorway of George's room, they watched a nurse's aid feed him soup. George laughed at something the girl said; and Beryl, seeing that his sense of humor and mental acuity had not been affected, suddenly weakened with relief and leaned against the wall.

The doctor came into the room and looked at George's empty lunch tray. "I hope you don't get motion sickness," he joked. Then he reassured the visitors, "He'll be carefully monitored at Jefferson. Head wounds like his are nothing to turn your back on. He had a few nightmares, so I want that problem looked at. Post traumatic stress is something we can nip in the bud." He looked at Beryl. "You, too. You should talk to a professional when you get home."

"All right," Beryl said. "If that's what you think is best, I'll do it."

Chief Mallory called Lionel to tell him that the Lodge was no longer "yellow-taped" and that Beryl's gun and phone could be picked up at the police station. "Could you all come by now," he asked. "I'd like to ask a few questions before you head on out of the jurisdiction. You understand."

They piled into the limo and went to police headquarters. Beryl signed for her phone and gun as Ron Mallory had extra chairs brought into his office. "First," he said, "I'd like to know who is the official owner of the Lodge?"

Lionel answered. "My grandson Groff Zollern Eckersley owns the Lodge. Brunton and the detectives were in his employ at the time of the incident. After the violence there this past spring, I obtained additional insurance. Brunton has a daughter somewhere in Pennsylvania. She's listed as the beneficiary. I'll notify her when I get back to my office; but if your office is in contact with her first, tell her to call me. He was a good man. Let's just get the lunatic son of a bitch who killed him off the streets."

Mallory addressed his next question to Beryl. "You mentioned Madeleine Eckersley's doctor. Now, Aubrey Euell who's been at the Lodge many times with the Colonel... hunting and some fishing, too... he always was her doctor. I know he's still alive and in practice, so I want to know if Aubrey Euell could be involved in this bizarre incident in any way."

Beryl answered simply, "Mrs. Eckersley was considering moving into the Lodge, using it as her primary residence. Her son Groff, here, had graduated from college and was probably going to attend Law school in Philadelphia and would be living at The Hollyoak. Maybe she just wanted the peace and quiet of this beautiful area. I don't know. She was not medically estranged from Dr. Euell. He was in attendance when she died. He signed the death certificate. But geographically he was too far away, and she wanted a local physician."

"After her husband's death, she was seen up here several times with a long haired gentleman. Was she planning to live here with that man?"

"To my knowledge, she was planning to marry him in June and to live here with him as man and wife."

"I'm glad to hear that. We didn't know Mrs. Eckersley. We always wished we did, but this was the Colonel's 'den' so we never had the pleasure. Brunton liked the two of them... her and the new man. We always regarded her as a lady of quality." He turned to Groff. "My condolences on the loss of your mother. She looked so happy the last time I saw her."

Groff muttered, "Thank you."

"Will you all be going up to the Lodge now?" Mallory asked.

"Yes," Groff said. "I've never seen the place. Sad that this has to be the occasion of my first look at it."

"It's an ugly thing to see. We have a company in town here that specializes in cleaning up death scenes. The sergeant at the desk can give you the name if you're interested."

They shook hands and left the station. Groff did not ask for the name of the cleaning service.

Since the limousine could not possibly drive up to the Lodge, the chauffeur was left at the motel to watch football games on television. Sensei, Groff, Lionel and Beryl took George's pickup truck to the base of the hill where, once again, the snow chains had to be put on the pickup. It was after 2 p.m. before they got to the Lodge.

Lionel unlocked the door and pushed it open, revealing in the sunless light a gory scene of blood streaks and smudged footprints on the floors. Beryl's bloody handprints were all around the doorless closet. In the kitchen, a splintered table and more blood... pooled and in footprints. Groff went to the hutch cabinet and opened the middle drawer. "There's an envelope in here," he said, opening it. "It's got a U.S. passport and some letters to Mr. R. S. Porter in it."

"That's the medicine-man," Beryl said.

"That's all we came for," Groff said. "Let's go." He locked the house as they left.

They got into the pickup and stayed sitting there, waiting to read the contents of the envelope that Groff held in his lap. He stared at it, wondering if he wanted its contents disclosed to his grandfather.

Lionel said, "I'd like to have a look at those." Beryl, who was sitting in the back seat with Sensei, reached into Groff's lap, took the envelope, and handed it to Lionel who was sitting in the passenger seat. Groff, knowing that she wanted to avoid confrontation, said nothing. Lionel emptied the envelope into his lap. He picked up the passport. Is this the man who killed Brunton?" he asked, showing her the photo in the passport.

"No," she said. "Definitely not. This man has only one foot. We're looking for somebody who has two feet."

Sensei couldn't resist saying, "Well now, that narrows it. A two footed man, eh?"

Groff extended his hand. "Show it to me." The photograph was dark and did not flatter Sanchey. He returned the passport to Lionel and muttered. "This is all complete bullshit."

Lionel sorted the envelopes by date. He took the oldest one and opened it. "It's some kind of love letter."

"If it's a letter my mother wrote, I don't want you to read it," Groff snapped. "Give it to me."

Lionel handed him all the letters. Groff leaned over and showed Beryl the love letter Lionel had started to read. "It's not my mother's handwriting," he said. He looked at the envelope. "It's from X.C., no return address, but a Philadelphia postmark." He began to read:

August 20, 2008
Beloved Lord,

How often I have wondered why my life was empty. I did not realize that I was an empty vessel God was waiting to fill.

That magical June night I met you the world changed. God had put his plan into action. My heart had been broken. Once again the Beast had asked for my help. He was giving a party to celebrate his new swimming pool. It had a high board and as a kid I had been regional diving champion. He knew that I would love to attend the party; but my name wasn't on the list. I cried as I wrote other people's names.

I now know that it was part of your divine plan. If my name had been on that list, I never would have gone to the fair to get my fortune told. I was so desperate for guidance. I expected to find an old gypsy. Instead I found a young lord. What Power brought me to you, an Aztec God-Priest, who would make me his consort? What divine force lifted me up to vanquish all my enemies?

I agree that word-of-mouth is the best way to gain new devotees. I have created files on eight more women. Their sordid little stories will assist you in your ascendance. I have also included notes on events in their lives that are not in anyone's files. When I meet you on Friday at our Manor Temple, I will give everything to you. We are on our way to glory.

My Obsidian Lord. We shall prosper together. I shall be lying next to you on the white beaches beside the blue ocean waters. Our hearts shall beat together. I will wear a crown of bright feathers. Oh! since I started writing this note an inspiration came to me! I will dive off La Quebrada Cliff at Acapulco just for you! This will be my special offering of gratitude to you.

Your Loving,
X.C.

"Is this some kind of religious cult?" Lionel asked.

"Yes," Beryl said. "In a manner of speaking it is. It's a fake Mexican god-priest and his followers. But what does the author mean about assembling files? He or she must be passing him useful information for the 'fortune telling' con. 'X.C.'? Arturo Rosales told me that Xipe Totec's consort was Xilonen Chico... something. The writer thinks she... or he... is his wife... and she's obviously his confederate. Read the next one."

"Have you ever seen those cliff divers?" Sensei asked. "That's the Mount Everest of diving. Insane. She or he - I guess it's not politically correct to eliminate males - definitely is not playing with a full deck. *La Quebrada?*"

Groff returned the letter to its envelope and opened the next one. "This one is dated November 19, 2008." He read the letter.

Beloved Husband,

How delighted I was to see how our bank account is growing.

I'm taking note after note and with each one I think about the rewards we will receive and the future we will have together. I have addressed more letters for you. Tell Pablito to be prepared. I cannot wait until I see you on Friday. I'll bring all the notes and a new disposable cellphone, too.

I am so glad that Pablito has succeeded in getting new ingredients for the tea. It cheers me to think of these "holier than thou' witches acting like maenads. Once they are in your arms, those dried-up old weeds bloom like passion flowers.

Your loving wife who needs no aphrodisiac to melt into your arms,

Xilonen

Groff looked around to see if the words meant anything to anyone. No one responded to his expression. He opened and read the next letter which was dated December 1st.

Beloved Lord,

I can't tell you how wonderful the feedback has been. These women always get maudlin around the holidays. Planting a little of your seed in them makes them bloom with praise for their new master. They don't pay honest people who work for them. But they love to throw money at the people who exploit them. I ask only that you think of me when you take them into your private chambers.

Your loving wife,

Xilonen

Groff looked at the next letter and said, "Uh huh. Here we go! This is about us. It's dated December 16th..

"My Husband, Lord Tezcatlipoca,

Please have Pablito mail the enclosed letter and envelope to Madeleine Eckersley. I just received word that she will be in town soon. Tell him not to delay because this woman moves around a lot. But she has money and lots of fine jewelry.

There isn't much in the files about her. We can stick with the 'Easing the trouble in your heart caused by a loved one' pitch. She may call right away after she gets Pablito's mailing. Her husband is Colonel Dalton E. They have one child, a nitwit named Groff who's been committed to a Swiss asylum. She takes him around like a pet dog to museums and the pyramids. Her mother-in-law is a senile old meddler named Alicia and her father-in-law is Lionel E., a high-priced lawyer who has never seen the inside of a courtroom because he's so incompetent. The two of them hate M. Her parents are dead. She's an only child. She is so crazy about her son that she lives with him inside the asylum! Here, she lives in a mansion called The Hollyoak. She was born in New Hope, Pennsylvania. If I think of anything else, I'll let you know. She's mainly worried about her son. He's around 20. She's an Aries. But play this one carefully. She doesn't suspect that anyone knows she's having an incestuous relationship with her son, but everyone knows, even her husband who has vowed to kill them both if he finds them together. So win her confidence before you bestow your sacred essence upon her."

Your beloved X.

Lionel shook his head. "Well, let's remember to vet anyone who wants to write our family bio very very carefully. Jewelry? Last December? Could this have anything to do with that affair in Ireland?"

"I know better than to say 'No,' definitely. I can't see how it could, but what do I know?" Groff returned the letter to its envelope and opened the next one.

January 9, 2009.
Heart of Heaven, Beloved Lord,

What a wonderful weekend we had. My heart rejoices to see you so happy. I knew that our time would come. Six more months of this and we will have enough to free ourselves from all this secretive behavior.

Not being able to touch you all week is my punishment for my previous life's sins. I am able to withstand it only because I know my pain will bear much joy. I imagine that it must be like a labor pain. I will deliver a new life.

I'm glad you've got M.E. in the palm of your heavenly hand. I will get you whatever additional information about her I can get. She should be good for at least 20 or 30K or more! Our best approach is to continue to advise her about her brat.

Your loving wife,
Xilonen

"What I don't get is why Tonto would give these letters to my mother. Did she know about this scam? This is crazy!"

"Continue reading," Lionel said. "We may yet get a clue. Your mother had a chambermaid during this period. She had a hairdresser and dress shop women with whom she chatted. Read on. Read on."

Groff said, "This one is dated February 23rd."

My Lord,

Please do not be angry with me. You cannot imagine how distressed I was to see that woman with you. Yes, I struck M. I would fight Heaven and Earth for you. Without you I am desiccated, a parched desert in which nothing grows. She thirsts and a thousand fountains offer her cool water. Yet she comes to my desert and drills down for whatever water she can find deep below my barren surface. All I have ever asked of you is that every once in a while you fill my cup. I know it takes time to set up a big score. I have been fighting my impatience and also my jealousy. Forgive me for doubting your motives.

I confess that knowing that she has not paid you for your attentions distresses me deeply. You have assured me that your investment in her will profit us greatly. I have no choice but to trust you.

I wish that I had not acted so harshly. You make me pay for my sins. You show your anger to me but you do not show your displeasure to her for not paying you. The longer she does not pay, the longer we must wait to gather the money we need to live as we were born to live.

Your loving wife,
Xilonen.

"And the next to last epistle from the goddess to the god is dated May 11th. Groff read:

My Lord and Husband,

Seven times I have shed my skin. My last rebirth was beautiful. I am still glowing from our Easter weekend together. Death and Resurrection. Sleeping in your arms was my rebirth, my Spring. The beating of your sacred heart - was the drumbeat that the happy victim marched to as she ascended the steps of your temple. All I know is that when I saw the blessed moon rise on Easter Morning, I rejoiced. I was reborn. New wine in old skins. Xipe!

But just when I was finally able to free myself from being jealous of M., you told me that she was trying to renew your relationship and that you still have hope that she is good for a big score. She is dangerous and perfidious. Please do not fall into her trap.

Do you care about the truth? Constantly Pablito lies for you. He says that you are out looking for spring flowers for me or you are looking for a piece of jewelry for me. Yet I get no flowers. I receive no jewelry. You sleep late in the mornings and he will not disturb you. And every evening he says you are with someone and he cannot enter your chamber.

Now you tell me you need to spend another weekend with that new woman who came unannounced to the Manor. I know nothing about her. You say she spent thousands of dollars on you in Florida and that you really needed the break away from our business. You say she has promised you the deed to a home in California, a home for us to enjoy together. I do not know what to believe.

Please remember your vows to me, your loving wife,
Xilonen

"Why would anyone commit such thoughts to print?" Sensei asked.

"People in love act like fools," Lionel answered. "Phone calls show up on phone bills. You can burn a hand written letter or claim it's a forgery, but just try to get rid of an email or any electronic trail. It's damned near impossible."

"She could have called him on a prepaid phone," Groff offered.

"Yes," Lionel said. "But what was the point? He didn't want to talk to her. She says Pablito would lie."

"If she met *Sitting Bull* at a carnival," Groff said, "chances are the dwarfs were there, too, and that's where they joined up."

"Let's get to that last letter," Beryl said.

"It's dated July, 2009. No specific day." Groff read:

My Lord of the Smoking Mirror,

Fate has intervened. I am told that M. has run off with a married doctor to Switzerland. It's a big hush-hush affair. Lots of lies circulating. Well, she has burned her bridges behind her and I pray that you were not on one of those bridges. No doubt she will resume her sick relationship with her son.

How could she leave you? How could she lie to you about helping you in your ministry? The last thing I heard was that she hoped no one would besmirch her good name. What a joke.

I beg you to never mention her name again to me or to anyone else. Her deceitful behavior has caused other people to hire private detectives to investigate her life. She is the subject of much scandal. If you discuss her with anyone, you will put us all in jeopardy. You have wasted so much time with her. Now she laughs at you for thinking she would donate money to your ministry.

I know in my heart that you were only trying to help her to reform. If she had stopped sinning, you could have absolved her of her transgressions.

Your loving wife,

X.

"I can't handle this," Groff said. "Let's get the hell out of here." He began to speak in an authoritative manner. He turned to Beryl. "You're in no condition to travel. And you need to be looked at, too. I'll stay with you at your place. Since the letter mentioned Hollyoak we won't be safe in any 'witness protection' program there.

"Who were the 'private investigators,' X.C referred to? It can't have meant Wagner & Tilson. I didn't meet you until October and I'm the one who called you. So there was no setup. We need to make a list of possible candidates. What about Euell's nurse? She knew you were coming here."

Beryl nodded. "Yes, she would have all kinds of information at her disposal and she also knew we'd be here. But then so did Loretta, that quiet receptionist in her office. She has the same access to information. And Aubrey Euell. He can't be more than 5'8" tall. And Clive Trask knew we'd be here and he also had a tendency to record things, as I recall. He would have fit into that skin suit and so would the astrologer. He had files on all the women."

"I take exception to your including Clive Trask," Lionel said.

"You're not my client," Beryl said. "You can object to anything you like. But please don't subject me to your opinions about anyone's guilt or innocence."

Lionel apologized. "I had no right to voice an objection and you're right. For all I know it was Clive Trask. I'd just like to say that idle speculation won't get us anywhere. Let's think about the whole situation, about every aspect of it. We need to take precautions... to protect ourselves and the people around us. The only thing we know for certain is that someone we know is limping badly." He looked at Groff and Sensei. "Beryl is emphatic about puncturing the killer's foot. Tomorrow we'll be thinking more clearly, and very soon we'll have George's account of the incident. Let's go back to the Motel now. It's time I returned home. I really don't want to leave my wife alone. Everything's paid for." He opened his wallet and gave Groff several bills.

Groff stuffed the money in his pocket and started the pickup.

Sensei watched the limo pull away. "Is it me or did he not want to discuss the possibility that the files were Euell's?"

"It's not you," Groff said. "They cover each other's ass. It's the coterie of 'them that's got.'"

"Let's all go home," Sensei said. "I've got to get back to my class. So, unless there's an objection, I'll drive the Jaguar back and you two can take the pickup." He waited for an objection. None came. He got into the car, waved, and called, "I'll see you back at the Vatican."

Groff waved back. "*Pax Vobiscum.*"

MONDAY, OCTOBER 19, 2009

After a night of fitful sleeping, Beryl staggered into the bathroom feeling more tired than when she went to bed the evening before. She took the splint off her hand and tested her fingers and wrist. Movement was tender and stiff but without any pinpoint of pain. She tossed the splint and bandages into the trash.

On Sunday evening the air ambulance had taken George to Jefferson Hospital in Philadelphia. There was no need to stay in Emmaus any longer. She had to be able to think clearly about the case, and to do that she needed to be able to sleep; and to sleep she needed to be home in her own bed. The weather had worsened, but the chains were still on the pickup. At least that much was done.

Groff was sleeping in the next bed, his head turned away, half-concealed by covers and his unbound long hair. She brought fresh clothing into the bathroom and closed the door quietly. With such a premium on sleep, even if he got only ten minutes more, it was worth it.

At dawn, they checked out, had breakfast at a truck stop, and began the slow drive home.

Everything was a mottled grey around the pickup. It had snowed again through the night and the morning traffic had not yet started to draw ridge lines in the highway. The horizon disappeared into the fog and the fog disappeared into the lowering clouds. In the headlights, tiny snowflakes swirled in the wind.

They had no way of knowing whether the day would be clear or overcast. To Beryl it felt as though not even the sun could break through the gloom.

It grew lighter. The snowflakes grew bigger and slower to melt as they lay on the windshield. "More snow," Groff said, turning on the defrosters; and then the flurry ended, a broken-off threat that left them wary of commenting about it. The horizon returned, the asphalt became black again, and Groff pulled into a gas station and asked an attendant to remove the chains. He bought a six-pack of *Mountain Dew*. "We need the caffeine," he said.

As the day brightened, the answers and the questions in Beryl's mind also became clearer. The letters had been a revelation, but what they revealed most was the vast area of unknowns. Yes, Revere Sanchey was a fake spirit-guide or health guru or shaman - by any name he was a fraudster. He, Pablito, and Doña Maria preyed upon rich women. The fourth member - and at the very least there had to be one more person involved - had supplied him with information about the women; and his knowledge of their private lives would have made him seem godly in his omniscience.

Yet, even if giving them aphrodisiacs and hashish had some long-term negative effect, the women currently had to be healthy and sufficiently improved in body and mind to recommend his services to their friends. "Word of mouth" Member Four or X.C. agreed was the best way to gain new devotees. Harming the clients did not help their cause. But when the fourth member became jealous of Madeleine Eckersley sometime in January, everything changed. The timeline had to be established.

Madeleine had been physically attacked in February. Member Four apologized for the attack, and as the letters indicated, Member Four was more than neurotic. This was a strange schizophrenia. The letters were florid but reasoned. If a person in a "legitimate" religion had written those florid passages to a saviour figure - to Christ, for example - the language would not have seemed unusual. With that thought, the possibility that X.C. was Isabel McAndrew grew stronger.

Madeleine had come home from Switzerland before Christmas. Groff had gone to Ireland and spent Christmas in the hospital. Madeleine saw Euell on December 22nd. She bought the first case of wine on December 23rd. Why didn't she plan to spend Christmas with

Groff in Switzerland? "When did you go back to Zurich after you were hospitalized in Ireland?" she asked.

"On December 30th. I had to sign some legal papers. The lawyer drove me to the airport. Why do you ask?"

"I'm trying to establish a timeline for your mother. By Christmas she was with Sanchey. She had to have seen him on or before the 23rd, the day she bought the wine. When did she leave Cairo?"

"It was a Thursday, the 18th or 19th."

"I'm wondering why she didn't plan to spend Christmas with you."

"That was my fault. Don Don left me the only thing he owned: that little house west of London. He had a son but they had had a falling out when he was in his crazy period. He showed me where his son lived. He had kids in high school. We'd sometimes ride our bikes past the house to see if we could see them. But Don Don wouldn't forgive him for some of the things he had said. So he left his house to me and I transferred title to his son. I was due to sign the papers on December 30th. For tax reasons it was best done in 2008. I also had a lot of his books I wanted to give him. I don't think my mother was feeling a hundred percent. She had a bladder infection. She saw a doctor in Zurich and then she called Euell's office from Switzerland - before she went to Cairo."

"Ahhh."

"What about the the gender of the letter writer? It could be a male. Euell knew she'd be in town, so he could have set her up with that initial baiting call or letter to go see the Mexican Wizard about me."

"No, think from both sides... like victimology. The fourth member's letters were written to Revere Sanchey Porter. But there is no doubt that Revere loved your mother. He was a heterosexual male. The letters spoke of what the writer considered a loving, connubial relationship. They were written by a woman because Sanchey would not have led-on a male just to make money."

"Why not?" Groff snarled. "He's already proven to be a low-life scum, bilking rich women. You think faking a homosexual love attraction is beneath him?"

"Your mother bought the wine on December 23rd. She fell in love with him as fast as he fell in love with her. Being married to Dalton might have prevented her from marrying Revere Sanchey, but it didn't make her poor. She had plenty of money in her own right. If it was money he was after, he already got it by December 23rd. He wouldn't have continued to string a male lover along to make a few bucks servicing women. And give your mother some credit. She loved him. And the letters indicate that he did not get any money from her - at least that went into the fortune telling business. They also indicate that he was paying less and less attention to his Aztec 'business' and was trying to distance himself from it. No. Number Four is a woman... and an older woman, at that. She calls him, 'a young lord.' A young woman doesn't praise a young lover for being young."

"Member Four had to know you'd be at the Lodge this weekend. How many older women knew?"

"Don't jump to conclusions. We don't know that the Flayed person and Member Four are one in the same. The desk was cleaned out. If the Flayed person wanted to get back the love letters he or she had written to Sanchey, he didn't look very hard... or maybe he found what he was looking for in the desk."

"All right. Humor me. What older women were privy to files of fortune-telling information?"

"Groff... at this point I don't give a rat's ass about Sanchey's Aztec baloney. I'm after the man or woman who killed Brunton and nearly killed George. Do I think they're the same same person? Yes. What bothers me is that I can't say with any certainty how tall the Flayer was. You didn't see the way Brunton's hair had been pulled up into points, stiffened with blood and gore. I was in flat shoes and the Flayer was shoeless. I thought the Flayer was taller than I; but I was scared. When we're scared we tend to enlarge the size of our attacker."

Groff tried to affect a patient and gentle attitude. "I understand your reticence. But don't you think you're losing valuable time by deferring any attempt to identify the person you stabbed with that little screwdriver?

Wounds heal, and by the time you get around to looking for a limp, the limp may be gone."

"I've already asked a photographer who does a lot of work for us to film Euell, his nurse, and the astrologer. You can check the Trasks when you get home. If you know how to reach your mother's chambermaid, by all means go watch her walk."

"You already hired a photographer? Would it have killed you to tell me? When did you hire him?"

"Why do you assume the photographer is a male?"

Groff tried to engage Beryl in light conversation. He asked how she became a widow when she lived in Arizona, what her early life was like when she grew up in Philadelphia, and why she came back. She was thinking about the case and gave only brief answers. Finally, as he got into the exit lane, he asked, "Why did Jack go back to Arizona to go to school?"

"Because," Beryl answered, "he inherited a nice house trailer in Chandler, Arizona. It's nice to go back to a place that you were tormented in - when all your tormenters are dead."

"I'll have to remember that." He did not ask any more questions.

At ten o'clock, Beryl talked to Sensei - and indirectly to George - at Jefferson Hospital. "George is very angry about the whole business," Sensei reported. He's sitting here fuming because he just saw how much of his scalp was shaved so that the plastic surgeon could do a beautiful job of suturing his wound."

"Finish the shave, then," Beryl suggested, "and let him take Holy Orders." She could hear George mumble something but Sensei would not repeat it.

The house phone rang. Groff answered and called, "Ted wants to talk to you."

Beryl held up her hand. "I've got another call." She quickly asked, "When will George be released?"

"Tomorrow," Sensei said. "He says not to come and visit him. He's not seeing anyone until his hair grows back. 10-4."

Beryl laughed and disconnected the call.

Ted Fiorentino had video of all three subjects and told her to open her laptop so that he could upload and discuss them. As Groff sat beside her, Ted narrated the images that appeared on her screen."This is the astrologer Daniel Moor. I got him Saturday afternoon, grocery shopping. It's October but as you can see, he's wearing sandals. The temperature's at fifty degrees, and he's barefoot in sandals. He ain't your guy."

The video changed. "This," the photographer said, "is Dr. Euell out jogging with his dog Saturday afternoon. As you can see, he's running with even steps. Nothing's pierced this guy's foot either."

The footage changed. "I couldn't get the nurse until this morning. She's walking to get the bus or get to her car. She's in her nurse's uniform so I assume she's going to work. She's walking naturally."

"How come you couldn't get her until this morning? Were you unable to get to it, or wasn't she coming outside?"

"I was covering the doc, so I had one of my guys watching her house. He waited a couple of hours and then tried the delivery boy routine and rang her bell. He had a camera in his visor cap. She didn't come down and the landlady said she wasn't home and that was usual for weekends. So I went myself this morning and got her leaving her house to go to work."

"Thanks Ted. Send us the bill. You did a nice job."

Groff grumbled. "You could have told me you were moving on this."

"No... what I could have done was tell you and then let you screw-up my train of thought with your own theories and prejudices. George and I are the ones who have to solve this. So please.. don't try to get me into a debate about this. You're used to academic debates. 'Pick a side, any side.' This isn't rhetoric. In short, shut up and let me do my job. I need to call George back so I want you in the bathroom with the water running."

"I am paying big bucks for this abuse."

"Go!" She called Sensei who put his phone on speaker so that she could discuss the videos with George.

At eleven, as they ate an early lunch, Groff's phone tinkled *God Save The Queen*. Lionel Eckersley was calling. Groff answered and repeated Lionel's message as he received it. "He says to tell you that he has important evidence that he can show you. He's also inviting us to come along with him to Haddon Manor. He's already at the Shell Station, but as a courtesy to Beryl, he will wait 'if she wants to come.'" He grinned at Beryl's angry expression. "Should I tell him to shut up and let you do your job?"

"Sure... if you're ready to hire another P.I. Other than that tell him we'll be right there."

"We'll be right there," Groff told Lionel. Then he listened to Lionel's final comment and disconnected the call. "He says that I'm to bring the letters and passport."

"The base of the Buddha statue on my altar functions as a storage place for incense. Put the letters and the passport in it and let's go."

The limousine was parked at the side of the gas station. As they pulled up beside it, they could see Lionel sitting in the back, studying the screen of a laptop computer. He rolled down the window and told them to get in.

"Before I show you this," he said, attempting to deflect the angry questions that he could see forming in Beryl's expression, "I need to ask Beryl this: are you absolutely sure you wounded that creature?"

"Yes. Absoutely. And I am absolutely exhausted, too. What is this all about?"

"After hearing those wretched letters to this Aztec person, I tried to list the people I knew who could possibly have been the author. I realize that the author and the attacker do not necessarily have to be the same person. But we do know that files of information as well as gossip were given to the Aztec fortune teller. That would have put Dr. Euell and his staff at the forefront of suspects."

"We've all been playing 'whodunit,' Mr. Eckersley. What is it that you want to show us?"

Lionel turned the screen so that Beryl and Groff could see it. A video recording of Aubrey Euell came on the screen. "This was taken on

Saturday afternoon. Aubrey takes his Afghan hound to the dog park. I had one of the photographers who works for my firm film it. Aubrey is running without favoring either foot.

"And here," the video changed, "is his nurse coming out of the parking lot behind his office. She walks without the slightest indication of podiatric distress. There! Euell and his nurse can be eliminated as candidates for your Flayed attacker." He signaled his driver and the limousine pulled onto the road, heading for Haddon Manor.

"Did you lock the pickup?" Beryl asked Groff.

"Yes," he said. "I don't know if they'll appreciate the way we're parked, but it's locked."

Beryl turned to Lionel Eckersley. "I'm going to ask you in a nice way to cease interfering in this investigation. Frankly, Sir, you don't know shit from Shinola. You've lived in abysmal ignorance of the principals of this case for years. Evidence? You haven't proven a damned thing with those videos. If one of them had limped, yes, that might evidence 'podiatric distress,' or that there was a nail or pebble in the shoe. Do I have to tell you... you, a lawyer... that the absence of evidence is not the evidence of absence? Both Euell and his nurse are medical professionals. They have easy access to novocaine. If I had a pain in my foot and I knew that by showing that pain I was giving visual evidence of my guilt, I'd take pains to conceal that pain. With or without novocaine, I wouldn't limp in public if it killed me! You haven't proven a thing. I already had the subjects videotaped. I learned what I needed to learn. You learned nothing!"

The limo pulled into Haddon Manor's driveway. No cars were parked in front. Beryl, still angry, ordered, "Tell your man to go around to the rear."

Doña Maria pulled a kitchen curtain aside and studied them as they walked to the kitchen door. Lionel, miffed at being told not to interfere, took the lead and knocked repeatedly before Pablito opened the door.

Doña Maria screeched, "It's that investigator again. Shut the door!"

"Well," Pablito smirked, looking at Beryl, "if it isn't Laura Orsini, or whatever you are today."

"Whoever," Groff corrected.

"We'd like to see Mr. Sanchey," she said. "Mr. Lionel Eckersley would like to ask him a few questions."

Pablito looked around to receive instructions. Sanchey came to the door. "Let 'em in," he said. As Pablito stepped back, opening the door wide, Doña Maria shouted, "Don't tell them anything!"

The three visitors filed into the kitchen and watched Sanchey, bloated, hung over, and so weary that he could barely hold his head up, proceed on crutches to the booth-style kitchen table. He dropped down onto the bench, squinted, and muttered, "What can I do for you today?" The clip that had secured his long braid had fallen off, letting strands of uncombed hair straggle down into his crumpled collar.

Groff's tone was vicious. "*This* is The Heart of Heaven?" Beryl silenced him with a look.

Addressing Sanchey, Lionel spoke in a gentle unofficial tone, "Someone associated with your religion went to the Lodge in Lehigh County this past weekend. Do you happen to know who that person was?"

"No. I don't. Is this Madeleine's boy?"

Beryl put her hand out and poked Groff indicating that he should shut up. "Yes," she said, "this is Groff, and this is Madeleine's former father-in-law, Mr. Lionel Eckersley."

Sanchey looked at Groff. "You have your mother's eyes. Sit down."

Instead of sitting across from him, Groff went to the little table in the center of the room and picked up a chair. He swung it around to the booth, turned it backwards and sat on it.

Beryl sat in the booth. Lionel took the another chair from the table and positioned it correctly next to Groff's.

Lionel asked, "Does the name 'Euell' mean anything to you?"

Doña Maria again shouted, "Don't tell them nothin'!"

Sanchey stared at Groff admiringly. Groff looked back at him with disgust.

Lionel continued. "Does the name 'Isabel McAndrew' mean anything to you?"

Pablito positioned himself between Sanchey and Lionel. "You ain't got no authority to ask us about anything. I signed the lease to this joint and I'm tellin' you to leave."

"Unless I'm mistaken," Beryl said, "if he signed the lease he has the right to ask us to leave. So, shall we go?"

"Stay!" Sanchey said. "I'll tell you whatever you want to know. But Groff has to ask me."

"No. No. No." Beryl stood up. "We're leaving."

"Ok," Sanchey relented, "*You* can ask me."

Lionel looked up at her. "Ask him the questions, Miss Tilson. For my sake. Please."

Beryl sighed and sat down. "Do you know Isabel McAndrew or Dr. Aubrey Euell?"

"Her, I know. Him? I've never had the pleasure."

"Did you receive secret information about your clients from anyone other than Isabel?"

"Directly, she was the only one; but sometimes a woman would be so explicit that I'd know who she was talking about."

"Can you tell us when you saw Isabel last?"

"I drove to the shore this weekend. I didn't see her at all. She was gone by the time I got home last night. Ask Pablito. She was here all weekend.. or most of it." He looked at the dwarf. "Tell her what she wants to know!"

"Did you see her Friday?" Beryl asked Pablito.

"Friday," said Pablito. "Revere left in the middle of the afternoon. My wife and I were in the trailer watching television. Isabel showed up around eight o'clock. On Friday night after work she does the grocery shopping."

Doña Maria clarified his statement. "She's supposed to work only half a day on Friday, but that doctor keeps her late a lot of times. Sometimes she comes at six, and sometimes she works until six and doesn't get here until nine."

"Was Isabel limping?"

Pablito and Doña Maria looked at each other and shrugged. "Not that we saw," Pablito said.

"Was her behavior any different Friday night from what it usually was? Beryl asked.

"Before or after we had the argument?"

"Why don't you start at eight o'clock when she arrived."

"She was putting away the groceries. We went to help. She asked where Revere was. We said he went away for the weekend with his girlfriend. That's what he told us to say. She went nuts. Then she argued with my wife about getting cheese cake. She didn't buy cheese cake and my wife was looking forward to eating some while we watched the late movie."

Sanchey scoffed. "Tell them what they want to know. 'Cheese cake.' Jesus."

Lionel stood up. "We didn't come here to learn about your domestic disputes. It's enough for us to know she wasn't limping."

"No, it isn't," Groff said. "Sit down. This party was your idea. Let's get the whole story."

Sanchey looked at Beryl. "Isabel checked the week's receipts and saw that there was only your thousand dollar donation in the bank deposit. She started to scream about having made only a thousand dollars for the four days. After I saw you Tuesday morning, I told Pablito to cancel all my appointments. I was finished with the scam. We had more than 300K in the bank. A friend of Pablito's had a mobile home for sale... it was outfitted with pedal extensions and Pablito wanted to buy it. We split the money three ways. I paid up the lease - it runs to next July - out of my share; and Pablito took out their 100K and put it in their personal account. I took mine in cash. We left the remaining 118K in the bank for Isabel. I knew she'd go crazy when she found out so I went to Atlantic City... where Madeleine and I went a few times. That's all I know." He grimaced. His eyes filled with tears. He covered his face with his hands and bent over, nearly touching the table. He tried to stifle a sob. It came out as a kind of hiccup. He wiped his eyes and lamented, "The only good thing that ever happened to me... and now she's gone... ashes in a jar."

"Stop it," Groff said sarcastically. "You're breaking my fucking heart."

Pablito looked at Groff. "Isabel knew you were onto us. She told us you hired a private dick and were snooping around. Yeah... we knew all about it. We didn't break no laws. We'd be outta here already if we didn't have to get the Winnebago inspected and registered. Rev says he'll be gone as soon as he gets his passport."

Doña Maria tugged at his sleeve. "Don't tell him any more. He got no warrant!"

Beryl asked Pablito, "Did she stay here the whole weekend?"

"No, she drove down to the shore looking for Revere. It's a big place. She didn't find him and came back. She was acting nuts. She really believes that Aztec god stuff. Tezcatlipoca would never let her down. Xipe Totec would never let her down. She had seven snakes - one was sweet and harmless and three were constrictors that she would choke the life out of us with, and three were poisonous and she would have them strike us with venom. On and on it went. We just wanted to leave."

"I think we can help," Lionel said. "We've got your passport." He looked at Groff. "Did you bring it?"

Beryl barked at Groff. "Say nothing!" She turned to Lionel. "This is my case, Mr. Eckersley. My client and I do not require your assistance. Nobody will be leaving town. There was a murder at the lodge and the police may want to question Mr. Sanchey and his associates."

Sanchey looked up. "Who was murdered?"

"Brunton. And the person who murdered him is extremely dangerous. So take precautions. Protect yourselves." Beryl looked at Sanchey. "I know this is hard for you to talk about. But how is it that you didn't know Madeleine was dead? Isabel knew Madeleine was dead. She worked for Euell and Euell signed the death certificate. But why didn't other people know Madeleine was dead?"

"We have a rule. No names. A client can say she's having trouble with her husband, but she can't call him by name. It has to be 'My H.' She can say 'my friend,' but she can't name her. So how could I ask about Madeleine? And I don't have any outside social life. Isabel knew I loved M. but she would act like she didn't know. It was crazy. She'd say, "Do you remember Madeleine? You know, she had a son in Switzerland. Well, I heard she's getting medical treatments in France." And then it was Brazil. Once she laughed and said she heard a silly rumor that Madeleine had gotten married to some doctor. I was supposed to gossip with her... to say, 'Oh, really?'" He leaned back and closed his eyes, and the muscles in his face relaxed. He was alone with his thoughts.

Groff, disgusted, said, "The point is that as long as Isabel thought she could bait Rasputin, here, with the hope that my mother was still alive, she could control him."

Sanchey groaned. "You got that right."

Beryl saw a clean towel on the counter near the sink. She drenched it in cold water, wrung it out, and handed it to Sanchey.

"How did you get this racket started?" Groff asked.

Pablito answered. "Doña Maria knows the secrets of fortune telling - how to recognize a mark's 'tells.' She's got 'the gift.' She knows how to ask the right questions. But we were small stuff. We needed a front man. That's why we got Revere to go in with us. We went all over the U.S. and Canada with Charity Productions Inc. We got top billing. People came in droves."

Sanchey gestured to him to be quiet. "I was billed as a Sioux Medicine Man. Pablito was my barker. We made money. Bought that mobile home, the one outside. When a lady looked like she wanted to hook up, Pablo would tell her that for a donation she could have a private audience after the show. Doña Maria always put fresh sheets on the bed and candles and stuff around. They'd go wait in the truck until I put a signal light on. We were doing good business.

"Then we came to town here last year. It was raining. Business was lousy. Everybody set up on a parking lot near the hospital. So in comes Isabel. I went into my routine. 'Tell me, Beautiful Lady, what is in your heart.' She puts her head on the altar and cries.

"Nobody was in line waiting, so I gave her all the time she wanted. She told me about Doctor Euell. She said he tantalized her with love and friendship and used her as cheap labor. She had been in love with him for twenty years."

Sanchey stopped talking. Doña Maria took the wet towel, filled it with ice cubes, and returned it to him. Everyone waited, saying nothing. He held the cold towel against his face for a few minutes and seemed more sober when he continued. "I felt sorry for her. I told her she was sensitive and intelligent, and she ought to find another job. I admit it. I felt sorry for her. She was alone. Forty-five years old, never married, overworked and underpaid. Same old story.

"I told her I understood her grief. Then she turned and said, 'How could you possibly understand my pain?'

"I told her to come behind the altar. I showed her my missing foot. She asked me how it happened. I told her and then she dropped to her knees and kissed the stump. I felt her tears on it. When she looked up, I could see how sex starved she was. She asked me where I lived on the lot and I told her. She asked if she could see me later, and I said, 'Sure. Eleven o'clock.'" He held the towel to his face again. No one said a word.

"When she showed up at eleven, she had it all written out. She came to the trailer and talked to the three of us. She said she had unlimited access to private information about the rich women who had made her life so miserable. She had a generation's worth of dirt on them. She knew their secrets. Who had an abortion. Who had a venereal disease. Who had been treated for alcoholism or drug addiction. The scam was brilliant. We were sold right away.

"She also got all the lab reports when they came into the office. That information was solid gold in a fortune telling con. I would know in advance what the test results would reveal. It was beautiful."

At the mention of lab reports, Beryl interrupted him. "That was in June of 2008. When did you put the scheme into action?" she asked.

"Right away. Last summer. Isabel knew that one of the patients got gonorrhea from her cheating husband. The guy was making a play for the daughter of another patient, so Isabel got a disposable cellphone for us, and in Pablito's name she sent a letter to that lady saying her daughter was in danger of contracting a terrible disease from a married man and she should contact me immediately. I would give her the information free. She called. Isabel rented a hotel suite. I wore plain white cotton

Indian clothing for the interview. I even gave her the guy's initials. She had been suspicious of him, and I had independently confirmed it. I told her to take the girl out of town as quickly as possible. She took my advice and got the kid away for a long cruise. While they were away, the scandal broke. The Health Department had notified dozens of people. It was a bad kind of gonorrhea... really resistant. The woman wanted to show her appreciation. We rented another hotel suite. She believed in me and wanted to help my ministry. She laid 100K on me. With that money we got the white peacock headdress and the jewelry, rented this place and bought the sets and props. She's still a regular client." Sanchey hiccoughed a few times and began to cry again.

Lionel interjected, "I remember hearing about this scandal. No wonder the scheme worked."

Pablito asked, "Is this gonna prevent us from leaving? We're getting ready to head south. We ain't broke no laws! Those women made donations by their own free will. And they were all consenting adults!"

"I'm sure they were," Beryl nodded. "But I want to know more about those lab test reports. Did she ever alter the reports?"

Sanchey shrugged. "Not that I know of." He looked at Pablito. "You would know. She filled out the 'tip' sheets with you."

Pablito affected an 'I'm no stool pigeon' attitude. Doña Maria spoke for him. "Isabel said that sometimes if she didn't want to see the patient again she wouldn't send out requests to come back."

Sanchey asked Pablito. "Did she ever mention Mrs. Eckersley's lab reports?"

The dwarf folded his arms and stood defiantly silent. Sanchey lunged for him and grabbed his collar and shouted, "What did she say about the reports?"

"She said she sent only one request out. She didn't know who you were sneakin' around with. She believed the lies you told her but then she found out who it was. So she said, 'We won't be inviting her back to the office any time soon.' I didn't know what she meant and she said, 'No more requests for retesting for that whore.'"

Sanchey released the dwarf. "I knew one day I'd find out that she died because of me." He covered his face with his hands and bent forward, nearly touching the table top.

Beryl asked Pablito, "How did you get women to come out here?"

"Different ways. World of mouth mostly," he said proudly. "We helped people! Sometimes Isabel bought classy paper and she'd send a letter to a woman, feeding her some line."

"My mother would never have fallen for that crap," Groff declared, shrugging off Lionel's restraining hand. "How did you lure her out here?"

Sanchey looked up defiantly. "That's exactly how! We played on her concerns about you!" He looked at Beryl. "But as I told you, I took one look at her and the scam was finished - for her and me, anyway. Isabel went crazy with jealousy."

"What's the story about her hitting my mother?" Groff asked.

Sanchey groaned. "It was Valentine's Day, Saturday, a long holiday weekend. The sixteenth was a national holiday. Isabel was asked to help one of the patients run errands or something at her house for a big party. She was so sure she'd be invited to the party as a reward for helping that she said she'd see me Sunday, but then it started to snow and she said she'd see me the following week. Your mom and I decided to spend the holiday weekend here.

"We lit a fire in the living room and I got out my guitar and she sang. The four of us. We ate a Jamaican dish Pablito made. Plantains and fish, papaya, mangos, in a really hot sauce. We laughed every time we took a bite.

"Isabel splurged on new clothes and went to help with the party, and when she was done and the guests started to arrive, the woman pressed a twenty dollar bill in her hand and thanked her. She was so furious she came right here.

"I was in the bedroom getting the Valentine's present I had gotten for your mom. I had hidden it at the back of a closet shelf so Isabel wouldn't find it. While I was out of the room, Isabel burst in and began cursing Madeleine, hitting her, pulling her hair, kicking her. She hit her on the side of her face with the guitar. She was screaming all kinds of insane shit.

"Madeleine had been sitting on the floor and was taken by surprise. I pulled Isabel off her and picked her up. It was like holding electricity. She was flinging her arms and kicking and screaming. I had her wedged under one arm and my crutch under the other. Pablito opened the kitchen door and I tossed her out. She was banging on the doors and windows. I had to get your mother away. Isabel wanted to kill her and I wanted to kill Isabel. We tricked Isabel, letting her into the house and then locking her in a room while I got 'M' out to my car. Her face was scratched bad. She was bruised all over. She had plans to go visit you in Switzerland, but until she was healed she couldn't go anywhere. I got her home and she called your grandmother. She wanted to give her some kind of excuse for suddenly dropping out of sight. She didn't want the Trasks or the chambermaid to see her like that so she rented a motel room. I saw her every night."

"So that's why she didn't come to Zurich. Why the hell didn't she tell me?" Groff looked around for an answer, but no one had anything to add.

"Isabel thought that when we made enough money we'd retire as gods on Mount Olympus. She'd book so many hook-ups, like, four or five a day! And this wasn't whorehouse, assembly line service. I had to do the whole, 'You're so special,' love-making grind. And I had no desire to do any of them. Madeleine was a married woman. A scandal would have hurt her. If I walked away from the scam, Isabel would have destroyed her. She was so jealous. I had to make it appear that nothing had changed." He looked up forlornly. "So I took those blue pills.

"And then on weekends, to preserve the deal, I had to do Isabel. I couldn't take being near her. She always smelled bad. It got worse. You know how paranoid people smell so bad? Her suspicions covered her like a mold... a fungus of some kind. When I touched her I'd sometimes look to see if I scraped any of it off under my fingernails. Perfume couldn't cover the odor. Neither could booze."

Pablito disagreed. "She didn't smell funny to me!"

Sanchey snapped, "You didn't have to lay with her!"

"You could have been nicer. She tried to please you in every way."

"You're all pigs!" Groff said.

Lionel put his hand on Groff's shoulder. "Easy, son. Let's get it all." He turned to Sanchey. "Was Dr. Euell involved in any of this?"

"I don't know. He liked to make money. Isabel said he'd give hormone injections instead of pill prescriptions. It kept the women coming back for expensive office visits. He had pills that increased a woman's libido. I don't know if she stole them or bought them from him. She worked out the tea ingredients with Pablito and the 'Aztec' cookie ingredients with Doña Maria. Some women wanted to come back three or four times a week."

"Did Isabel ever call you on Euell's office phone?" Lionel asked.

"Not that I know of. She said she always used a prepaid cellphone."

"How much money did you get out of my mother?" Groff asked.

"She paid only for that first visit. She had already given Pablito the money before I saw her. Look," Sanchey pleaded, "you can believe what you like, but I loved your mother. To keep Isabel from snooping, I'd take care of as many women as I could all day so that when she called in the evening, Pablo could tell her I was busy with a client and the cash receipts would cover me. I bought a little Honda. Pablito said it was his. But at dinner time, when I was finished here, I'd drive down to The Hollyoak and on the way I'd pick up sandwiches at a deli your mother liked.

"I'd never call first. I didn't want phone records. Isabel was nutty to begin with, and when she was jealous, she was worse than insane. In the evening when I was with Madeleine, going up to her bedroom was like climbing up to heaven."

"How did you get in?" Groff asked.

"When I got to your house, if I saw lights on in her bedroom, I'd turn the car lights off and follow the driveway up and park at the far end of the house. I always carried a morral that I put the sandwiches in. I had a key to the front door but there was a vertical floor bolt. She'd leave the door locked but she'd release the floor bolt. I'd let myself in and go down to the wine cellar - she always left small lights on - to pick up a bottle of wine, put it in my morral, and then get two wine glasses from the china cabinet and go on up to her bedroom. We'd eat and watch TV. Smoke a little grass and talk and laugh. Sometimes I'd recite poetry to her. I learned a lot of poetry when I was a kid. Or else I'd just fall asleep with her head on my shoulder. We'd sleep like babies. She didn't know how exhausted I was. I didn't know how sick she was." He began to gasp and whoop and then he put his head down and sobbed, banging his head against the table.

"Nice," said Groff, glaring at his grandfather, "that somebody had a key to *my* house." He walked to the table and placed both hands on it. "Stop your bawling." Snidely he added, "It's unbecoming to a man of your stature." Groff indicated that Beryl should move over to let him sit. When he was directly across from Sanchey, he affected the attitude of a warlord. "What else do you have that belongs to me?"

Sanchey wasn't intimidated or offended. He answered unemotionally, "Some jewelry and bonds are a safe deposit box in Allentown. We can go up now if you want and get them. It's all yours. I'll give you my key." He reached for a coffee can on a shelf behind him. He opened the can and removed a ring of keys and a Jaguar key-pod. "Here's your house key," he said, sliding the key like a quoit towards Groff. He slid two others across the table. "The steel one opens the lock to the cellar door at The Hollyoak. The brass one is the front door key to your Lodge. All I want are my papers and some photographs of your mom and me." He slid another key. "This is the safe deposit box key, and this," he pushed the Jaguar key pod toward Groff, "is the key to your mother's car."

Beryl expected Groff to respond with civility. Instead, his face distorted into an expression of stunned disbelief. "What the hell are you doing with the key to my mother's car? How can you drive a stick shift?"

Sanchey closed his eyes and nodded, alone again in his thoughts. Rousing himself, he said simply, "When she went shopping she put things in the trunk of the car and left the car parked near the cellar door. I'd open the door and the car trunk and bring the things in. It was usually wine."

Groff did not soften his tone, which now indicated that he thought he had caught Sanchey in a lie. "And how did you manage to carry a case of wine, on crutches?"

"I have a prosthetic foot. I can walk without crutches when I need to."

"In the letters Isabel sent you, she mentions another woman... and a house in California."

"That was all bullshit to keep her off M's case." Again, he began to sob, shaking so hard with each gasp that the table moved in cadence with his shuddering grief.

Lionel stood up. "We've taxed this man enough. He doesn't know anything about the murder and there's been no criminal complaint about anything that went on here. Euell won't violate doctor-patient confidentiality. And if we continue to poke around and embarrass people, we'll only compromise any investigation that might be planned.

"The likelihood that any of the victims will come forward is nil," he conceded. "People would prefer to lose money than subject themselves to ridicule."

"And if she manipulated medical records or fabricated them?" Beryl asked.

"We have no evidence of that. It will be up to Aubrey Euell to determine if any records were disturbed. If Isabel says she sent your mother requests for retesting, who's to say she didn't? There have been no complaints filed.

"There is nothing here that concerns us."

"I don't want to seem obtuse," Beryl protested, "but instead of focussing on potential or silent victims, how about giving a thought to some actual ones. George nearly got his head bashed in and there's a killer out there, a lunatic who could flay a man like a deer and squeeze inside his skin!"

Sanchey raised his head. "What the hell are you talking about?"

Groff sneered. "Are you worried that somebody else is horning in on your 'She-pay' Totec act? More Aztec gods runnin' loose? Call Animal Control!"

Lionel apologized. "I got carried away with legal minutia. It's a lawyer's disease. I'm too emotionally involved to think objectively. I shouldn't jump to conclusions. We must defer to the DA's of Montgomery and Lehigh Counties and, I guess," he concluded, "Philadelphia County, too."

Sanchey broke in, "I want to know what you're talking about. Flaying a man? Who's George?"

Beryl didn't want to revisit that nightmare, but it occurred to her that Sanchey, Pablito, and Dona Maria might also be in danger. She briefly related the story of the encounter with Brunton's killer.

Pablito and Dona Maria screeched and hugged each other. Sanchey groaned and covered his face with his hands. Doña Maria wailed, "I knew that crazy woman was going to cause trouble. Now she's got us involved in a murder! We're gonna end up in jail!"

"So what?" Sanchey said. "I don't give a shit where I end up."

Beryl advised, "Start giving a shit! Where you end up, Madeleine's reputation ends up."

Sanchey looked at her, alarmed. "What should I do?"

Beryl spoke sincerely, "Do yourself a favor and get yourself a lawyer." Then, still resentful that Lionel Eckersley had interfered in the investigation, she taunted, "Mr. Eckersley's a lawyer. Ask him."

"He'd love to take you on as a client," Groff exclaimed. "But you'll have to give him a dollar first. I can lend you the money."

Sanchey looked at Lionel Eckersley. "Madeleine said nice things about you. Will you take me as a client?"

Eckersley stared down his grandson and then turned to Sanchey. "I'll need a dollar for a retainer," he said.

"Wait a minute," Groff said, his joke having backfired on him. "Isn't that a conflict of interest?"

"Is there a matter before the courts that you'd like to tell me about?" Lionel challenged him. "Do I have a fiduciary relationship with Euell or his nurse or any of these people? Am I representing the interests of anyone else that would be compromised by my representation of this man?"

Sanchey reached into his pocket, withdrew a crumpled dollar bill, and gave it to Lionel who accepted it and looked around at the others. "Would all of you mind letting me speak privately with my client?"

Pablito had been listening. "What about us? Don't we need a lawyer, too? Or can we just leave tomorrow and head for Mexico or Canada?"

Beryl pushed Groff and the two of them got out of the booth. "Didn't you say you just bought a mobile home from a friend?" she asked Pablito. "Try thinking about that check you wrote him. If that account is frozen or if Isabel manages to stop payment on it, your friend may be stuck. Do you care? So don't leave town until you're sure there won't be any warrants out for you. And yes... get yourself another lawyer. Try the Yellow Pages. And don't try to conspire with anyone to obstruct any investigation."

Doña Maria put her hands on her hips. "We're going to be the scapegoats for all this trouble. The rich take care of themselves. We little people always get the shitty end of the stick."

Groff answered. "Of course you'll get the shitty end! Why do you think the wise old attorney is representing his daughter-in-law's rent-a-stud? So he can manage the case and keep quiet whatever needs to be kept quiet! And place the blame wherever it is most likely not to damage privileged reputations."

Groff took Beryl's arm. "Show me Rasputin's bedroom and then let's get out of here."

Beryl led him back through the altar room and into the tea reception room. When he said that he had seen enough, they went out to wait in the limo for Lionel to finish his consultation.

No one spoke as they returned to the Shell Station and changed cars. In the pickup, Groff called Sensei who was still sitting at George's bedside. "Can you stay there and wait for us?" he asked. Sensei said that he hadn't planned on going anywhere and neither did George. "See you soon," Groff said.

Beryl again put the pieces of the case together in her mind. She saw clearly what had already happened, but she had no way of predicting what would happen next.

Groff pulled into Jefferson Hospital's entrance and asked Beryl to go on without him. "I have a few things to do. Sensei's here. He can take you home. Tell George I said, 'Hi,' and that I'm taking good care of his pickup. I'll talk to you later."

Annoyed and confused, Beryl watched him drive away. "A loose cannon on the deck," she muttered as she entered the hospital.

It was dark when Sensei dropped Beryl off at the front door of her office. "Don't even think about coming to services tonight," he said. "Get some rest. Call me if you need me."

Wearily, she climbed up the stairs to her apartment and flopped on her bed. The case, as far as Wagner & Tilson was concerned, was over. The recent murder and assaults were police matters; and the fortune telling scam was not their problem. She put her Colt under her pillow, kicked off her shoes, and pulled the comforter up. The last thing she remembered thinking was that George's prognosis was said to be excellent with no expectation of problems... except, of course, for the time it took to regrow hair.

At seven o'clock the office extension phone rang. Startled, she answered and fumbled for the lamp switch.

Groff spoke hurriedly. "Now don't get tight-assed about this, but I'm taking Isabel McAndrew out to dinner tonight, at Angelo's. I'm picking her up at her place. We have a reservation at seven-thirty. She likes Italian food. Don't even think about objecting. I know what I'm doing. I just wanted you to know in case Xipe shows up." He disconnected the call.

Immediately Beryl called Lionel and told him. He was angry. "What put that fool idea in his head?"

"I don't know! When we left you, he dropped me off at the hospital. I thought he was going to see George. But he just said that he had things to do and he'd see me later."

"What can that boy be thinking? She may be a homicidal maniac. And he's going to her residence? How did he get her address?"

"It's in the phone book." Beryl gave him the address.

Lionel's limo was conspicuously double-parked a block away from Isabel's address on Reid Street, a derelict, overcrowded broken chain of row houses. The street was so rundown that she doubted that she had gotten the correct address. Some of the houses had chunks of glued-on fake stonework that stubbornly clung to the old brick. None had been painted in years. Several that were burned out or abandoned lacked doors. The onlooker could see through to their back yards. Broken windows were filled with cardboard. Trees that once lined the street had all been removed, and the squares in the sidewalk where they once grew were filled with trash and clumps of grass. Car wrecks took the best parking places. Kids played while drunks slept on the 'stoops.' Generations of graffiti defaced windows and walls.

Beryl drove around the block. She spotted Lionel's limousine and parked behind it. They dispensed with greetings.

"Did you see the pickup truck?" Beryl called.

"No," he answered in a worried voice.

"We're either early or late," Beryl said, adding, "and it wouldn't be past him to have changed the time. Let's go directly to her address."

"Yes," said Lionel, "let's go. The devil loves a coward."

They walked together until they found her address. Lionel insisted that Beryl remain on the sidewalk while he went up the steps and opened the vestibule door. He rang the landlady's bell.

Beryl followed him and opened the outer door as the landlady opened the inner vestibule door.

"Who you lookin' for?" the landlady asked Lionel.

"Miss McAndrew. I didn't see her name on the mailboxes."

"The kids sneak in and try to rob the mailboxes. For spite they take the names off. Hers is the bell on the end. You her big date tonight?"

"Not exactly." He rang the last bell.

She looked at Beryl. "Who you lookin' for?"

"I'm with him."

There was no answer to the bell. The landlady tried to help. "Maybe it's broke or maybe she's down the hall in the bathroom. Go on up and knock on her door. It's the rear apartment. Third floor."

She let them pass through the vestibule and into a foul-smelling hallway that led to a worn wooden stairway. They were both out of breath when they reached the third floor. "How," Lionel asked rhetorically, "can people live in a place like this?"

They heard a commotion downstairs and then the sound of steps being climbed several at a time.

"He's here," Beryl announced.

They waited for Groff at the third floor landing.

"What the hell is this?" Groff whispered angrily.

"What has gotten into you?" Lionel hissed. "Are you insane? Coming here like this?"

"I'm taking Dr. Euell's nurse to Angelo's for dinner. What's wrong with that?" His tone turned threatening. "Don't interfere." There was an open door at the front end of the hallway. He pointed to it. "See if you can duck in there." They retreated. The door was to a bathroom - which they determined more from the stench and from the sound of a running toilet than from what they could see in the dim hall light. Groff knocked loudly on Isabel's door.

They heard the door open. "Come in," Isabel said sweetly. The door closed behind him.

Ten minutes later, Groff and the nurse emerged and descended the first few steps. Groff, in gentlemanly form, took a step down first. Isabel, wearing high heeled boots and a pants suit, followed, taking Groff's upraised hand as she descended. She was not limping.

Lionel and Beryl waited until Groff and Isabel had left the building. They then rushed down the stairs, but by the time they reached the street, the pickup was nowhere to be seen. They separately drove to Angelo's, but the pair had obviously gone elsewhere.

TUESDAY, OCTOBER 20, 2009

At three-thirty in the morning, Groff shook Beryl awake. "Get dressed," he said urgently. "I think Isabel may head out to Haddon Manor to settle a few scores. I want to get there before she does."

Beryl, still buttoning her shirt as they sped away in George's pickup, asked, "What makes you think she's going to do something crazy? What did she tell you?"

"I got a quick course in Aztec mythology. I also got told about the devil's advocate. She told me that when a person was nominated for sainthood there were always people who'd be happy to run that candidate's name into the ground. These people truly were those who advocated the devil's interests. They needed to be stopped before they could do his dirty work. She was serious. I got a little nervous.

"She asked me if I knew that Xochiquetzal was another name of the Virgin of Ocotlan. I said I didn't know that. She said that Xochiquetzal used to be her name. That was the first X-name she used. The second was her married name, Xilonen.

"Then she mentioned entering a convent in Michigan. So I began to think that maybe in her craziness she imagined she'd be canonized some day and wanted to be sure the people who could testify about her sex life with Revere Sanchey would be silenced. She seemed completely unaware of the murder at the lodge. I mean... she never mentioned it at all."

"She told me that she wanted to enter a convent," Beryl said. "But this business about the devil's advocate sounds like she has an even higher ambition in mind. She may need to do a pre-emptive strike."

"My gut told me she was gonna do a little house cleaning at the Manor."

Beryl agreed. "Those three can not only prevent her from being canonized, they can prevent her from entering the convent in the first place. Tell me everything that happened after you left Isabel's apartment."

"I took her to a French restaurant in Media. She told me about Amerindian contributions to agriculture. That part was nice. I didn't know that pineapple was native to Central America. She talked about how the Aztec nuns made aphrodisiac sauces. It was kind of funny and we laughed. But then I asked her how come she was so informed about pre-Columbian culture. She said it was a hot topic at work; and she was inclined to get interested in it because that charlatan Daniel Moor was badmouthing the American Indian shaman who had done a lot of good. Moor, a fake, was calling him a fake. She had led the charge against Moor. 'Finally,' she said, 'his reputation is now totally destroyed. He can't even pay the rent.'

"We lingered over dinner. It was after eleven when I paid the check. She said she had some jewelry she wanted to show me, so when I took her home I parked on that goddamned street she lives on and followed her up to her apartment. I went to the bathroom. What a rathole! The tub's faucets aren't connected. The toilet runs. The washstand has only cold water. I mean... it was too fucking dirty to piss in."

"Forget the bathroom. What was the jewelry?"

"Silver stuff from Mexico she got at some flea market. I said it was nice and tried to get her to talk about my mother. So I asked her if she had any tea. She made a pot and we sat and talked. I asked her how well she knew my mother. She says, 'I hardly knew the dear lady. I wish I had gotten to know her better.' And right away she starts talking about saints and the devil's advocate. She said that my mother would be on the path to sainthood if it hadn't been for her devil's advocate.

"I got set for some wacky monologue about my mother; but she just wants to discuss the devil's advocate. 'People will tell terrible lies about you,' she said. I give a dumb-ass 'fresher' response: 'it doesn't make any difference as long as you know the truth.' And then she looked at me and her eyes filled up with tears and she says, 'Groff... No! It is so much worse to be accused of something when you're innocent than it is to be accused when you're guilty.' And I ask her why that would be worse. And she says, 'If you are called a thief, and you are a thief, you can obtain forgiveness. You can repent, declare yourself remorseful, and rejoin society. People love the redeemed sinner. A Parole Board will put its imprimatur on your early release. But if you are charged with being a thief and you're not a thief, how can you ask for forgiveness? You are the one who should forgive the liars and those who falsely or incompetently brought charges against you. You can't lie and say you were guilty and are repentant. And so people will continue to believe you're guilty, an unrepentant sinner. They will shun you and scorn you. You will continue to suffer the accusations. *You can't forgive innocence.*'

"I babbled, 'Your only hope then is total faith in God's judgment, faith that is strong enough to withstand temporal hardship and not give way to bitter recriminations, because then you'd have to face a judgment for your own enmity.' Blah, blah.

"We kicked God's Will around and just when I start to fear that the discussion was devolving into Lapsarian drivel, she mentions the Ethics of Innocence. I ask her what she meant by that. I swear, I've never even heard the term before. Maybe I was absent the day they taught it. Anyway, she gives me some unusual examples - loosely based on the Sydney Carton predicament - and we talk for a couple of hours.

"I'm no philosophical wunderkind, but I know enough to recognize the logic in her cockeyed arguments. I'd have loved to see that woman at some of my tutorials. Well, fuck Kierkegaard. We talked about a lot of things. But when I got up to leave and she walked me to the door, she started advising me about the need to silence liars before they had a chance to lie. She had the weirdest look on her face. It scared the shit out of me."

No one was parked outside when they arrived at Haddon Manor. Either Isabel hadn't arrived yet or her car was inside the garage or parked in back. Beryl looked in the garage window and saw only Sanchey's Honda. Groff motioned for her to get back into the pickup. He wanted to drive to the rear of the house to be sure she wasn't there and, if not, to park the pickup so that they wouldn't be seen by anyone.

It was nearly 5 a.m. when they began to knock on the kitchen door. It took ten minutes before Doña Maria opened the door. She tried to block them from entering, but Groff pushed her aside and shouted for Sanchey. In a few minutes Pablito came into the kitchen.

"Go get Master," he ordered his wife. "I'll start the coffee."

There were piles of clothing on the booth's benches. Beryl sat at the kitchen table in the center of the room. They could hear Doña Maria trying to awaken Sanchey with her shrill voice. Pablito put a filter and several measures of coffee into a coffee maker and poured bottled water into the machine.

Groff leaned against the kitchen door and waited until he heard the shower run before he sat with Beryl. Pablo put three cups on the table and filled them.

Sanchey, on crutches, but looking better than he had looked before, entered the room. "You guys are here early," he said as he swung his leg forward and dropped into a chair at the table.

Grudgingly, Groff related his dinner conversation with Isabel.

Sanchey looked at him intently. "And you give a shit whether or not she kills the three of us? You've walked into the lion's den, my man. If she shows up, she'll just as easily kill you. In fact, she probably hates you two more than she hates the three of us. But thanks for the warning."

"You are quite welcome," Groff said sarcastically. "Too bad such solicitude didn't extend to my mother."

"I see that you take after your father," Sanchey countered. "What is it you want? You didn't come all the way out here because you were worried about us."

"Well, since you mentioned it," Groff pointed to the dwarfs, "tell them to go get everything - I don't care how small or insignificant you think it is - everything that belonged to my mother. Clothes, combs, photographs, perfume... everything. I don't want anything of hers to be in your possession. I want it all, and I want it now." Sanchey nodded to the dwarfs who went into the inner rooms, arguing about the location of various items.

"After you get your mother's things, you need to leave. I don't mind tangling with Isabel, but she's dangerous and your mom would expect me to look out for you. So take her things and go someplace safe." Sanchey spoke without emotion.

"I need some answers," Groff replied with an equal lack of emotion.

"You want to know about your mother and me. How we hooked up. You resent me. I get it. So in case Isabel manages to put me out of my misery, I ought to tell you while I still can."

Groff nodded. "That sums it up."

"All you need to know is that you were her reason for living. It began and it ended that way. What she cared about, I cared about. She became my life. And she's dead now, and so am I." He slumped in his chair and began to stare at his fingers.

"I'm touched," Groff said. "But could we have the gory details of the seduction."

Beryl objected. "What went on between your mother and this man is their business, not yours. Your mother would never pry into your sex life. Your father might."

Groff suddenly looked as though he were going to cry. His mouth shut tightly, its corners turned downwards. His eyebrows furled. He turned away and supported his head with his hand. Beryl looked at Revere Sanchey and shrugged.

Sanchey closed his eyes. "He has a right to know. Madeleine should have told him." He opened his eyes and spoke directly to Groff. "I used to think 'love at first sight' was just something people said... an exaggeration. But I loved her the moment I looked at her. It was December. I watched her through the mirror window. She said she felt ill and didn't want to drink the tea. Pablito wanted to cancel. I told him to lead her back and to cancel the rest of my appointments. She seemed to be in pain or something. She denied it, but I took her into my bedroom and made her lie on my bed. I sat beside her on a chair. We talked awhile, and I just stared at her while her eyes closed and she fell asleep. I stayed with her but after a few hours, I worried that it was getting late. She might have been expected somewhere. I found a feather on the floor, so I tickled her nose with it. She opened her eyes." Once again he lapsed into silence. Groff seemed to sense that he was going to hear something he didn't want to hear. His facial muscles tensed.

Sanchey's tone changed. He began to talk to some spirit presence no one else could see. "She said, 'Well, hello. What are you doing?' and I said, 'I'm dusting your nose.' She said, 'You'll make me sneeze.' And I said, 'No! No! Don't sneeze! A sneeze makes the devil come out of you. That's why we say, "God Bless You" when we sneeze.' And she asked, 'And you want the devil to stay in me?' And I said, 'I want you and your devil to run off with me and my devil so that the four of us can be good or bad whenever we want.'" He shuddered and gulped, folded his arms and put his face down.

"Don't leave me hanging, Bro!" Groff sarcastically insisted. "This is such a great story. Then what did she say?"

Sanchey raised his head and stared at Groff. In a strong clear voice he said, "'Should I pack or will we be wearing fig leaves?'" The remark had a stinging effect.

Groff's head jerked to the side. After a moment, he smirked. "I cannot tell you how moved I am by this tender tale. Is this 'The Early Years' of your apotheosis?"

Sanchey ignored the rudeness. "We talked about you and your life. I told her about my life in Belize... and how a shark bit my foot off."

"Too bad it didn't bite your cock off," Groff said simply as he tilted the chair back.

Sanchey's tone softened. "You don't think your mother loved me. She did. You think it was a sexual thing. It wasn't. And I don't give a shit if you believe that or not. At first, whenever I went to Hollyoak I was so totally fucked out that I was useless. I was sore and I was exhausted. And she always had these damned bladder infections. They were painful. But I would hold her in my arms and kiss her for hours. The smell of her... like all the flowers in Eden.

"Later on, when I changed my schedule, and wanted to make love to her to make her happy, she was too tender and had these mysterious stomach pains. We knew she wasn't pregnant. She thought that if anything serious was wrong, Euell would have found it. I begged her to see another doctor and I even made an appointment for her with a specialist in Norristown, but she had that run-in with Isabel and she cancelled it."

Groff waited a moment and then clapped his hands. "Great story."

Sanchey was suddenly angry. "She told me personal things about herself that you don't know. You're sitting there expecting me to tell you personal things she told me, just to prove she loved me. Kid, it ain't gonna happen. I'm not betraying her confidence just to gain your sympathy."

"This is bullshit. Confidence? Trust? Did you tell her how you were always a whore, with or without feathers? How you took advantage of a frustrated old maid and made her your pimp?"

Beryl, trying to ignore the unpleasant exchange, had been staring at the kitchen door. She thought she saw the knob begin to turn. She raised her hand, signaling 'quiet.' Everyone watched the knob turn. The door opened and Isabel McAndrew stepped into the room. "Isabel!" Beryl said in a friendly way. As Isabel walked silently towards the table, Beryl could see that she was carrying something under her coat.

Beryl's shoulder bag was hanging from the back of her chair. She slid her hand down the strap, trying to reach the gun slot.

Isabel caught the movement and hissed, "Keep your meddling little fingers on the table where I can see them!" Then she removed a shotgun from under her coat, took a few steps back, and pointed the gun at Groff. "I could blow his pretty little face right off." Beryl kept her hands on the table.

She stopped beside Groff's chair and bent forward to look into his face. "Madeleine's little *coq au vin*. How sweet!"

Then she began to sing, "Madeleine's got something in her tum-tum." With the shotgun still pointed at Groff, she walked to Sanchey's chair and kicked the crutches that were propped against it. "Now, Hopalong Revere, let's all hear how your rough sex hastened poor Madeleine's death." She looked at the ceiling. "What a pity that was," she said in a maudlin singsong voice. "I had my heart set on one of those aristocratic death-bed scenes. The old family retainers standing by, wiping their eyes, wondering if they've been mentioned in the will. A priest! Extreme Unction! Paving the path with gold and flowers all the way to heaven. Oh! What am I thinking? Madeleine wasn't Catholic! Wasn't she a member of some Aztec religion?" She began to cackle.

The noise of the metal crutches hitting the floor brought Pablito and Doña Maria rushing into the room. They carried some of Madeleine's possessions.

Doña Maria was frantic. "Don't do anything foolish, Isabel. He's not worth it." She tried to put the items into a paper bag but she dropped a bottle of Chanel No. 5. It fell against the foot of a metal radiator and broke. Instantly the room filled with Madeleine's scent.

Pablito dropped a pair of Madeleine's shoes and put a pile of photographs on the kitchen sink. "That's right! Put the gun down, Isabel. We can all walk away from this! No harm's been done."

Isabel stared at them, pretending to not know who they were. "We can walk away? We?"

Doña Maria ignored the remark. "You always knew the truth about Madeleine. If she hadn't married into the Eckersley family, she'd be a hash slinger. She had no class. You have class... class and brains."

"Yes," said Isabel. "She married well. So did I. But she didn't have to work. Humanity was my work. That's why she always smelled so good. Work makes a person sweat."

Doña Maria jumped in front of Pablito. "I always thought you smelled nice. You got class. Revere's a dog from the gutter. Look, we can walk away from this. We made plenty. Pablo and I are gonna buy a condo in Orlando. Come with us. You can buy one, too. Who knows? If we ever run short, we can work the con again... with somebody better, somebody with more brains. We don't need this toad. We're a team. Isabel! Don't break up the team!"

Isabel looked up at the ceiling again. "Hah! Listen to this little freak! A condo with pygmies? Oh, my! I will be moving in high society!" She pointed the shotgun at Dona Maria. "Get out of my sight or I'll splatter your itsy-bitsy body all over this room!"

Pablito raised his hands and pleaded, "Isabel, none of them's worth dogshit. And don't worry about those society weirdos. They'll never go public. Nobody will file a complaint. The only bad thing is that you won't ever get the pleasure of telling the world how stupid those rich bitches are. You're home free, Lady."

"What are you saying?" Isabel's eyes grew wide. "Those ladies are my friends. My dearest friends. And you little freaks dare to insult my friends!" She suddenly shouted, "You wiggly little maggots!" and pulled the trigger. An immense blast of fire left the shotgun with a deafening noise. The two dwarfs were hurled backward, buckshot in their faces and chests. A mist of blood and smoke filled the room. The shotgun's recoil forced Isabel backward. Groff, seeing that she was off balance, immediately lunged at her, knocking her to the floor.

Beryl leapt for the shotgun, pulling it from her hand as she shouted, "I have zip-ties in my purse." Sanchey opened the shoulder bag and tossed the plastic strips to her. Groff held Isabel in a headlock as Beryl tried to secure her flailing arms and legs. Sanchey picked up a crutch and swung his body into the action. He knelt on Isabel's legs and held her hands together so that Beryl could secure her wrists with the tie. She screamed and writhed. Sanchey saw a length of clothesline in the corner of the room. He crawled to it and tossed it to Beryl.

Not until Isabel's feet were bound together did anyone take a deep breath. Beryl removed Isabel's left shoe and sock. The tell-tale wound was there.

Sanchey looked at Isabel with a kind of wonderment. He softly pleaded, "Why didn't you tell me Madelaine was dead? All these months I've been waiting to hear from her."

She smiled sweetly and then hissed, "Tell you? The ventriloquist's dummy? I don't have to tell you anything. You don't get it, do you? You were just the oracle's mouth. I was the oracle! Without me you were nothing!"

Beryl called Lionel and related the events. He was firm. "Revere Sanchey is my client, but I'll get immediate representation for Groff." He asked Beryl who her attorney was. She said that she and George didn't have a criminal attorney - just an attorney for their contracts and such. He asked if she wanted him to recommend someone. She didn't think she needed one but if he thought so, yes, by all means.

"Call the police right away," Lionel insisted, "but give only one-word answers. Volunteer nothing. I'm on my way. Try to delay everything until I get there. Meanwhile please put my client, Mr. Sanchey, on the phone."

Groff wanted to see the photographs Pablito had put on the sink. He picked them up and brought them to the table. He took a napkin and wiped spattered blood from the top picture. Then after he studied each one, he passed it to Beryl. In all of them, Madeleine and Revere Sanchey were laughing and obviously in love. Revere had a suave and genteel look about him. He was, Groff realized, a handsome man... a man who, a mere half year earlier, was thin and healthy in appearance. Madeleine looked up at him with an adoring expression. Her joy was indisputable. When Beryl finished looking at the last one, Groff gathered them together and put them in his jacket pocket.

Lionel finally arrived. He had already called Dr. Euell who was at home, nearby in Montgomery County. Lionel gave a brief summation of the events and advised Euell to call his attorney and if he were so obliged, to get one for Isabel. "Get over to Haddon Manor as quickly as you can."

As Lionel sat at the kitchen table, Euell called on his car phone. In swift and clear sentences Lionel gave him directions to the old house. Euell wanted more details about the shooting. Lionel said, "Isabel McAndrew has just shot and killed two people... tenants of Haddon Manor. You'll need to talk to your attorney about questions of liability. It is alleged that she used private information from your patient files in a fortune-telling scheme. I can't advise you since my services have already been retained by Mr. Revere Sanchey Porter, the man she claims was her partner in the scheme."

In fifteen minutes, Aubrey Euell's car pulled into the driveway even before the police arrived. In obvious distress, he, too, bolted into the kitchen.

Isabel shouted, "Aubrey! I knew you'd never let me down. Oh, Aubrey!"

"Put some tape over this bitch's mouth," Aubrey responded.

Beryl was still trying to process the events. She rubbed her face repeatedly. A police car pulled onto Haddon Manor's driveway. "Time for Isabel to go," Beryl said.

Two police detectives entered the kitchen. "Why is her shoe off?" one asked.

"To display a wound," Beryl replied.

Isabel suddenly shouted, "It's one of the stigmata, you fool. Can't you see that?"

Groff had not examined the wound before. He got up and looked at it carefully. "She needs medical treatment," he said to the detective. "See to it that she gets it." He turned to Beryl. "It's cold. Put her sock and shoe back on."

As she prepared to put the sock on, a police photographer entered the room. "Here," Beryl called, "document this wound." The photographer took several photographs of the injury.

The detectives agreed to complete the questioning at the police station. "Let's get out of the way of the crime scene people," one said. The coroner's deputies put the bodies of the dwarfs into a van, and the forensics' technicians continued to measure, bag, and take their own photographs.

Lionel indicated that Sanchey should accompany him to the police station. Sanchey went into the private rooms to put on his prosthetic foot. He reappeared in the kitchen, and to Groff's discomfort, he stood eye-level with him.

Beryl said that she and Groff would follow. They left the house as the coroner's van was pulling away. A shiny new blue Buick that it had hidden from view was suddenly revealed.

"That Buick is Isabel's car," Groff said.

"She lives in that squalor and drives a new Buick?" Beryl asked incredulously.

"Yes... and that's one reason that she lives in squalor. She told me a long time ago she had an old car that she parked in the staff and patients' private parking lot. The ladies asked Euell what that disgusting wreck was doing in the private lot. Aubrey asked Isabel if she couldn't show more consideration for the opinion of others and get a more acceptable vehicle. She told him she couldn't afford a new car. Aubrey, *Largesse personified*, gave her an extra ten dollars a week. That was nearly twenty years ago. She gets a new car every three or four years."

"She can't possibly park it on the street she lives on. Does she rent a garage somewhere?" Beryl asked.

"Yes, and that expense is another reason she lives in squalor."

At Lionel's suggestion, Euell stayed at the Manor to wait for his attorney. Groff, Beryl, and Revere gave statements at the station.

As they prepared to leave, Sanchey called Groff aside. "I don't know what charges will be brought against me, but if you want your mother's property, the smart thing would be to get it now. We can still make the bank if we don't delay." Groff did not reply but instead told Beryl that it was a good idea to go to Allentown immediately. "Sanchey suggested it," he said. "We shouldn't compromise my grandfather by telling him."

Groff told his grandfather that he'd see him back at "the house" for dinner. As they went out to the pickup truck, a young woman from the public defender's office arrived to represent Isabel.

On the highway, there was no communication inside the cab of the pickup truck all the way to Allentown. They arrived at the bank before 3 p.m. Beryl waited in the lobby while Sanchey and Groff went back to the vault.

Groff returned with a large paper sack that contained Madeleine's jewelry and a stack of bearer bonds. Sanchey had wanted him to take the cash, too. Groff declined, saying that he didn't want anything that belonged to Sanchey.

All the way back to Philadelphia not a single word was spoken. Groff dropped Beryl off at George's house and continued on to Rittenhouse Square with Sanchey. He stopped in front of his grandfather's brownstone and called him. When the old lawyer appeared on the door step, Groff leaned over and opened the passenger's door. He called to his grandfather,

"Here's your client. I figured you'd want to brief him as soon as possible." Sanchey left the pickup truck, and Groff sped away from the curb.

By the time he had driven back to George's house, Alicia Eckersley was on the phone telling Beryl how she was caring for Madeleine's "beau."

Groff came into the 'orchid ranch' and tossed the bag on the kitchen table. "What's in it?" George asked.

Unceremoniously, Groff dumped the contents on the table. "A few mil in diamonds and another few mil in bearer bonds." He looked around. "You got anything to eat in here? Do you want me to go out and get something?"

Sensei made spinach omelets and a pot of tea and nuked some pastry. While they ate, Beryl told him what his grandmother was doing. "She had 'Lionel's man' commence the god's demystifying process by getting him to take a variety of measurements - 'inseams, out seams, sleeve, neck, waist, and chest,' so that he would know precisely what sizes to buy when he went downtown, 'to buy suitable attire for the next few legally eventful days.' She had asked him if he still wanted his long hair and he said that he didn't care one way or the other. She immediately called her hairdresser, who also cut and styled men's hair, and asked if she could bring her an important client for an early morning appointment. Revere Sanchey Porter's return to the world of the ordinary has begun," Beryl announced.

That evening, Lionel called Beryl to tell her that he and two other attorneys would meet all three clients for lunch the next day in Drexel Hill, at a mutually convenient location, a restaurant. From there, everyone would go out to The Hollyoak for a strategy session.

Beryl and Sensei returned to the office. Sensei had to prepare for services.

Groff stayed with George and the orchids. "I need the family environment," he said.

WEDNESDAY, OCTOBER 21, 2009

At noon, the three lawyers, who evidently had not seen each other in years, and their three clients met at the Wilmouth Inn in Drexel Hill. They ordered lunch, and as they ate, Groff, Beryl, and Revere Sanchey seemed to vanish. The three old men talked about old times, unusual cases and unforgettable clients. At the end of the main course, they declined to order dessert - a decision, Beryl assumed, that was made because they had exhausted their repertoire of anecdotes.

Lionel called ahead and told Clive to light the fire in the living room, make a samovar of Darjeeling tea, and buy a large box of pastries at the bakery.

It was nearly 2 p.m.when their cars pulled into The Hollyoak's driveway. Beryl had not yet had a conversation with her attorney, an elderly gentleman named Horatio Falk, and Groff had not talked yet to his attorney, an even older gentleman named G. Tryon Bache.

The three clients were not at first discomfited by the lack of attention paid them. Beryl and Groff were not in any legal trouble. By then, Revere did not care whether he was or not. But once the physical presence of the old stone house stimulated their senses, and the old lawyers were able to recall more events from prior decades, Groff could tolerate no more nostalgia. "Jesus!" he growled, "can we get on with it?"

Hushed, the guests awkwardly sat on sofas and chairs that Beryl's memory refused to clean.

Lionel Eckersley tried to restore the group's conviviality. He stood and asked, "Say, Gentlemen, unless I miss my guess, Clive is guarding some fine 30-year old single malt scotch back in the study for the private use of old friends. Who is going to join me?" The other lawyers were in jovial accord with the invitation. "Clive, it's time to break out the good stuff!" Clive smiled as he bowed.

Suddenly Groff stayed the order. "No! This, I believe, is my house. That makes *me* the host. If you don't mind, I'll tell Clive what to serve... and we won't be serving alcohol this early in the afternoon."

Everyone sat in stunned silence. The wild boy was preventing his civilized grandfather from taking a drink! Nobody knew how to respond. Then Groff said, "Clive, we can serve ourselves tea. Bring my mother's portrait - the one in the green feather headdress - here. It's in her dressing room."

"Yes, sir," said Clive, bowing his head again.

When Clive returned, carrying the portrait, Sanchey gasped. "Is this the portrait she had done for my birthday?" he asked. "She said it would be funny, but I knew no artist would paint her as a joke. It's so beautiful." Tears began to run down his face.

"I'm so glad you like it," Groff said. Then he turned to Clive. "Put the portrait back where you found it."

"That was cold," Beryl admonished him.

"All right, boy," demanded Lionel. "Out with it. What's bothering you?"

"Why we're here is bothering me. A strategy session? What do we have to strategize about? We're not going to sue anybody. We're not going to have a criminal trial. Why are we having a strategy session?"

Lionel was indignant. "Isabel will be tried for the murders of two people, the ones she just committed in Montgomery County. Her fraudulent activities are a separate matter. It's a bit premature to predict civil actions, but rest assured that Aubrey Euell will do the honorable thing and compensate all those who have been damaged in any way."

"Of course," Groff said sarcastically. "And what about Brunton's murder and the attack on Beryl and George up in Lehigh County?"

Lionel responded stiffly. "A murder trial in Lehigh County would likely be obviated by Isabel McAndrew's responsibility for two deaths in Montgomery County. Out of consideration for the innocent, we'll see to it that Brunton's family and Beryl and George are generously compensated."

Groff sneered. "So, what you're saying is that Lehigh County doesn't have to investigate Brunton's murder. Isabel hasn't even been charged with a crime, but no matter, Lionel Eckersley says she's guilty, so they don't need to try her. Isn't there something about that in the Constitution... I thought I read someplace that you're not supposed to do that."

"You know very well that she killed Brunton. You, yourself, saw her kill two people down here. Why are you seeking a scandal? Why are you so anxious to re-open terrible wounds and bring discredit to the Eckersley name?"

"Open whose terrible wounds? Not Brunton's. He's one *big open* wound. There's nothing to be *re-opened*. Ah. You mean the bullet-ridden ass of my father... the wounds he got during one of his routine statutory rapes. You don't want to call attention to another murder at the lodge. You're gonna disappoint the folks up there. Quite a few got rich... the girl, her father, and God knows who else. Protecting the Eckersley name has become a growth industry in Lehigh County!"

"I don't regret the actions I took to protect this family's welfare," Lionel countered.

"What did you do to protect my mother and me from my father? Weren't we members of the family?"

"What protection did you require? Your father was a forceful man - too forceful, I concede; and as a Christian he should have left retribution to God. He did not always act with forethought."

"That's it! *That's what I mean!*" Groff shouted. "We were never victims. We were always perpetrators. He was simply imposing a harsher punishment than was needed. His wife and son were incestuous lovers. Poor Dalton! Madeleine was Eurotrash and Groff had to be put in a mental hospital. Poor Dalton! He got the sympathy. We got the bruises. If her belly was distended and she bled to death, well, now... that sounds like a botched abortion. Poor Dalton!

"And that is precisely what you're doing to Isabel. Turning the guilt inside out and dumping as much of it on her as you can... all to protect the honor of the Euell and the Eckersley family names, not to mention the family names of the idiotic women who were ready to worship... I can't even say it! *an Aztec god!*"

Lionel was distracted. He seemed not to have heard Groff or else, Beryl thought, he didn't like his friends hearing what Groff was saying. When he spoke, it was in a scornful tone. "Your mother was a married woman when she began her affair. Does your contempt for Mr. Sanchey overwhelm your concern for your mother's good name? Or haven't you thought of that?"

Groff's response was not detoured by Sanchey's name. He sneered at his grandfather, "My mother's good name doesn't require anyone's protection. And don't refer to her love for this man as an affair. But I compliment you on finding a new way to gain sympathy for the bullying rapist." He scornfully recited, "Madeleine committed adultery with a fortune teller. Poor Dalton!"

"I did not excuse Dalton's behavior any more than I excused yours. We burdened him with too many expectations. *Someday you may learn that it is much easier to hate your father than it is to hate your son.* But let's leave him out of this.

"Nobody is making Isabel guilty. She made herself guilty. She betrayed her employer's trust. What you want is a scandal that will penalize dozens of innocent women and their families. What is to be gained by public disclosures? Aubrey will make full restitution and he will compensate all possible damages.

"Say what you will, Aubrey Euell is an honorable man. As to Isabel, I know he was angry when he came to the Manor. But I also know that he will not simply throw her to the dogs."

Groff stood up. "*You still don't get it!* What you are doing is one of your 'shifting blame connivances.' And *that* is the purpose of this 'strategy session'- Isabel's automatic guilt for anything and everything she can possibly be charged with - while mitigating Aubrey Euell's negligence.

"*My mother is dead!* Euell saw her cervix. He palpated her abdomen. He heard her complaints. When the lab report came in *from a lab that he owned*, he read the results. He was your good old friend and Dad's. When she didn't come in for retesting, why didn't he pick up a phone and inquire? What does Isabel have to do with his criminal indifference to his patient? Tell me that if it had been Alicia Eckersley on his examining room table and he callously *ignored* the testimony of her complaints, the documented suspicions of a lab report, and the evidence provided by his own hands and eyes, you wouldn't have gotten out that Glock 9 and drilled him a third eye!"

Lionel fumbled for a moment. "Of course, Euell had been remiss not only as a physician but as a friend to treat so casually... the evidence of cancer. I can't deny that Aubrey failed to respond with the appropriate degree of... caring."

"I guess you can't, counselor." Groff suddenly spoke with ironic emotion. He whined, "Isn't one evil woman enough? Why involve Aubrey and his patients in such unnecessary notoriety! Why make people of quality seem like idiotic victims of peasant schemers.

"Ah, genteel Aubrey will make a cultivated appeal to aristocratic sensibilities. I can hear him now." He mimicked Euell. "In good faith did he employ that wretched woman. She was a trusted employee and she revealed confidential information for her own personal gain. Oh, how she not only damaged him professionally, but she harmed the very people he loved most. Naturally his first concern was with them, his patients! How he thanks God that no one's health was compromised. 'Servants! Are we not all at their mercy?'"

Lionel stared quizzically at him and said nothing.

Groff became livid. "Strategy? Let's prepare for her trial? *Trial? What trial?* She will never go to trial! You and Aubrey have enough friends and sycophants to declare her unfit for trial and she'll be committed to a state asylum *for eternity*! No scandal. No embarrassing disclosures. And naturally no investigation or trial for Brunton's murder.

"You hypocrite!" he said scornfully. "For decades Aubrey Euell exploited Isabel. Christ! How she looked at him when he came into the kitchen! Tell me he didn't tantalize her with romantic possibilities. Tell me that twenty years ago when he was strong and she was pretty he didn't bang her regularly. Whose imagination would be challenged to visualize him flattering her, telling her how indispensable she was, how it was she who made his practice so successful? *Nobody's*! You know in your heart that that's exactly what he did! But instead of a decent salary - enough money for her to get a life of her own or move out of the slum she lived in, he led her on, dangling in front of her future decades of locking the office door and spreading her legs for a bona fide member of 'American Nobility.'

"And who will face punishment for everything that went wrong? One socially irrelevant, insane woman. You'll develop a strategy that never even mentions the *sane* people who were complicit in that guilt. Aubrey Euell will secure the cooperation of prosecutor, psychiatric examiners, and judges to see to it that Isabel is buried in an asylum and none of your lily-white thoughts will ever have to be soiled with the remembrance of the sight or the sound or the smell of her." He walked to a casement window, unlatched it, and pushed it open. He looked at his grandfather with disgust. "We need fresh air in here!"

Beryl expected Lionel to react badly. Instead, his eyes grew wide. His mouth opened dumbly as he turned to look at the others while he pointed at Groff. "Did you hear that?" he said. "Did you all listen to that? *That* is the gift of rhetoric! *That* is a talent for argument!" His voice was quivering as he turned again to Groff. "I had no idea!" Tears had filled the old man's eyes. He pulled a handkerchief from his breast pocket and began to dab his eyes. Then he bellowed, as if threatening his audience, "You cannot *acquire* talent! *No!* You cannot acquire talent! *It is a Providential Gift!*"

"Lionel, you better send that boy to law school," said G. Tyron Bache.

THURSDAY, OCTOBER 22, 2009

The knock on Beryl's kitchen door couldn't have come at a worse time. She had been sitting on her zafu in deep meditation for nearly two hours and had not noticed that her legs had "fallen asleep" until she tried to get up. She squirmed helplessly on the floor, waiting for the pins-and-needles sensation to respond to the sudden flow of blood into her legs. She heard another knock at the kitchen door and then the door being opened and closed. She heard footsteps coming towards the front room. "Who's there?" she called.

"It's Grasshopper. Can I come in? Don't worry. I'm taking my kicks off." The sneakers hit the floor with a thud. The shoji screens slid open and Groff entered the meditation room. He crossed the room and sat on one of the cushions by the low square table. "You should have stayed at Hollyoak last night. I had a place all picked out for you."

She laughed. "Where did you intend for me to sleep?"

"With me. What? Would you have preferred to lay beside the old man... or maybe The Heart of Heaven?"

"I'll never tell. Are they still there?"

"No. This morning my grandfather took Rasputin to Rittenhouse Square again so that he could continue captivating my grandmother with his magnetic charm. She's acting like he's Apollo. Poor guy can't get away from mythology."

"You were cruel to him yesterday. I don't think your mother would have appreciated it."

"I know. As soon as you guys left, I looked at him and, believe it or not, I felt ashamed. Seizing a moment of such rarity, I gave the portrait to him. I also offered him the job of caretaker at the lodge. Lionel approved."

"Did he accept?"

"He needs to think about it. He wants to, but he's a staunch member of the Moral Majority, and his law-abiding sensibilities are challenged somewhat by all the criminal activity that went on there. He's also an illegal alien, technically. But what the hell. Maybe one of Dad's girl friends is old enough now to get married and make him legal. He has to stick around for all the legal stuff, so why not? What I want to know is what law school should I go to?"

"Will they take you at the U of Pennsylvania?"

"If I pass the tests they give me. I'm a 'legacy' admission. That's where Lionel went."

"That sounds like the course you should follow. When will you apply?"

"Lionel's determined to fast-track me. He's hiring a flock of tutors so I can take the LSAT admissions test. Don't worry. I won't be too busy to see you."

"I'm relieved. You can keep my house keys."

"It may interest you to know that my little tirade on behalf of Isabel moved my grandfather sufficiently to pressure Euell into getting her quality legal representation. He'll push for innocence by virtue of mental defect or some such reason. For whatever it's worth, she'll get psychiatric treatment at a first-rate private facility. And get this - I heard him on the phone telling the *Employer of the Year* that a private hospital shouldn't cost him too much."

"By 'cost *him*' you mean Aubrey Euell?"

"Naturally. To quote my grandfather as he spoke to him on the phone this morning, 'Aubrey, I know you are anxious to do the right thing. You and your family have always taken well-deserved pride in being just and fair. And Isabel did do a lot of unpaid overtime work for you.'"

Beryl had to laugh. "I can see how he earned his reputation. He compliments him as he intimidates him and then he threatens him with a Labor Department Wage and Hour Board investigation - just in case."

"We're slick, we Eckersleys. How's George?"

"He's ok. Sensei's up there with him in his house. He's almost back to normal... a little stiff... some headaches. Furious that so much of his beautiful hair was shaved off. Sensei shaved his head, 'to show common cause,' with him. He's trying to get George to shave off the rest. He says that if George attempts some kind of comb-over, he'll shut the temple doors to him."

"Sensei's a great guy. Can he teach me karate?"

"No. It ain't in Blackstone or the Revised Statutes... or whatever you study. Besides, he may have extra studying of his own to do. George will have to take it easy for a while; and we'll need Sensei to get licensed. He likes the excitement. He says, 'Zen is a great getaway, but sometimes you need to get away from the getaway.' He's already worked on many of our cases, so it won't be a great stretch to get licensed."

"Listen, I want George to know that we have a hothouse behind the carriage house. The hothouse is empty and the glass is filthy. It hasn't been used since they kept fresh flowers in the big house, decades ago. I'll fix it up for him. He can move all his plants - regardless of social standing - into our Crystal Palace. I'll even hire a gardener to assist him. George can live at The Hollyoak for as long as he wants, steadily or on a come-and-go basis. I've already ordered the installation of a complete physical therapy room - equipment... weights... sauna... mats... the works. The pool's been covered up for years. I intend to refurbish it and build a room around it so that it can be used all year-round. Swimming will be good for him. If he wants a chauffeur, I'll get one. I'll hire a chef." He squinted, "Don't think I'm having an attack of altruism. If I go to Penn, I'll be home every night. I'd really like the company."

Beryl thought it was a good idea. "Well, then," she said. "Let's go tell him, but keep in mind that if he intends to stay in the P.I. business, your house is too far away. Maybe he'll join you for weekends and one night a week. Just don't press him."

Her legs were back to normal and she was finally able to walk. She ushered him out of the meditation room. "Go wait in the kitchen and give me a minute to change."

"A minute? Let's not get carried away. Oh, and don't forget to tell Jack that when I'm here I'll be sure to leave a necktie hanging on the door knobs... both doors."

Beryl tossed a slipper at him and went to get dressed.